ANYONE
BUT
RICH

OTHER TITLES BY PENELOPE BLOOM

The Objects of Attraction Series

His Banana
Her Cherry
His Treat
His Package
Her Secret

Stand-Alones

Savage
The Bodyguard
Miss Matchmaker
Single Dad Next Door
Single Dad's Virgin
Single Dad's Hostage

BDSM Themed

Three-Book Stand-Alone Series

Knocked Up by the Dom
Knocked Up by the Master
Knocked Up and Punished
The Dom's Virgin
Punished
Punished by the Prince

Mafia

Two-Book Stand-Alone Series
Baby for the Beast
Baby for the Brute

Three-Book Stand-Alone Series
His
Mine
Dark

ANYONE BUT RICH

PENELOPE BLOOM

Montlake
Romance

Text copyright © 2019 by Publishing Bloom LLC
All rights reserved.

Published by Montlake Romance, Seattle

www.apub.com

Amazon, the Amazon logo, and Montlake Romance are trademarks of Amazon.com, Inc., or its affiliates.

ISBN-13: 9781542014151
ISBN-10: 1542014158

Cover design by Caroline Teagle Johnson

Printed in the United States of America

ANYONE
BUT
RICH

SEVEN YEARS AGO

We parked our cars at Overlook Point. The hills surrounding our little town were so small that it would've been more accurate to call it Mosquito Bite Point, where the hill was barely big enough to see over my uncle's bald spot, let alone the school that blocked most of the view. If you leaned just right, you could sort of see the chapel and the river near the center of town, but my friends and I never came here for the view.

For as long as I could remember, this was where we came to talk when something had gone seriously wrong. And not *I tried to hover pee and accidentally blasted the entire toilet* wrong. Not even the *I mistook my mom's hair removal cream for conditioner* event of two years ago. No, Overlook Point was for the big-drama moments. It was for life-and-death situations, and if the King brothers weren't a life-and-death situation, I didn't know what was.

Iris would have normally been wearing her soccer uniform. She'd have her hair pulled up in a sporty little ponytail, and she'd be in a hurry to get back to school in time for practice. Miranda would have a stack of textbooks open on her passenger seat, because she was so nerdy that her idea of texting and driving involved chemistry books instead of a cell phone. She'd be chewing on the nearest object, because some life-altering exam was looming. My own car would have usually been burdened with folders full of the work I'd been doing on my latest story for the school newspaper and scripts full of highlighted lines to study for the next school play.

We all had our things. Iris was going to head butt her way into a college scholarship. Miranda was going to outbrain everyone in the state and get a free ride to any college she wanted. And me? Thanks to Rich King, I was probably going to be picking gum off the bottoms of tables while customers tried to pinch my ass.

My friends and I had been happily making our way through life when the King brothers—with their chiseled jawlines, six-pack abs, and obnoxiously gorgeous smiles—collided with us like freight trains.

One by one, the Kings had managed to smooth talk their way into our lives and throw a wrench into the perfectly oiled machine that was my friendship with Iris and Miranda. Since kindergarten, the three of us had survived disputes over who was going to hold Brady Hall's hand during skate night and arguments over who got to wear that black-and-white dress to the formal, and we'd even managed to stage the school's greatest cover-up when my first period came in seventh grade while I was wearing white jeans. It never mattered how big the obstacle was. The three of us were unbreakable, and we'd find a way to overcome it. Only this time, I thought maybe the rift between us would be too serious to fix.

For as long as I could remember, the King brothers had been the royalty of West Valley. The oldest two were twins, and the younger was only a year their junior. They could've had any girl in town. Everybody knew they'd go on to bigger and better things after all this. Movies, professional sports, megabusinesses—whatever they wanted. There was just an aura about the three of them. They seemed invincible, like some greater power had accidentally dropped them into a frothing pot of good luck and stellar genetics before they left the assembly line. Landing a date with one of the Kings was like stealing a slice of something larger than life. For those few hours—days, if you were lucky—you were carving out your moment in the life of someone who was almost certainly going to be special. It was a moment in the spotlight, and I didn't know any girl who didn't want it.

We hadn't been any different. The Kings were distant and unattainable—even Nick, the youngest, seemed out of reach. He'd been friends with Miranda ever since middle school, but he was always dating someone else. Three weeks ago, that someone else was me, and that was how I stupidly set off the chain reaction that brought us to the hilltop and nearly to the breaking point in our friendship.

We all sat on the hoods of our cars, and no one seemed to want to be the first to talk.

"I really am sorry," I said to Miranda.

She was looking down at the school and the little piece of West Valley she could see below.

"You seriously didn't know I liked him all this time?" she asked.

Iris chimed in. "You *did* say, 'Ew, Nick is like a brother to me,' pretty much every time we teased you about liking him. So you can't really blame Kira for not realizing you wanted to fuck your brother. *Brotherfucker*," she added. "Besides, if you wanted to get Kira back for dating Nick, I think Rich kind of beat you to the punch."

I covered my mouth so Miranda wouldn't see me grinning, but thankfully, Miranda was smiling too. We could always count on Iris to say something dumb at the right time. I didn't think Iris could even help it if she'd wanted to. That was just how she was. And saying Rich had beaten her to the punch was the understatement of the century. I didn't need to dig deep to know why I'd dated Nick. The King brother I'd always dreamed of had been Rich, but he was untouchable. Nick was my pathetic attempt to get his attention. If only I'd realized a single day of Rich's attention would be enough to turn my world upside down.

"Just because you're right, it doesn't mean you're not an asshole," Miranda said.

"I'm the nicest asshole you've ever seen," Iris said. "Admit it."

The stony look on Miranda's face finally softened. "I'm proud to say I have only seen one asshole. And I think you'd have to be a little demented to call it 'nice.'"

"You get that, Kira?" asked Iris. "That can be your front-page story for the next school paper. Miranda Collins has a disfigured, terrifying asshole."

Miranda rolled her eyes, but she was still smiling. "Just make sure you put an asterisk after that sentence. *And her name is Iris.*"

"You named your asshole after Iris?" I asked.

Miranda threw up her hands and shook her head. "I thought this was supposed to be some kind of cease-fire meeting. You two are just teaming up on me and my poor asshole."

Her words reminded us all why we'd come to Overlook Point and of everything that had happened. Nobody was smiling anymore.

"I had an idea," I said. "It won't fix what happened, but I think it's the best way to move forward."

Iris nodded. "I know what you're going to say, and you're right. We leave the gas on in their house and then lob cherry bombs in the window. If science doesn't let us down, only their teeth will survive the explosion."

I stared at her. "Surprisingly, that wasn't what I was about to say."

Iris shrugged. "If your idea isn't good, we're going with mine."

"I hope your idea is good," Miranda said, "because I'm scared by how much I like this cherry bomb plan."

"I say we make a pact. We all swear that no matter what, even if the King brothers come begging us for forgiveness on their knees, even if they end up becoming megafamous billionaires, we'll never date them again. No matter what."

"That's it?" Iris asked. "Can we at least slash their tires? Maybe shove a potato in their exhaust pipes?"

"What the hell?" I laughed. "I don't see how any of that would help."

"It would help," Iris said quietly.

"You can vandalize whatever you want, but I think we all need to swear it," I said.

Miranda nodded. "I swear."

"Fine. Me too," Iris said.

"And me," I said.

Chapter 1

KIRA

Seven Years Later

"Friendships are a lot like kindergarten art projects: without glue, they all fall apart." Surprisingly, my father had said that. Granted, he'd also gone on to rant about how he never understood the stigma of eating glue and how scented glue sticks could have been like candy if people only tried them. It was always a little bit shocking that the man had ended up becoming a mayor, even if it was of a small town in rural North Carolina.

What he said had stuck with me. The first part, at least.

Maybe that was why I couldn't help feeling like my friends and I were growing apart. Our promise to stay away from the Kings had brought us back together all those years ago, and it had held us together since. The Kings had left right after high school to launch some tech company out in California. Unfortunately for us, they'd found enough success and money that they *had* become billionaires and they *had* become national celebrities. Their shocking good looks, antics, success, and money made them household names. Go figure. When you made a solemn vow and filled it with a bunch of "even if" clauses, you didn't really expect every last one of them to come true.

The way things had turned out also made our promise seem silly. It wasn't like back then, when we had to hold each other accountable. The Kings weren't walking the halls of our school and parading right in front of our faces day after day. Now they were just gorgeous faces on tabloid magazine racks in the grocery store checkout. They were occasionally spotlighted on TV, but they were as distant and untouchable as Brad Pitt and Ryan Reynolds. Pretending we had to even think about trying *not* to date them was beyond silly.

To make matters worse, we'd all been struck by adulthood. That inexorable internal shift when people started judging the success of a day by how *productive* they were instead of how much fun they had. Fun was the enemy, and it was only allowed if the production quota was met. Our common interests were dying a slow death, and it was becoming more and more clear that we were clinging to the last, decaying wisps of the promise.

I let out a long sigh through my nose, because that wasn't as dramatic as a mouth sigh. I was sitting at our usual table by the windows in Bradley's, a local-bakery-slash-coffee-shop-slash-comedy-improv-venue-slash-gossip-nexus for the entire town. A dose of routine felt good when everything else was changing, and Bradley's for coffee before work was our routine.

As a longtime eavesdropper, I saw all the signs that some particularly juicy bit of news was circulating throughout the store. I knew it *had* to be something good, because Landry Miller had actually set down his newspaper and hobbled all the way across the restaurant to lean into the conversation. There would've been no shame in getting up to listen in, but I wasn't in the mood today, no matter how interesting the news was.

Tomorrow, I had to find a way to stand in front of classrooms full of high school seniors and try not to make a fool of myself. Seven times in a row. *Yay for the seven-period school day.*

I was almost driven out of my disinterest when I heard a collective gasp from the gossipers and saw a few wide eyes. *What the hell are they talking about?* I was usually disappointed by what passed for juicy gossip in West Valley. I'd seen the same group of people practically frothing at the mouth when somebody caught Franklin Moore with one of his sheep. It didn't help that Franklin had tried to defend himself by saying it was actually a goat. As it turned out, his wife didn't care much which it was, and she promptly left him. The real kicker was when her divorce lawyer managed to get her custody of the goat, and it had been revealed that the goat was a male.

Thinking back, I realized that had actually been a pretty juicy story. It made me want to get up and dive into the gossip circle even more, but then I saw Iris come in through the front door. Rumors could wait a little while longer.

The bell above the entrance gave a half-hearted jingle to announce her presence, but nobody so much as turned to look at who had come in. I distantly wondered if it was the Frank-and-farm-animal-romance saga part two that had everyone so transfixed. Maybe he'd moved on to bigger game—*cows and horses, beware.*

Iris was clad in her police uniform. She had graduated from the academy four months ago, and now she even got to carry around a gun. I still wasn't quite used to the girl I grew up with packing heat instead of soccer cleats, but we'd all changed, and I had a feeling the differences were only going to continue to grow.

Iris sat down before getting herself a coffee. She flashed me a quick, friendly smile. She had her black hair trimmed short in a pixie cut, and her cute pointed chin made it somehow both adorable and sexy. I knew she was always trying to look more tough to fit in with the guys at the station, but unfortunately, she was blessed and cursed with highly feminine features.

"Something big going on today?" she asked with a nod toward the crowd of people at the other end of the store.

"Something," I said.

She turned her eyes on me, expression growing serious. Iris always saw straight through me, and she clearly could read my stress. "You're going to be fine, Kira. Those kids are going to love you. You're impossible to hate. You've got that innocent little small-town librarian thing going on."

"What the hell?" I asked, half-mad and half-amused. "It's only seven in the morning, and you already get the award for the most back-handed compliment of the day."

"You can be butt hurt all you want. Librarians are hot. Especially when they have sweater puppies." She yanked her nightstick from her belt and jabbed at my boobs with it.

I laughed, dodging and swatting it away. "I'm going to call your boss and get that thing taken away from you."

She did a stylish twirl of the stick and slid it back into her belt without looking. "Call my boss? I *am* the law, bitch. So leave a message."

I rolled my eyes. "That's impressive. The part where you can say that with a straight face."

She cracked a smile and shrugged. "I've been practicing. The guys at the station aren't really taking me seriously, so I've been practicing my tough faces in the mirror."

Iris's voice was light, but I thought I sensed a touch of real sadness there. The bell above the door jingled again. Iris and I were the only ones who turned to see Miranda walking in. She had always been a good dresser, even back in our school days. She had a way of finding creative ways to put together ordinary clothes. Thanks to her new job, she also had the money to straight-up *buy* fancy clothes. Of course, she managed to wear them well, too, which normally drew all sorts of eyes everywhere she went.

I was surprised when nobody in the gossiping crowd at the other end of the store seemed interested.

Miranda skipped ordering a coffee and joined us at the table. Her blonde hair was in perfect order, as usual, and tied into a braid she wore to one side. It had the enviable effect of making her look like some sort of Amazon warrior. She glanced between the two of us like she was waiting for us to say something.

"What?" I asked.

"You guys *have* heard, right?" Miranda asked.

My eyes went to the gossiping crowd for the hundredth time. "I literally walked straight from my house and plopped down at this table. No pit stops and no phone. So no, I haven't heard anything except my stomach grumbling, because you assholes think thirty minutes is fashionably late."

"They're coming," Miranda said.

I didn't even know who she was talking about, but the tone of her voice and the look on her face made my stomach clench. "*Who* is coming?" I asked, a little annoyed by the theatrics of saying something like that and waiting for the obvious question.

"Hemorrhoids?" guessed Iris. "We're getting closer to thirty. They say that's when you really have to be careful. No more than five minutes on the toilet and definitely no straining."

I gave her a disgusted look.

"What?" she asked. "Google it."

"The Kings," Miranda said. "All of them. Not just them either. The entire crazy tribe is coming. Mom and Dad. Media. Probably a wagon of ex-girlfriends. *Here,*" she added, tapping her finger on the table.

"To Bradley's?" Iris asked.

Miranda shot her a look. "No. To West Valley. *Here,*" she said again.

"Why would they come here?" I asked. I wore the perpetual creased-eyebrow look of somebody who was hoping to argue their way out of the inevitable.

"Yeah," Iris said. "They've been perfectly happy in California all this time. It was like they couldn't leave West Valley fast enough after high school. I don't buy it. Not until I see them with my eyes."

"Buy it or not, they're coming," Miranda said. "They're building a new headquarters for Sion, and they're putting it *here*." She tapped the table again, like she couldn't say the word *here* without both a whisper and a tap.

I shook my head, still frowning. "No. Silicon Valley is like a mecca for tech giants. Have you ever heard of a Google headquarters in North Carolina? Where would they even find employees?"

"When is this happening? *Allegedly, that is*," Iris said.

"Any day? I don't know. It's just all over the local news. They announced it last night. And think about it. That massive construction site they've been working on out in the hills? The one everybody was having so much fun speculating about a few months back? I think I have a pretty good guess what it's going to be."

I was rapidly working my way through the five stages, starting with denial and moving to anger. "What gives them the right?" I demanded. "They want to turn our hometown into a circus? Is that it? They didn't get enough satisfaction from all the shit they pulled in high school?"

Iris whipped out her nightstick and started stroking it in a way I thought was probably unconscious. Her fingertips ran down its length, and her eyes were distant. I knew she was visualizing *some* kind of beating.

"We need to agree again," Miranda said. "The promise still stands, right?"

"Of course it does," I said.

"Like it matters," Iris scoffed. "There's probably going to be an influx of supermodels applying for any and every part-time job they can find around town in the next few days. It's going to be like a hunting ground around here, and the target will be the King brothers. If you think they'll even remember us, you're kidding yourselves."

"She's probably right," I said. "If you made billions of dollars and dated celebrities, would you still be thinking back on high school drama? Would you even give any of us a second glance? No offense to us, of course."

Miranda shook her head. "It matters. We need to all swear it again. No matter what, we won't date the Kings."

I watched her, feeling my stomach lurch at the memory of the last time we swore. I nodded. "I still swear it. No matter what," I said.

"I swear it," Iris agreed.

Miranda breathed out, then puffed up like the life was suddenly returning to her. In seconds, the in-control businesswoman was back. "Well, I'll grab coffees and some food for that rumbling belly of yours."

I sat back in my chair and stared at the table, mind racing. Five minutes ago, my biggest concern was how I'd avoid embarrassing myself in front of my students. Now I had to wonder what was going to happen when the Kings came storming into West Valley like horsemen of the apocalypse—except these horsemen didn't bring plague and pestilence. They brought ladyboners, bad decisions, and enough money to make my head spin.

I *was* being dramatic, though. And Iris was right. It wasn't as if they'd remember us, let alone be interested if they did. I'd be fine. *We* would be fine.

Chapter 2

RICH

I tapped my finger on the armrest of my seat. I knew we would just be passing over the North Carolina border, thirty thousand miles below. I hadn't expected to feel the sharp tingle of anticipation in my chest when we arrived. I could have played psychologist and tried to dig into what *that* meant, but I was more focused on work.

Establishing a headquarters on the other side of the country was a massive risk. It was a risk we didn't need to take, but I'd let my brothers goad me into it, even though I was highly suspicious of their motivations. In all honesty, I was suspicious of myself for agreeing to something so idiotic. My brothers and I all played our parts in the success of Sion. My twin brother, Cade, was good with people. He was our negotiator and our salesman. Our younger brother, Nick, had a stroke of genius in him. I could always count on him to think us out of a pinch, but he could also be too kind for his own good. He would let us shoot ourselves in the foot to avoid catching another business in the cross fire if it was up to him.

Then there was me. I was supposed to be the one with the head for business. I was the one who filtered their ideas and made the ultimate decision on whether a certain move was the right call. I pushed Nick to give me the best answer and not the nicest answer with the least potential fallout. I made sure Cade talked to the right people at the right times and got the right results. It was my job to make the tough decisions. My responsibility was to bear the burdens and be the asshole when it was necessary.

So when they pitched the idea of setting up a headquarters in West Valley, it was my job to say no.

But here we were. The building was nearly finished. We already had a stack of résumés and files on the new employees who'd be coming to North Carolina.

My brothers liked the idea because it felt right, according to them. We'd be back home. We'd be bringing business and growth to our hometown, and they missed the hills of West Valley. Nick wanted to get away from the bright lights and the crush of the paparazzi in California. Cade wanted a fresh hunting ground for women, and he liked the idea of seeing how many of our pseudostalkers were going to relocate across the country to follow us here.

That was what they told me. I thought I knew them well enough to know the truth. The three of us had done our fair share of damage growing up here. Even though we never talked about it, there were three girls who had stuck with all of us in their own ways. They were also the three who had the most reasons to hate us.

I couldn't speak for Nick and Cade, but I knew I'd never stopped thinking about Kira and what I'd done. Not entirely. I could lie to myself all I wanted, but she was the reason I agreed to this. I had no illusions about coming back to sweep her off her feet and rekindle the relationship that never was. Seven years was a long time, and people changed. I knew I had. Chances were the girl I'd secretly longed for would be unrecognizable now. Guilt welled up in my chest when I realized I'd probably be the reason she was so different. Like everyone else who crossed my path, she'd been left with a life that was a burned ruin of what it had been before she met me.

I wondered if she could forgive me or if her forgiveness would fill the void I'd been carrying inside for so long. I'd been too proud to come here without an excuse before now, but I apparently wasn't above risking tens of millions and the future of my company when doing so had provided even the flimsiest reason to return to West Valley. I could laugh at myself if it wasn't so sad. It was the billionaire version of leaving your coat at a girl's house on the first date so you had a reason to see her again.

We were on a private jet that was technically owned by Sion. Maybe it was only because I was back home, but I kept catching my mind wandering. I thought about how strange it was to own a private jet when the guys we'd gone to school with were still trying to land their first salaried jobs. I thought about how I would've never believed you could get used to so much excess. I even thought of Kira, who still looked seventeen in my mind's eye, and I thought of what she'd think if she saw me now. I wondered if she'd let life run her down already. If she had bags under her eyes and was waiting tables in some crummy diner. It was possible, but I didn't think so. The Kira I knew was too driven. Too strong.

I put it from my mind when Stella took her seat beside me. She rested her hand on top of mine. It was cold and stiff, but I figured it would look convincing enough to anyone who cared to pay attention, most of all my parents. We hadn't even told my brothers the truth about our farce of a relationship, which was for the best. My brothers didn't see our parents the way I did, and I couldn't be sure they'd keep the truth quiet.

My parents sat a few seats over, but they seemed more preoccupied by their drinks and the plate of appetizers they were sharing.

"Airsick?" I asked. Stella looked a little more icy and pale than usual.

"A little," she said. "Or maybe it's just touching you."

I grinned and lowered my voice. "Asshole. Just because you're not interested in men, it doesn't mean you can't hurt my feelings."

She made a tittering sound. "I wasn't aware you *had* feelings."

"Careful. If you provoke me too much, I'll put my hand on your thigh and make you puke."

"If you make me puke, I'm aiming for your eyes."

I laughed. "Heterophobe."

"That's not even a thing," she said dryly.

"I'm screwing with you." I lowered my voice until it was barely a whisper. "I get it. This arrangement is weird, but it's keeping both our parents off our backs. Yours can stop setting you up with guys who try to paw you, and mine can stop harassing me about how I should get to know so-and-so's daughter because her parents have a great estate or because they're very well regarded at the country clubs."

She sighed, and the amusement faded from her face. "You know I'm kidding too. I still feel weird about all of this. We can't pretend we're together forever. Sooner or later, my parents—"

"What's up, lovebirds?" asked Cade. He came walking down the aisle with Nick trailing behind him. Cade gripped a beer bottle by the neck and tipped back a sip while grinning at me. "Jesus." He laughed. "She looks like she's got a flagpole up her ass, and you look like someone took a dump in your cereal this morning."

Nick nodded.

"We're launching a new headquarters, not going to a funeral. You told him, right?" Cade asked Nick.

Nick's hair was always a tousled mess of raven black. He wore glasses because he still refused to get corrective surgery. He was the smartest guy I knew, but he could also be a paranoid idiot when it came to medical things. Everything came easy to him, and he'd gradually learned that he had to try only half as hard as everyone else to do twice as well.

Cade and Nick slid into the seats across from Stella and me.

"I have an idea," Cade said.

"No," I said without hesitation. "Whatever it is, it's going to be borderline suicidal, and it probably also has the potential to kill somebody else."

He frowned, but from the grin on Nick's face I could already see I was spot-on.

"Okay, while both of those outcomes are technically possibilities, they're highly unlikely. I was just going to say there *are* parachutes onboard. That's it. We checked earlier, and they're definitely here. Wasn't gonna say another word." He waited with his hands spread and his eyebrows up, as if he had just given me information that would be highly relevant to me.

"Okay," I said. "Jalen," I called to my personal assistant, who was at the back of the plane. He posed for a selfie by one of the windows, flashing his phone a cringeworthy duck face and narrowed eyes.

"Sorry," he said, stuffing his phone in his pocket. "I'm going to use that for my Tinder profile. It's crazy how many matches I get when I take selfies in front of your stuff."

I glared at him, and from the way he shrank into himself, he got the message.

"I need you to find any and all parachutes on the plane and barricade yourself in the bathroom with them. You can try taking a selfie with those and see if it gets you any matches too."

"All the—yeah, the parachutes. Right. Probably could find one over—" He reached for the door that led outside.

Nick stood, stopping him with a barrage of "whoa whoa whoa."

"That door goes outside," Nick said.

Jalen was looking at him like he didn't understand the problem.

"Like we're thirty thousand feet in the air, and it goes *outside*," Nick said. "You'd depressurize the cabin, and we'd all get sucked out to our deaths."

"Not if we had parachutes," Cade added, as if he'd just made the winning point in an argument.

Jalen pulled his hand away and gave a half smile. "My bad. I thought it was a closet."

Cade looked at me with pursed lips. "What makes you think I didn't already stash a few in my bags?"

"The fact that you haven't packed your own luggage in years."

Cade reeled his head back and clutched at his heart. "You make me sound like some sort of rich, entitled asshole."

"And you make it sound like that's not true."

Stella laughed softly beside me. It was rare to hear her laugh genuinely, and it was enough of a surprise to draw my eyes. She quickly looked away and focused on her hands, which were motionless in her lap.

"How's this for capturing reality?" Cade asked. "You're a *dick*. And I'm stronger than you."

I screwed up my face at him. "There's no point. Arguing with you is like arguing with a five-year-old."

"Yeah, well. If you can't win arguments with a little kid, why would you expect to win them with me?"

I briefly thought about explaining to him how he'd entirely missed the point, but there really wasn't such a thing as winning an argument with Cade. He was too bullheaded to ever admit he was wrong, and he was an expert in twisting reality until even he was so confused that he thought all the facts had aligned in his favor.

"On a serious note," I said, "can you promise you'll at least stay out of trouble for a few weeks when we land in West Valley? The mayor technically still holds a few permits for the construction and traffic regulation that could be real pains in our asses. I'm pretty confident legal could eventually overpower him if he actually tried to stop us, but we'd be talking months, if not years, of delay."

"*Trouble,*" Cade mused. "Are you trying to tell me to keep my dick in my pants? Because you *know* I'm very responsible when it comes to my *extracurdickular* activities."

I nearly corrected him but decided even Cade wasn't dumb enough to think *extracurdickular* was a real word and that he was making an attempt at humor.

"I'm telling you to avoid getting tangled up in the normal dumb shit you usually do. At the very least, don't get caught if you're going to do something idiotic."

He sighed in relief. "Got it. I promise I won't get caught."

I knew it was likely the best I could hope for from him, so I let it go.

"You know, she's hot and everything," he said suddenly. He pointed toward Stella, then leaned in like he was trying to catch her eyes. "But it's pretty weird how she's always so quiet. And if a girl ever touched me like *that*," he said, nodding toward where her hand sat limply on top of mine, "I think my dick would retreat so far into my body you'd have to start calling me Cadealina." He raised his eyebrows at Stella and raised his voice. "Blink twice if he's holding you hostage. Blink three times if he's shit in bed. Cross your toes if he's a barbarian who likes ketchup on his grilled cheese."

Stella stiffened, then turned toward me. "I don't think it's actually possible to avoid blinking, and I'm wearing closed-toed shoes, so . . ."

Cade crossed his arms and smirked. "You dirty dog. Shit in bed *and* you've taken a hostage. So that's why we've been lugging the silent sister around with us for weeks now?"

"You told her to blin—"

"I got it. I'm not an idiot," Cade interrupted. "But hey, I'm not judging. If you're into weirdly quiet women who kind of give off a Viking princess vibe, then have at it. But if you do eventually decide to fuck her, let me know. I'll knit you a little sweater for your dick. Wouldn't want it freezing off inside the Ice Queen. *A really little sweater.*"

"We're identical twins," I said dryly. "From our feet to our cocks."

He gave me a grudging nod. "Yeah, you're lucky you got my huge cock. If you weren't my twin, it'd be as small as Nick's. I guarantee it."

Nick spread his hands in a silent *what-the-hell* kind of way but knew stepping into the conversation would be like stepping neck-deep into a pool of idiot. He wisely stayed out of it.

As if he'd successfully concluded the conversation, Cade excused himself and left—most likely to see if he could beat Jalen at finding the parachutes.

"So," I said quietly once Stella and I had relative privacy again. "You're sure pretending to be my girlfriend is actually your least painful option? Remember, I can't make my brothers go away."

She sighed and sank into her seat. "No. Every time Cade opens his mouth, I'm not even sure living on this planet is my least painful option anymore. Maybe I can convince Jalen to open that door after all."

"All joking aside, Cade is kind of funny, once you get used to him."

"And I'm sure you would also get used to the smell of shit if you lived in a sewer, but why would you want to?"

I grinned. "Didn't you ever want to have a dog?"

"Yes, but I don't see your point."

"Actually . . ." I sighed. "I was going to say Cade was like a dog, but better because he won't piss in your house. But then I remembered last Christmas when he got really drunk."

Stella finally cracked a smile. "I find myself wondering what I got myself into with this whole arrangement."

"Then you're finally starting to see clearly."

Chapter 3

KIRA

There were a few ways to describe the outfit I was wearing on my first day as a high school teacher. You could call it a tasteful arrangement of clothing procured from a wide variety of retail establishments. If you wanted to brush on only a little of the sugarcoating, you might say I had mixed together some great finds from Target and Walmart. *And* if you were an ass, you could just say I was poor.

Considering I needed all the confidence I could get, I was absolutely rolling with the first option.

I stood at the front of my empty classroom with my feet twelve inches apart. *The legendary power stance.* My body formed the strongest shape in nature when I stood like this. I was a pyramid. I was a symbol of strength and dominance. My body, which had been chiseled from literal *days* of exercise over the years, was an immovable object. *I was awesome.* I also had to pee, but according to the guide I'd read while sipping coffee from trembling hands this morning, "simply standing in the power stance releases chemicals in the brain to improve confidence and helps others perceive you as more imposing."

In practice, it made me feel a little bit like I was trying to casually let gravity and time handle a stubborn wedgie, or maybe like my water had broken and I was trying not to get any on my shoes.

I was clutching my materials like lifelines, while my eyes were locked on the door to my classroom. The hallways were flooded with students who all wore their West Valley High uniforms in varying states of rebellion. The boys wore white button-down shirts with yellow-and-silver ties, while the girls wore white button-downs tucked into yellow-and-silver plaid skirts. The boys either had their ties worn comically short or long. Short seemed to be the trend among upperclassmen, while the freshmen had ties dangling inches below their belts. For the girls, rebellion had two forms: cleavage and short skirts. They'd either wear their shirts in such small sizes that their chests were trying to burst out from between the buttons, or they'd roll their skirts up as high as they dared. Teachers were handing out pink slips left and right.

Me? I was standing my ground. Dress code was a battle for another day. Today, I just needed to survive. For a moment, I thought I knew how soldiers in war must have felt moments before the enemy came bursting from the fog with rifles in hand and screams in their throats. A moment later, I decided I actually had no idea how those soldiers felt, but I was definitely scared.

My door opened, and I immediately abandoned the power stance to turn wide eyed to see who it was.

Principal Lockett.

He was shorter than most of the freshmen, but the shiny patch of bald skin on his crown and the drooping bags under his eyes meant there was no mistaking him for a student. "Just wanted to say good luck on your first day, Kira."

"Thank you," I said. I hoped my smile looked genuine. I'd expected to need to try very hard to make a good impression on my new boss, but from the first day of preplanning two weeks ago, it seemed like *he* was the one sucking up. It wasn't the first time being the mayor's daughter had given me some unwanted advantage. No matter how much I protested, some people in West Valley were dead set on the idea that getting in my good graces was the same as getting in my father's good graces. Unfortunately, my objections went unnoticed, and people had never been quick to believe that favoritism wasn't something I secretly encouraged.

So I did what I always did. I pretended I still needed to bust my ass to make a good impression. I refused to sit back and let my father be an easy pass, and I hoped for the best.

"Is everything okay?" I asked when he was still standing there with a smile plastered on his face. From the corner of my eye, I saw students start pouring into my room from the back door.

"There is just one thing. A slight hiccup, really. Nothing that you would need to worry your father about," he said. "There's a very influential businessman in town. He got on the phone with the right people a few minutes ago, made some very interesting promises, and . . . *well* . . ."

"Well, what?" My eyes were darting between Principal Lockett and my rapidly filling classroom.

"He's apparently an old friend of yours. Said he'd like to be able to stop by today and say hello. He promised it would be quick."

"It's my first day," I said slowly, hoping I wouldn't need to explain any further.

"And you'll do great!" Principal Lockett seemed to sense my inevitable eruption, so he ducked back into the hallway and flashed me a quick thumbs-up before the door snicked closed.

I turned my eyes toward my students and made a weak attempt to mentally rally. *I can do this. They're just children in bodies that have grown faster than their brains. They aren't as mature as they look.*

"Do you see how red her face is?" whispered a girl in the front row. I wasn't sure if it was intentional, but I was pretty sure I would've been able to make out every word of the "whisper" from the parking lot.

The boy beside her smiled cruelly. "Maybe she's PMSing."

The girl frowned at him and slapped his arm. "That's not how it works, you idiot."

"What do you mean? There's all the blood issues. Some of it must end up in their heads."

The girl rolled her eyes, crossed her arms, and gave up on him.

I cleared my throat. "I'm Miss Summerland." I paused, swallowed, and willed my windpipe to grow a little bigger. "This is—"

The bell signaling the start of first period rang deafeningly, cutting me off and making me realize I was already showing what a rookie I was.

I cleared my throat again. "This is—"

The announcements began, instructing the students to stand for the Pledge and the anthem.

I turned my back to face the flag and pretended I didn't hear the snickering students behind me. I also pretended I didn't remember being a high schooler not so long ago, and how quickly I would've decided a teacher like me was the kind students were going to eat for breakfast.

A few minutes later, the announcements ended, and I finally turned to face the students again.

"Okay. This is—"

The door to my room opened. I spun, hands balled into fists. All the frustration of the last few minutes boiled over into an embarrassingly squeaky outburst. "I would love to finish my sentence!"

And that was when I saw my visitor.

Richard King.

Distantly, I heard the excited whispers of every girl in my classroom.

"Is that him?"

"Oh my God, is my hair okay?"

"This is going on my Snapchat!"

Their voices faded into background noise as I looked at him in person for the first time in so many years.

"Please," he said. His voice was so deep and rich I could feel it rumble through my chest. "Finish your sentence. I'll wait."

He knew damn well there was no way I could think about anything else with him standing there. The corner of his mouth had twitched up into the suggestion of a smirk, and his eyes were locked predatorily on me. He knew *exactly* what was happening to me, and he was enjoying it.

I tried to picture a normal human being in his place. I tried and failed to unsee the broad, powerful shoulders and long legs, to unmake every cruel and perfect line of his face, from the sharp jaw to the dark eyebrows and burning green eyes. His nearly black hair was cut short and neat. He wore a suit that would've made most men look overdressed, but he seemed perfectly at ease. Here I was with my legs spread out like I was trying not to step in a puddle, pretending I was in control. Meanwhile, Rich's pinkie toe projected more confidence than my entire body.

I wanted him and his obnoxiously cocky pinkie toe out of my classroom and out of my life. I was perfectly happy seeing him in a dirty dream every few weeks, where he couldn't screw up my reality any more, thank you very much.

"Out," I said.

"That was the end of your sentence? 'This is . . . out'?"

The students acted like his sitcom laugh track, and I already wanted to give them all detentions for being traitors.

I turned, annoyed, and gestured to my students. "This is English Four Honors." I looked back at Richard. *"Out."*

"I'll go out in the hallway, but you're coming too."

I gritted my teeth, wishing I could throw something at him without looking like a psychopath. I'd rehearsed what I would say to Richard a thousand times in the shower, but I should have known the mere sight of him would make me feel as powerless as I had seven years ago. If that wasn't bad enough, he'd managed to undermine me in front of my students on their first day in my room.

I settled for stomping out into the hallway and throwing a warning look at my class. Some of the students stopped grinning, and others even shrank into their seats.

The door closed behind me, and I was suddenly alone with him. "This is so like you," I said. "You show up after seven years and think the world revolves around you, so why should you even *consider* waiting until my first day of teaching is over? Why would it even occur to you that calling in favors and smooth talking your way past protocol would be ridiculous and unnecessary? God forbid the great Richard King has to wait a few hours to get what he wants."

He waited patiently for me to finish, and he even paused a few seconds, as if giving me a chance to add any final thoughts if I wanted.

"I still prefer to go by Rich," he said.

I could have punched him. "And I would've preferred not to have my first day of my new job interrupted by you."

"I came to say I was sorry. I thought you'd want to hear that."

I shook my head. Every passing second made me feel less starstruck and more aware of how much I hated the man. Yes, in biological terms, my ovaries and my vagina were having a sidebar about how nice his genes would look all tangled up with mine, but I was perfectly capable of focusing on the obvious: Rich was an entitled asshole, and I needed to say whatever it took to get him out of my life. "Congratulations. That's the most self-serving, insincere apology I've ever heard."

He let his eyes drop. For the first time since he'd showed up in my doorway, he looked a shade less than supremely confident. In the quiet seconds that followed, I thought I saw genuine regret creep into his features. "I really am sorry, Kira."

I never expected Rich to apologize. If I'd thought about it, I would have guessed it would feel good. Like some kind of vindication or maybe even like justice had been served. Instead, it felt only hollow, and that made me all the more furious with him. Did he really think a few words could wipe away everything he'd done back then?

"Thank you," I said robotically. "I'm going to go back to work, and it'd be great if I never had to speak to you again."

"Kira," he said, taking a half step toward me.

I held up my hand to stop him. "Have a good life, *Richard*."

Chapter 4
RICH

I spent most of the limo ride to my parents' new house brooding over my interaction with Kira. What stung the most was that she was right. When I thought back on how everything went to shit seven years ago, I automatically assumed I was such a vastly different man now. I believed an apology would magically make that clear, and she'd jump into my arms with happy tears running down her cheeks.

Maybe not that exact scenario, but I certainly hadn't expected a door slamming in my face or the way she'd been so cold toward me. I also hadn't expected her to look so damn good after seven years. She was supposed to be run down by life. Just a shadow of her former self. She'd already haunted my memories with how perfectly unforgettable she'd been, and yet it still looked like she'd blossomed.

She had grown into a woman, and not just a run-of-the-mill, straight-off-the-assembly-line kind the universe liked to flood my life with. She'd looked like she was ready to rip the American flag off the wall and run me through with the pole, which meant she had brains. Of course, everything going on *beneath* the brains was very much to my liking too.

I had foolishly told myself I could take care of the old emotional scar as easily as running an errand. Now I knew it wasn't going to be nearly so easy.

Stella yawned. "I'm surprised they had a home big enough to suit your parents in this little town."

"Yeah, well, my idiot brothers promised they would pay a premium to have renovations and expansion projects rushed along. I'm sure we'll hear how much they hate it when we arrive."

She nodded, but her eyes said her mind was elsewhere. "Rich," she said suddenly. "What really happened with this girl? Kira?"

I stiffened. I hadn't told Stella what I was going to do that morning, but I'd learned a long time ago to stop being surprised when nothing I did was private anymore. As long as there was money to be made in reporting every little detail of my life and the lives of my brothers, I wouldn't have privacy. "She was an old high school friend. I was . . . kind of horrible to her back then. I thought I'd go and apologize."

"And how did that go?" Stella was watching me very closely. She didn't say it, but her eyes spoke volumes about the real questions running through her mind. She was looking straight through me, and somehow, seeing the truth in another person's eyes was worse than feeling it in my own heart.

"I think if she'd had a live hand grenade, she might have shoved it down my pants by the time I was done."

"I see." She looked back out the window, and after she'd waited long enough for it to seem like a randomly occurring thought, she spoke again. "Was it serious? I mean, after all those years apart, she was still the first person you went to see in West Valley. She must have left an impression for you to be in such a rush to apologize."

I finally cracked a smile, but I sneaked a look at the driver before speaking. He didn't look like he was listening in, at least. "You're not jealous, are you?"

Stella looked toward the driver, too, and then back to me with a wry smile. "Maybe I'm just curious if she's my type."

I laughed but leaned forward and lowered my voice. "Be careful how loudly you say things like that. If our parents even heard a *rumor* that you weren't straight, we'd be under way more scrutiny, and things would start failing to add up. And then we'd be right back where we started in the game of whose parents are the shittiest matchmakers."

Stella wiggled her eyebrows. "Come on, now. Give them a little more credit than that." She lowered her voice to barely above a whisper. "If I was into penises and men, you would absolutely be a great match for me. They couldn't have known."

"That's flattering, Stella. And for the record, you had better keep your sights off Kira, or our fake courtship is going to come to a screeching halt."

"And maybe you should remember the same thing. If they see you going out of your way to spend time with this girl, what are they going to think of our suspiciously loveless pairing?"

She was right. I knew she was, but I also knew I wasn't about to give up getting Kira to forgive me. "You just worry about you."

Stella looked thoughtful. "So this girl is going to be what ruins everything, isn't she?"

"What? Why would you say that?"

"Because I can already see it in your eyes. You're going to do something stupid because of her. More likely, several stupid somethings."

I crossed my arms. "She's just a loose end, and I hate loose ends."

"You're also a bad liar."

♥ ♥ ♥

My parents welcomed us into their home, which already bustled with "help." The average American believed society had become too progressive for things like butlers and maids to still exist, but my parents hadn't gotten the memo. Neither had my idiot of a twin brother, for that matter. I still wanted to shake my head in shame when I remembered the saga of "Jeeves," the college kid he had dressed in a tuxedo and white gloves and paid to stand in his foyer for parties.

A man wearing a black suit—not a tux and white gloves, but not far from it—took our coats as we came in, and we had to squeeze past a team of women who were polishing the floors. Another team of men was debating the ideal height to hang a massive oil painting of my parents, and I could smell chicken and vegetables cooking from deeper in the house. I had no doubt it was their chef cooking the meal, and that every ingredient was gluten-free and organic. A soundtrack of pretentious classical music softly played over all of it.

My father, Harper King, was dressed as if he were on break from a busy day of running his own company. He had a button-down shirt tucked in neatly with his sleeves rolled up to his forearms. It was the kind of look that told you his idea of a hard day's work was a phone call and some stern words to an underling. Of course, my father had also never worked a real day in his life.

My parents were blue bloods. My great-grandfather had earned a significant fortune in a handful of successful business ventures, from restaurant chains to real estate and investments. His son, my grandfather, had inherited more money than he could spend in a lifetime, but he had made a valiant effort of burning through it. Still, he'd ended up passing before he could squander the fortune he left to my father. Like his father, mine had made spending the family fortune his full-time job from a young age.

In the world of big money, there were two types of wealth. Old money and new money. The older the money, and the further removed you were from having had to work to earn it yourself, the more prestige you carried in high society. And no, it wasn't supposed to make sense. It was simply meant to preserve the egos of the men and women who loathed the idea of doing anything useful but still wanted to feel like they were superior to everyone else.

Self-made millionaires and even billionaires were seen as upstarts. They didn't just get skipped on invitations to the most exclusive parties and events; they didn't even know about them in the first place. The blue bloods looked down on them because the self-made millionaires had to suffer the indignity of earning their fortunes. It was a little pocket of the aristocracy that was still alive and well in the dark gold-lined corners of the world.

So the success of my brothers and me put my parents in a strange place. They were old money. True blue bloods. But they also didn't have a whole lot of that old money left. Conveniently for them, we had so much money coming in from Sion that we were practically overflowing with it. It was more than we could figure out what to do with. For my brothers, that meant giving my parents whatever they wanted was no big deal. Compared with what was in our bank accounts, it was pennies.

Maybe it made me a cold bastard, but I would rather have watched our parents struggle for the first time in their lives. I thought it might be the only thing that would humanize them. Instead, my brothers made sure our parents had their lifelong philosophy that things would always fall perfectly into place validated, and all they had to do was keep being obnoxious snobs.

My father patted me on the back and flashed his overly white smile. "Let me take you on a tour. We've got a lot planned in this old dump, but with a little hard work, I think we can get it looking respectable before long."

I nodded and gave him a tight smile. The hard work, of course, would be from the men and women he hired with money from my brothers. And the old dump was a multimillion-dollar mansion on a sprawling property full of gorgeous landscaping.

My mother, Edna, made no attempt to hide her distaste for me. She stood a few feet behind my father with chin tilted up so high I could've counted her nose hairs. She wore a white turtleneck and a pair of jeans. She dressed up the outfit she probably saw as a casual, get-your-hands-dirty kind of style with pearls and diamonds.

"What's this nonsense I heard about you visiting some young, local tramp?" My mother practically spit the last three words out as though each were a curse word.

I spread my hands. "Is there a response you're looking for, or did you just want to insult her?"

"I'm looking for my goddamn son to show that he has some sense in his head. *Stella* is your future wife." She thrust her arm at Stella. "*Stella* comes from good breeding."

I nudged Stella. "Hear that? You were bred well. I'm sure your owners will be so proud to show you off. Maybe I can even ride you to victory in the Kentucky Derby if you stay healthy."

Stella shot me a warning glare. The look in her eyes told me not to mess this up for us by poking fun at my mother, but there was also only so much I could take.

"Son," my father said softly. It was almost like a plea. He knew my mother and I butted heads at every opportunity. Instead of talking down his wife, he always tried to get me to lay off.

"God forbid you got involved with the local girl," my mother continued. "Just imagine what people would think."

"Yes. It's almost inconceivable," I agreed. "They might think I liked her. Worse, they could even speculate that I loved her."

Stella elbowed me hard in the ribs. I needed the jab of pain as a reminder. What the hell was I trying to accomplish here, anyway? Even if Kira didn't hate my guts, she was probably the one woman on earth I had absolutely no chance of winning over. The look on her face at the school had told me as much. There were burned bridges, and there were burned bridges over rivers that had run dry, and *then* there was Kira and I.

"We're throwing a party tomorrow night," my mother said. If it was possible, she tilted her chin even higher. "I expect you and Stella to make an appearance. Many influential friends of ours will be there, and it's important for you to show everyone you're still committed to Stella even after all the turmoil of uprooting the family and moving back here. Especially after your ill-advised stunt at the school."

"Of course I'll be there. I'd never miss an opportunity to spend time with my family," I said.

My father clearly read the danger dripping from my words, if his bulging eyes were any indication, but my mother just nodded importantly.

"It goes without saying that you will *not* invite this local girl to the party. Yes?"

"I understand that would make you very unhappy. Yes," I said.

Stella turned her head a fraction of an inch to glance at me, and I knew she could sense where my thoughts were going.

Chapter 5
KIRA

"Whoa," Iris said.

There was already a steady morning hum of conversation at Bradley's. The smell of fresh coffee and bagels was doing wonderful things in my nostrils. I *should* have been feeling relieved to have my first day as a teacher behind me. I'd survived, even if it was with a few bumps and bruises.

Instead, I was watching Iris and Miranda run their hands over the invitation as if it were a letter from Hogwarts that had just propelled itself from the fireplace in a puff of pink smoke.

"The lettering is even engraved," Miranda noted. "Not cheap, at least as far as invitations go."

"This part seems handwritten," Iris said, tapping where my name was added to the typed invitation in flowing cursive letters.

"Is that coming from your extensive knowledge of crime scene investigation?" I asked.

Iris chuckled. "It's coming from the fact that it seems handwritten. Just look at it. Fonts don't work like that. See? The letters don't even line up perfectly at the bottom. And this little jagged part here is where they slipped."

Penelope Bloom

"Still way fancier than my handwriting," I said.

"If you put a pen between a monkey's teeth and asked it to sign its name while violently masturbating, *that* would be fancier than your handwriting too," Iris said.

"Jesus." I laughed. "That's part of your problem. Masturbating monkeys shouldn't even be in your vocabulary bank when you're trying to make analogies. It's not normal."

"Violently masturbating monkeys, at that," Miranda said.

"Don't look at me like that. I was at the zoo a few days ago. I watched the bonobos for like two minutes, and in that time I saw sex, betrayal, bribery, a monkey eating its own puke, and yes, even violent masturbation."

"Bribery?" Miranda asked. "I'm pretty sure monkeys don't understand the concept."

"Well, actually . . ." I started, and I cringed when I saw the looks they were both giving me. "Oh, come on. I have a good one this time. Let me use some of the useless knowledge I gained while getting my degree in sociology. Please?"

Miranda and Iris looked at one another, collectively sighed, and then Iris motioned for me to go on.

"I was just going to say they did an experiment where they gave monkeys a vending machine that accepted these coins. Monkeys could get things like bananas from the vending machine if they had the coins. And guess what happened once the monkeys grasped the concept?"

"Bribery?" Iris asked in a bored voice.

"Even better. Prostitution. Assault. All kinds of crimes we normally thought were uniquely human. Turned out, it's not being human that makes us suck. It's money."

Miranda laughed. "I get it now. You're just trying to convince yourself to stay away from the King brothers by any means necessary. I'm impressed. You even brought a relevant monkey story into it. That was subtle, but I'm not fooled."

34

"Ugh," I said. "Trust me. Richard King showed up yesterday for my first day and—"

Iris slapped her palms on the table, eyes wide. "What do you think this is, some fucking radio show where you bury the lede to sucker people into listening all day?" She pegged me with a rolled-up napkin. "I *saw* you yesterday. I pulled you over for old times' sake, and you didn't think that would be something I'd find interesting? We're here puzzling over why he'd invite you to this party, and you didn't think of mentioning that until now?"

I wrapped my hands around my cup, wishing I could sink into the liquid for a few minutes. "Okay, first of all? Pulling me over for old times' sake got old the *first time*. You are taking years off my life with that crap. Second of all—" I pursed my lips and swung my hand around in the air, searching for something that didn't sound like the lame excuse it would be. "I thought we should all be here. To hear it," I added quickly.

Miranda was watching me through narrowed eyes. "Hiding information about the Kings," she said slowly. "You're bordering on treason of the pact, Kira. You know what we do with traitors, right?"

Iris pulled out her nightstick and prodded me.

Miranda gave her a disgusted look. "Really, Iris? You have a Batman belt full of cool stuff, and you poke her with your oversize cop dildo?"

"What was I supposed to do? Set my pistol on the table? Also, cop dildo? Seriously? I've barely even considered using this thing for sexual pleasure before."

Miranda visibly shuddered. "Barely even considered? In other words, you've thought about it."

"What? You've never taken a long, lonely look at a cucumber or a banana before? Guys end up in the hospital with their dicks stuck in vacuum cleaners all the time. I'm not allowed to stick a nightstick up my—"

"I'm not a traitor," I said loudly enough to cut them off. "I told him I never wanted to see him again. I even said have a nice life. So you two can just back off. I handled it. I handled *him*."

"Handled him, did you?" Iris asked. She made a lewd hand gesture to show me I'd chosen my words poorly.

I laughed. "God, you can be such a perv."

"You call it perverted. I call it perceptive."

"Yeah," I said dryly. "It's so perceptive of you to realize that I totally gave Rich King a surprise hand job in the hallway outside my classroom."

Miranda held up the invitation and bonked me on the forehead with it. "Hand job or not, you 'handled' him so well that he decided to invite you to his fancy party tonight."

"Yeah. *Traitor*," Iris whispered.

"It's not like I'm going to say yes," I said. "Here. Give it to me. I'll tear the thing up. I just wanted you two to see how ridiculous it was."

"No," Miranda said. She was looking up and tapping her chin. "I think you should go."

"Why would I do that?" I hated that I could feel myself trying to act more indignant than I felt. The way my eyebrows were pulling together felt manufactured. Even the touch of outrage in my voice was forced. The only real irritation I felt was at how my friends seemed to push me toward what they thought was best for the situation and not what was necessarily best for me.

"Because it would be fun, and what better *fuck you* than to show up at his party and ignore him all night? He thinks you're going to show up and be on his heels, but you could just go to eat the free food and drink the booze. Dance with some other guy and then call it a night. Think about it. He'd be furious."

I chewed the inside of my cheek, mulling the idea over. "Do you remember when we were making that video in Iris's room? Freshman year of college?"

Iris put her palms over her eyes and started laughing quietly, but Miranda looked queasy at the memory.

"Why would you remind me of that?" she asked.

I grinned. We had just finished a night of partying and decided it would be a great idea to make an impromptu dance music video in Iris's room. Apparently, a few beers made me think I was suddenly Miss Booty Dropper, and when I went down for the showstopper, I ended up impaling the inside of my butt cheek on a protruding piece of furniture.

Iris had fallen over laughing, and Miranda had thrown up at the sight of the blood.

"Well," I continued, "once the stitches were gone and the wound was mostly healed, I kind of forgot about it. Then one day, it was a little itchy, and—"

"You spent all day scratching your ass?" Iris asked with an obnoxious grin.

"*No.* I mean, I might have scratched it in a very dignified, ladylike way once or twice. And then I guess I irritated it, because after that, I was miserable. I couldn't stop thinking about scratching it more, but every time I did, it made it worse. The only way to get it back to normal was to ignore it."

"As nice as it was to remember the time when you decided one butthole wasn't enough, I'm not seeing the point here. We were talking about Rich."

"Rich is like that scar. That's the point I was trying to make. If I go to the party, it'll end up making me think about him more, and then that'll lead to more, and so on. The only smart choice is to stay home."

Iris was grinning like an idiot.

"What?" I asked.

"I'm just making sure I understand the analogy, Miss Kira. So Rich is like your second butthole that closed up and scarred over, and you think scratching it would be a bad idea?"

I sighed. "It wasn't a butthole. I told you guys that a million times. The wound was only three inches deep, okay? And it was on my *butt cheek*. It wasn't even in the crack," I added quietly.

"Here's an analogy for you," Miranda said. She leaned forward with an evil glint in her eye. "When I get an ant bite, if I scratch it a little bit, it gets itchier. But I don't scratch it a little bit. I scratch that bitch until it bleeds. A few seconds of pain in exchange for no more itching. Simple as that."

"Oh, perfect," I said. "So you're saying murder is the answer."

Iris plugged her ears but nodded slowly to me and winked.

I laughed. "You two are idiots, and I'm not going. I'm also not murdering him." *Probably not, at least.*

♥ ♥ ♥

As it turned out, Iris had learned some torture techniques in her brief time with the police force. Chief of which had been the way she promised to help me cover up the murder of Rich and the disposal of his body. According to her, feeding the body to livestock was the way to go, but I wasn't sure about her idea of turning his bones into furniture. I thought a bone chair would be a dead giveaway if I was ever investigated.

So there I was. I was unfortunately incapable of murder, but I could at least piss the man off by showing up and ignoring him. That was the admittedly weak conclusion of the internal debate on whether I should come to the party.

This wasn't my first fancy party. Not by a long shot. There was my graduation party, which my father had treated almost like a wedding. He strung lights up around our backyard and had the whole thing catered. It was very *mayorly*. On the surface, it was generous and sweet. Unfortunately, I knew my father well enough to know it was a stunt for appearances, like everything else he did.

I'd also been dragged along to political parties he'd get invited to. Having my mom and me along reinforced the idea that he was a family man. It made him look relatable, or so he said. At the time, they seemed like parties thrown for royalty. Everyone wore expensive clothes, and the food was free. It was the height of privilege and class, or so I thought.

The party Rich invited me to made all of those look like high school parties in cramped living rooms with stained carpets and moldy couches.

I did a slow turn to take it all in while silently thanking Miranda for convincing me to come. The house was absolutely massive, and the decorations had a very Victorian feel to them. There was no piece of furniture or decor that wasn't absolutely loaded with fine detail and finishes. The end table in the foyer had claw legs with what I suspected was real gold gilding all along the edges. If not for the modern formal wear of the guests, I could've easily imagined I had been transported to some king or queen's palace two hundred years in the past. I almost expected a team of princesses in huge dresses to come parading down the staircase at any moment.

A woman in a uniform offered me some kind of food that looked like what you'd get if a doughnut had a baby with a chocolate bar, but a cupcake might've also joined in the love affair at some point and contributed a little DNA.

"Are these free?" I asked.

"Of course. The chocolate is from a remote region in South America. It's uniquely—"

"That's okay," I said quickly. "You had me at free." I took one from the tray and popped the whole thing in my mouth. I chewed through the waves of flavors, eyebrows climbing as it went from chocolaty and rich to pure sweetness and then finally finished with a hint of a flavor I couldn't have named if I tried. "Wow. Talk about a mouth-induced orgasm." I winced a little at the stunned look on her face. I had a very bad habit of talking too much when I was nervous.

From the look on the woman's face, she hadn't expected me to speak to her at all, unless it was to issue orders. Where had Rich and his family even found the staff for this? They must have paid to relocate employees all the way from California, and the cost had to have been staggering.

A man was passing by in front of me when he paused and did a double take. I only noticed him when he turned and started toward me. It was Nick King, the youngest of the trio.

"Kira?" he asked.

He pulled me into a hug before I could stop him, but it felt genuine, and I found myself hugging him back.

"It's me," I said when he pulled back.

Nick looked like his brothers, but with some noticeable differences. He had wavy dark hair that he wore a little longer. It fit his clean-shaven look and especially the glasses he always wore. The best way to describe the three brothers was what kind of movie they'd be cast for. Richard King would fit anything in need of a brooding but reluctantly charming leading man. As long as the movie later revealed he was a soul-sucking asshole who would stab in the back anyone who trusted him. Cade was a tougher pick. I couldn't quite decide if he'd fit the badass daredevil-type role, or maybe a more comedic, accident-prone but adorably sexy kind of thing. Then there was Nick. He was the kind of guy they always cast for those movies where you're supposed to root for the main character who is played by someone jaw-droppingly gorgeous, but because of the glasses audiences are supposed to believe no one realizes he's attractive. There would be the obligatory scene where he'd strip off his shirt and—*surprise*—he reveals he's absolutely ripped. Or better, the scene where he'd get some kind of makeover that was nothing more than taking off his glasses.

"Did Miranda come too?" His eyes moved past me, scanning the people behind me. "Or Iris?" he asked with less enthusiasm.

"You would've needed to send them invitations."

"Actually, Rich was in charge of all that. I just thought—"

"Well, it's just me, sorry."

"Sorry, I didn't mean it like that." He smiled, and it was a warm, inviting smile, just like I remembered from when we were kids. "Want me to let Rich know you're here?"

"No," I said. "I'd actually prefer that you didn't."

"Oh." He frowned down at me, eyes searching my face for answers. "I take it his grand apology tour didn't go so well?"

"You could say that."

Nick nodded but didn't look surprised. "I won't keep you. It was good catching up. And, uh, tell Miranda I said hi. Iris too."

"You got it." I hoped I sounded light and cheerful, but it felt strange talking to *any* of the King brothers after so long. It was almost stranger with Nick because I wasn't sure how I was supposed to feel. At least with Rich, I knew I was supposed to hate him.

Nick headed toward a group of men who were laughing about something and was welcomed with backslaps and manly shoulder squeezes. Something about sports and money made it okay for men to grope each other. I wondered distantly if there was some deeper truth buried in that but decided tonight wasn't a night for my mind to wander. I had to stay sharp, especially if I was going to avoid Rich.

I was playing a dangerous game. Be seen, but don't be seen. Be heard, but be silent. I would need to be like smoke between finger—

"Kira?" asked a man from behind me.

I turned and saw Cade, Rich's twin brother. Back in high school, I'd always been able to tell them apart at a glance because Rich never had a hair out of place, but Cade's hair was always a wild mess. Beyond that, the men were almost impossible to distinguish from one another. A woman was at his side. She was tall and stately, almost the spitting image of one of those imaginary princesses I'd expected to see.

She was watching me with a look I couldn't place, and I felt immediately inferior, like she only had to stand there and *be* to make me feel girlish and awkward by comparison. *Well, good for you, Cade.*

I squeezed out a smile instead of the grimace that was trying to rise up. "Oh, hey. I'm kind of in the middle of something, so . . ."

"Yeah?" he asked with an arched eyebrow. "Me too, actually."

The playful note in his voice tugged a reluctant smirk from me. "And what are you in the middle of, exactly?"

"Trying to get you to talk to me," he said.

"Last time I checked, we *were* talking."

"You're right. I guess my work here is done."

To my surprise, he and the woman turned and started walking away. I bit my lip as I watched them. I didn't know what was making me feel so impulsive, but I felt compelled to say something.

"Hey!" I called out.

Cade paused and turned to look over his shoulder. The woman was watching me too with those icy eyes of hers.

"You never asked what I was in the middle of."

He slowly walked back to me with his eyebrows raised expectantly. "Was it something exciting?"

"That depends," I said. "Everybody else looks like they want to dance, but I was thinking about seeing how many sweets at that dessert table would fit into my stomach."

"You had my attention, but now you have my interest."

I laughed. Cade had always been mischievous. Maybe it was the glint in his eye, or maybe it was just the stuffy, boring party, but I felt impulsive. "I wonder how much we could take before someone tried to stop us."

"Stella," he said. "Do you mind giving us—"

"Privacy?" she asked. "Are you sure that's the best idea?"

"I'm sure I don't need your permission," he said a little tightly.

Stella gave me one last look from head to toe and bit her lip. "Be careful with her."

A minute later, I was surprised to find myself giggling diabolically as Cade and I sneaked out the back door, across the patio, and down a small hill with our arms full of desserts. Even though the food was free, a waiter had tried to stop us when he saw we intended to stuff half the buffet table on our plates. We ended up ditching the plates and taking anything we could carry in our arms when our plan of a smooth exit turned into a mad, messy dash.

I sank down into the grass and looked at the pile of desserts in my arms, as well as the multiple places I'd smeared cream, frosting, chocolate, and fruit fillings on my clothing. From the looks of it, Cade hadn't fared much better.

"Looks like your dress is ruined," he said.

I followed his eyes down to my dress, not failing to notice how close his gaze was to my chest. I looked back up at him, hating how the sight of his eyes and cocky mouth in the moonlight were enough to rob me of my breath. He looked so much like Rich, which I knew was stupidly obvious, but even his expression reminded me of Rich. "It's fine. I have worn this thing like three times in five years. My dad doesn't really drag us along to his functions as often these days. I guess there's no legitimate threats to his seat as mayor, so he's getting lazy about it."

"That's right," Cade said. "You're the mayor's daughter. Somehow I'd forgotten that." He grinned a little wolfishly. "Some guys are into that sort of thing, you know. I bet the locals are crazy about you."

I laughed. I wasn't sure how to respond to that, so I decided to pop a chocolate tart in my mouth. Whoever catered this party was a wizard with sweets. I closed my eyes and groaned in satisfaction. "If this is what being rich tastes like, sign me up."

"Somehow you don't strike me as the kind of girl who chases after money."

I licked my fingers clean and shrugged. "I'm happy if I have enough money to get pizza once a week, go to the movies every once in a while, and buy materials for my . . ." I coughed and cleared my throat suddenly, realizing how pathetic what I was about to say was going to sound. "Wow, it's a little chilly out tonight."

Cade saw straight through my feeble deception. "Oh no. One, you're a terrible liar. Two, I will never stop until I know what you were about to say. I can see it in your eyes. It's embarrassing, isn't it?"

"You'll laugh."

"Yes, I probably will. I like laughing, so tell me."

"No. I mean you'll laugh *at* me."

"I promise, if I laugh, it'll be with you. But I also promise I will never drop this so long as I'm breathing. I need to know."

"I was just going to say as long as I have thread, I'm happy. I have a side hobby. That's it. So can we talk about something else now?"

"Not so fast. A side hobby? Do you make clothes or something?"

"Yep. Exactly."

He waited, eyes narrowing. "That's not the whole story. Spit it out, Kira. There's more. I know there is."

"I make rodent sweaters, okay? I sell them online. It's seriously not as weird as—"

That was as long as he lasted before throwing his head back and laughing.

I grinned as I watched him. His laughter was contagious, and pretty soon I was laughing right along with him.

"So, wait," he said, still smiling wide. "People buy them?"

"Some people do, yes. Hairless rats really like them, but some people just want something nice to put on their rodents for pictures or even just for wearing around the house."

His lips were quivering, and I could tell he was making an effort not to burst out laughing again. "Right. Because a mouse has to have something slick for those lazy days around the house."

"Don't make fun of it," I warned. "And people dress up their dogs, so it's really not as out there as you're making it out to be. Not everyone has a big enough place for a pet dog. Some people can only have a small pet."

He held his hands up. "I'm not judging. It just feels a little like someone opened a window up on a part of the world I never knew existed. Does this mean you have a pet rat with a massive collection of sweaters too?"

"I wish. I live in a condo with a strict no-pet policy."

"Do I even want to ask how you got started making rodent sweaters in the first place?"

"The first one was just a joke. I had a pet rat back in college, and I wanted to do a funny photo shoot for my profile picture. You know, the kind where someone's face is huge and kind of transparent in the background and everyone's staring off into the distance? Anyway, I realized that every time I got stressed about finals or just about life, making the little clothes helped calm me down. I liked it, I guess, and . . . yeah, the rest is history."

He was grinning. "History might be a slight overstatement."

I rocked sideways to bump him with my shoulder, but I was smiling too. "Jerk." My smile faded as a comfortable silence stretched between us. The sounds of the party drifted across the property to where we sat.

On so many levels, I felt guilty sitting here with Cade. It wasn't because of Rich. That man could go screw himself for all I cared. He'd proven what kind of person he was seven years ago, and I had no space in my life for somebody spiteful and cruel. I felt guilty because I knew what Miranda and Iris would think if they saw me here. I knew in my heart that I'd never let anything physical happen between Cade and me, but it felt like I was dangling my foot in the waters, just to get a taste of what it would feel like. It was the emotional equivalent of cheating, except I wasn't cheating on a person. I was cheating on the promise.

Cade popped one of the desserts in his mouth and smiled over at me, wiggling his eyebrows as he chewed. "Damn," he said once he swallowed. "That one was good."

"They're all good."

We sat for a few minutes longer, just eating and watching the sky while distant music and laughter washed over us.

"It's kind of romantic," he said finally. "Sitting just outside parties, I mean. I've always liked this. Even back in the high school days. Some of my favorite moments were the quiet ones when I'd slip away from a dance or beneath the bleachers after a football game. Just somewhere quiet." He laughed softly. "Not too quiet, though, I guess. I actually think I had to hear the sound of the party or the crowd not too far away. Like I needed to know it was there waiting for me when I was ready to go back. It sounds kind of pathetic when I put it like that."

"No," I said. I was surprised to hear Cade King opening up like this. I was surprised by a lot of what I'd seen from him tonight. The Cade I remembered in school was wild and always causing some kind of trouble. Tonight, he seemed more thoughtful and introspective. I guess I shouldn't have been so surprised that seven years could change a man. "I get what you mean. I think it's just human nature. Most people would feel weird just saying, *Hey, wanna go sit on a hill and stare at the stars while we talk?* Wandering off from the party gives us an excuse to do something we wanted to do all along."

He nodded slowly. "It's too bad it doesn't give us an excuse to do everything we've wanted to do all along."

My skin prickled a little at the tone in his voice, and when I met his eyes I felt all the unspoken promise there, dangling between us like candied poison. I looked away, smiling as if he'd said something funny. "What about the girl you were with?" I asked.

"What about her? She's in the party and you're here."

I bristled a little. "I'm not—" I clamped my mouth shut. I was about to say I'm not interested in being his *side chick*. What I should've been saying was that I wasn't interested in being his chick in any form or fashion. I had the pact to think of, and I knew Iris would probably jab me with something more sinister than her nightstick if I made a move on Cade. She could pretend to hate him all she wanted, but in her mind, he was still her first real love. I had let the party and the night get to my head enough, and it was time to come back to reality. "You know, I probably should be getting back to the party."

He looked at the haul of desserts still in my lap. He slid his fore-finger across my arm, gathering a small glob of whipped cream that he sucked from his fingertip. "Careful in there. With you looking like that, somebody might get the idea that you're on the menu."

"The kids' menu, maybe." I paused, replayed what I'd just said, and then frowned. "Wait. No." I laughed at my own stupidity. "Okay, that sounded really wrong. I meant like I wasn't—" I settled for sighing and pressing my fingers over my eyes.

Cade just chuckled. "I like that about you, Kira."

"What? That I sometimes say things that make me sound like a closeted pedophile?"

"No. That you don't always stop to calculate what you'll say. It's refreshing."

"Oh." Despite the thrumming warning in my brain telling me to step away from the King brother before I betrayed the pact, I blushed. "Well, thank you."

"Hey," a voice called from the top of the hill. "Nick said he saw you coming out here with Kira, and I—" He trailed off, and when I looked up, it felt like my eyes were playing tricks on me.

I saw Cade standing at the top of the hill. *And I saw Cade sitting beside me.*

Chapter 6
RICH

Kira was frowning between Cade and me. He still stood at the top of the hill with a confused look on his face. I was still beside Kira with my heart in my throat and the taste of whipped cream on my tongue. I'd watched the goose bumps roll across her skin when I touched her, and I knew she was feeling the same electrical buzz in the air that I felt.

"What the fuck were you two doing down here?" asked Cade. "Is this some kind of food porn thing? You should've got a kiddie pool, at least. That way the grass doesn't get all mixed in with the food." He started walking down the hill toward us, still shouting. "And next time, take off your clothes, you idiots. It's all fun and games until the cleaner tells you he can't get honey stains out of your tie. Trust me. I've been there."

He leaned down and plucked a chocolate-covered cherry from my lap. He stuck it in his mouth and made a kind of garbled attempt at speech while looking between us and smiling. I knew he was trying to tie the stem in a knot with his tongue, and I also knew he was too oblivious to realize Kira looked like she was on the verge of slapping me or laughing her ass off—I still couldn't tell which.

He pulled the cherry stem out of his mouth, but it was just chewed in two. "Shit," he said. "I swear I've done it before—oh, hey, Kira. Everything good?"

"You're Cade?" she said slowly, pointing to him.

His eyes darted once to the left and once to the right, and he nodded slowly with a widening smile. "Me Cade. You Kira?"

"And you're?" she asked my feet.

"Rich," I said. Reality hit me full force in the stomach. She'd gotten Cade and me confused. This whole time she thought she was talking to my goddamn brother. "You thought I was him?"

"Your hair," she said, finally looking up at me again. "It's all . . ."

"Oh." I touched my head and smoothed it out. "This idiot decided he was still a child and gave me a noogie right before I ran into you earlier, and I forgot to straighten it out."

She stood suddenly. "I'm sorry. I need to go."

"Can I see you again?" I asked.

"No," she said softly. "No," she said again, firmly this time. "I'm not even convinced you didn't just trick me on purpose." Her expression darkened. I could see her making up her mind, and it wasn't a good conclusion. "Congratulations. You got to make me look like an idiot one more time. I hope it was nostalgic for you."

She stood and let all the desserts in her lap fall to the grass. In seconds, I was left alone on the hill with Cade.

"Yikes," he said. "I've never seen you fail in person with a girl before. That was fun, man. We should do this more often. Kinda like a double date, but not exactly. Next time, I'd go with a little less of the clueless idiot approach and maybe try to project confidence. Just spitballing here, but what if you'd said, *Yeah, I know you thought I was*

Cade the whole time. But I'm basically the discount version of my brother anyway, so what's it going to be? Deal or no dick?"

I got up and brushed off what I could of the mess on my clothes. I felt and looked like an idiot. "*Deal or no dick?* Does that kind of shit actually work for you?"

Cade scraped some chocolate off my shirt and ate it. "Everything works for me. It's not about what you say. It's how you say it. *You're an idiot,*" he said with a big, goofy smile and a pat on my shoulder. "See? Didn't feel so bad when I said it like that, did it?"

"You're an idiot."

"Yep. When you say it like that, it sounds like an insult. But when you say it the way I did, not so bad, right?"

I shook my head. "I forget. Did I give myself the power to fire you?"

"One, you couldn't run the company without me. Two, I'm not the one who smeared chocolate and icing all over my clothes. I'm also not the one who got verbally ass blasted by a high school teacher."

"I didn't get 'ass blasted.' It was just a misunderstanding."

He laughed. "Actually, no, this is better than an ass blasting. You realize she was only talking to you because she thought you were *me.*" He punched my chest. "Bad news, bucko. We're identical. That means you can't even blame it on your looks. It's just you that sucks."

"Are you done?" I asked.

He scraped some frosting from my leg, some strawberry compote from my sleeve, and some more chocolate from my stomach. He squished the mess together into an impromptu sandwich and ate it with a satisfied sound. "Yes. Now I am."

I let him wander back to the party, but I had no interest in following him. I wasn't even trying to date Kira in the first place. The entire reason I endured the fake courtship with Stella was to avoid getting pressured into relationships by my parents. The only thing they cared about was playing an antiquated power game of family names and politics among friends. Women from the right families carried certain status, and that status would trickle back up to my parents. Stella was a Cartier, and the Cartier family was one of the biggest of the big. It was that simple.

I thought about Kira and the way she had looked just minutes ago. I couldn't say if nostalgia was clouding my judgment, but I had felt a kind of lightness with her. Some of the burdens I'd gradually taken on over the years didn't seem as heavy. I didn't feel like I had to choose every word with absolute care.

I refused to acknowledge the way my heart had been pounding when the thought of kissing her had crossed my mind—when I'd wondered if I would taste strawberry or chocolate on her lips first.

I wouldn't think about that, because it had been a mental glitch, like when you can't stop yourself from thinking about swerving into oncoming traffic on the highway. You know there's no way you'd ever do it, but some twisted part of the brain wants to explore the option—no matter how self-destructive it might be.

No. It wasn't romantic interest with Kira. I was competitive to a fault. I'd come to West Valley with a few goals, and one of the smaller goals was to apologize to Kira. She hadn't let me do that, and it was getting hard to think about anything else. That was all. I wanted her to accept my apology, even if she didn't forgive me. Her blatant refusal irked me, and I knew I wasn't even close to giving up.

I stepped out of the limo and took in our new headquarters for the first time. I couldn't help wondering if the massive structure was nothing but a monument to the folly of my brothers and me—like some misguided offering to the three women we'd all left a piece of our hearts with. Misguided or not, I knew we had to get it right. Our company wasn't so big that it couldn't fail if we botched this project.

We'd built a technology empire out in California. In a few short years, our business model had done exactly what it was designed to do.

We cannibalized the competition, used our custom software and training programs to make them more efficient, and then turned around to do what they already did, *only better*. We slapped the Sion name on them and watched the profits soar.

It had been a wild stretch of years since we left West Valley. Everybody we'd ever met had always seemed so sure that my brothers and I would go on to conquer the world. Whether we realized it or not, I think the three of us had bought into it. We drove ourselves so hard because anything less than extraordinary success would've felt like a massive failure. I'd always been driven to a fault. I set a goal to make a billion dollars, and I didn't stop until it happened.

That part had almost felt easy. I'd always known where I was headed. I had a target, and I had the combined capabilities of my brothers and me at my disposal. And then, two years ago, we reached our goal.

I never stopped to wonder what I'd do or what I expected when we made it. For so many years, the idea of a billion dollars had loomed in the distance. It stopped being a goal with a purpose. I didn't want a billion dollars to buy a yacht or build a mansion. It wasn't to impress people. I wanted it because I'd decided to chase it. Maybe that was what made me so good at chasing my goals down so relentlessly. I distilled them into their purest, most basic form. I let nothing cloud my vision. I never felt tempted to stop or that I'd done *good enough*, because the only thing that counted was the full realization of my goal.

After reaching a billion, I thought the next thing would materialize before long. Some new purpose and drive would strike me like inspiration, and the next cycle of blind pursuit would begin. Except it didn't. A month passed, then a year, then two. I was just going through the motions, and even as our wealth continued to grow exponentially, I felt numb.

Until West Valley. I hadn't realized it until now, but I already had my next goal.

Kira Summerland.

The thought made chills prickle across my skin. I knew myself well enough to know how dangerous it was to set my sights on a person—a woman. But maybe I could control it. I couldn't be sure, but I thought I might need only her forgiveness. With that dark chapter of my past closed, maybe then I could finally put my full energy back into the company and move forward. *Move on.*

My parents arrived a few minutes after me. They, along with a modest entourage of unrecognizable faces, arrived in a convoy of luxury supercars. Despite the heat, they all emerged wearing ridiculous outfits like we were going to walk the red carpet to an event instead of tour a construction site. A dozen or so local media members were already crouched around the parking lot and snapping pictures of everyone. I still couldn't understand why there was a market for pictures of people like us doing nothing but coming and going from places.

I only distantly became aware of the snapping of camera shutters and the glare of flashing lights. It was the kind of thing you never completely got used to but learned to tolerate.

I cut a straight path through the media and my family toward the building. My brothers were just as eager to break away from the crowd and join me.

"Nothing like slapping down a giant-ass building to assert your masculinity, is there?" Cade asked once we'd put some distance between ourselves and the crowd still lingering around the curb.

"It's not an exclusively masculine thing to do, though," Nick said. "A woman could do it. I'd say it's more about having money than having a dick."

"He has a point," I said.

Cade made a dismissive sound. "Nick always 'has a point,' but it's a flaccid one. It's simple. There's nothing more masculine than having a dick, dumb asses."

"That's not even what we were arguing about," Nick said. "You said—"

"Maybe you were arguing. *I* was making a point. And there's no bigger point than my dick."

I snorted and Nick shook his head in disbelief.

"The scary part is that he really thinks he just won," Nick said to me.

"If ignorance is bliss, being Cade is ecstasy," I said.

"Fuck," Cade said with a huge grin. "Thanks for the pickup line. I bet girls will eat that up. Maybe I'll change the last part to *banging* Cade is ecstasy, though."

"Anytime. Just let me know how it goes after you try it."

We were met inside by Mayor Summerland instead of the project manager I'd been expecting. Had it not been for the fact that he had Kira's eyes, I could've forgotten he was her father.

"Mayor Summerland," I said, reaching to shake his hand. "I didn't expect to see you here."

"No? The Beatles are in West Valley, and they're building their mecca. You don't think I'd want to see it in person?" He was smiling a politician's smile. Wide, toothy, and artificial. He even *looked* like a politician. He was clean cut and inoffensive in every way. His hair wasn't too long or too short, and it wasn't completely brown or completely gray. He wasn't ugly or attractive. He was a perfect, unassuming medium— the kind of guy the masses could settle on as a reasonable compromise. Yet there was a predatory glint in his eyes up close that would've stopped me from doing any kind of business with the man if I had a choice.

"We're hardly the Beatles," Nick said.

"He's right," Cade agreed. "We make the Beatles look like Bieber."

I shot him a look. "You can't even play a harmonica without getting a bloody nose."

He punched my shoulder. "One goddamn time. I told you too. It was an allergy thing. There must have been silver in it, and you know how I get—"

"It's quite all right," Mayor Summerland said. He still wore that plastered-on smile. "I like the bravado, actually. And hey, for West Valley, maybe you guys are bigger than the Beatles, right? Our own homegrown billionaires. It's quite the story." He was looking at Cade, who was eating up the praise. "I get the impression you boys like making a splash. Am I wrong?"

"We're not here to make a—" I started.

"Big-ass splashes," Cade agreed. "Belly-flop-off-the-high-dive-level splashes."

I saw Nick folding his arms beside me. He was probably the most perceptive of the three of us, but he was also the least confrontational, at least when it came to matters outside the family. I knew he was already reading Mayor Summerland like a book, but he probably wanted to wait and see how the conversation played out before jumping in.

Mayor Summerland winked and reached to shake Cade's hand again. He squeezed Cade's forearm with his free hand and laughed like he'd said something funny. "I'll keep my ear to the ground. Who knows, maybe some opportunities to get your name out around town in a good light will pop up."

"I think we'll be fine," I said.

"Oh?" he asked. "It's just that I've heard some rumblings. People upset about all the construction or the road closures while they worked on this headquarters of yours. Anger about the secrecy until now. And this isn't coming from me, mind you," he said, holding up his palms in innocence, "but I've even heard some unrest about all the techies this place is going to bring in to our little town. You know, people like their front porches and their rocking chairs. They just don't want to see farms getting turned into strip malls with computer stores and that sort of nonsense."

"We had all our permits approved and run through the state, Mayor Summerland," I said a little coldly. "So you can tell *them* we're operating completely legal. The employees we bring to the area should help local businesses and give a big boost to the economy around here. Maybe people should think about that too."

"Oh, sure," he agreed. "All I'm saying is a little act of good grace would go a long way toward quieting down those whispers. West Valley has grown over the years, but it's still a small town at heart, Mr. King. And a small town is like a pretty girl. You can't just show up with money and expect to grab her by the ass. You've got to win her heart first. Take her on a couple dates, *buy her something nice*, you know?" He laughed and slapped my shoulder with the back of his hand like we were old buddies. His voice lowered, and I didn't miss the menace there. "You wouldn't treat my *town* like that, would you?"

I knew we weren't just talking about West Valley anymore, but I wasn't about to let this devolve into a personal squabble involving Kira. "And what would pass for buying this town of yours something nice, exactly?"

"It's a bribe," Cade whispered. "He's asking for a bribe."

"No shit," I said.

"Easy now, boys. I'm no dirty politician by any stretch. I'm absolutely not asking for your money. I'm simply saying you fine young men have the resources to invest in a few projects here and there around town. Who knows, throw some money at the school football team, or the chess team, for all I care. I just think it'd go a long way toward getting the town on your side."

"Sure," I said. "You're not asking for our money, but you'd like some of our money." My hands were balled up tight with frustration. Just talking to the man felt like taking a bath in slime, and yet I knew on some level he had a point. It wouldn't hurt for us to make a few donations around town and boost our public image. Besides, his idea about donating to the school already had my gears turning.

Kira worked at a school. Unless West Valley High was a miraculous exception to the rule, it probably had dozens of programs that lacked funding. I was willing to bet whatever programs Kira was involved in could use more money too.

"You know, Mr. King," Mr. Summerland said. "A foolish man walks into a trap. A wise man avoids it. But a businessman? He takes advantage of it. Which are you?"

"A businessman," I said. *A wise one.*

Chapter 7

KIRA

I walked slowly around the classroom while my students worked on memorizing their scripts in small groups. It had been almost a week since I stormed away from Rich and Cade at the party. I'd been a lot of things that night. Embarrassed. Pissed. Ashamed. Even if I hadn't mistaken Rich for Cade, I'd sworn to Iris and Miranda that I'd stay away from *all* the King brothers. I wanted to believe it had just been the whirlwind of sights and sounds at the party throwing me off-balance, but I doubted that was true.

I'd had fun with Rich. Even worse, I knew I was secretly disappointed he seemed ready to let me go. I got exactly what I'd wanted, after all. He hadn't tried to contact me since the party. He'd probably already forgotten me for some supermodel, or maybe several supermodels. Besides, we both had our own problems to deal with. I had been saddled with the crumbling theater department no one wanted and a budget that couldn't even buy us a movie ticket, let alone props, costumes, and equipment to put on a respectable play. Of course, he had a national megabusiness to run.

It was better this way. I repeated that line in my head a few times, just like I had the last dozen times Rich and his arrival in West Valley had slid into my thoughts.

Thankfully, I had to pee so badly it was easy to distract myself. I looked at the clock and felt a surge of relief. One more minute until the bell. I could see the teachers' lounge from my window. It was separated from my room by a small, grassy courtyard and a stone table with benches where students would sometimes bring their lunches. I visualized myself fast walking through the crowds, bobbing and weaving to make sure I was the first in the lounge and wouldn't have to wait. I wasn't sure if I *could* wait.

An empty mug of coffee stood tauntingly on my desk. It was about the size of a toddler's head, and I had stupidly filled it to the brim and guzzled every last drop. Just over a week into being a teacher, and I'd already learned bladder management was an essential skill—one I was still failing to master.

Then again, I was failing to master a lot, it seemed. Being a teacher was more complicated than lesson planning and delivery. At the end of the day, I had to try to wrestle the attention and behavior of more than thirty wandering minds. On top of that, I had to try to work around the fact that the least important part of school for most of my students was what came out of my mouth. They were more concerned with who had a crush on whom, what was going on after the football game on Friday, or what the latest drama was.

The school year was a war between the teacher and students, and each day was a battle. Students tried their hardest to break down a teacher's defenses. They tested boundaries like swarms of foot soldiers smashing headfirst against a wall, sacrificing themselves for the greater good of their people. Once one made it through—like the kid who manages to talk without raising his hand—the rest would squeeze through the narrow opening until it was a gaping hole.

Unfortunately, my teacher walls had apparently been made of wet clay, because half my carefully planned classroom rules were already blown apart and forgotten.

"Miss Summerland?" asked a girl in a group that was practicing lines for our modified rendition of *Dracula*. "What kind of props are we going to have for this? Like, will we be able to make a castle out of cardboard or something?"

"Cardboard is cheap," I said cheerily, though the pressure of holding in my pee might have raised my pitch a few octaves. "We could try that."

"And maybe some dresses? Like old-school, medieval stuff." She grinned. "With corsets and cleavage."

"Cleavage?" asked her friend. "I doubt even a corset and medieval dress could press those mosquito bites of yours hard enough together to make cleavage."

"My mom says they'll come late, just like hers did, and they'll still be perky years after yours are dangling past your belt."

"Uh, I don't have to wear a belt, because I actually have these things called hips. You should try them sometime."

"Girls," I said tightly. My bladder was screaming for release, and their conversation was just one of many conversations I wanted to laugh at, but I knew I had to maintain a teacherly neutral. "I'm sorry, but I doubt we're going to have the budget for anything like that. We'll do our best, th—"

The bell rang, and I abandoned all pretense of authority, making a mad rush to be the first out of my room. "Study your lines. Quiz tomorrow," I shouted over my shoulder on the way out. I had made it halfway to the lounge before students even began leaving their classrooms and flooding the corridor.

I tried to walk while simultaneously squeezing my thighs together and praying I wouldn't pee myself. I probably looked like a constipated duck, but I didn't have time to worry about it. I had to go so badly that I thought there was a chance I might propel myself off the toilet when the time came, as if I had one of those water jet packs strapped to my back.

I wove my way through a final group of students before reaching the door of the lounge, knowing I had only seconds before the first wave of teachers would come bearing lunches and full bladders.

I fumbled my keys at the door, yanked it open, and stepped inside the lounge. I vaulted over a chair in my way and yanked the door to the women's restroom open. I took one huge step in before stopping dead in my tracks.

Something had gone terribly wrong. Terribly, terribly wrong.

It looked like a murder scene, except instead of blood, it was poop. On the walls. On the ceiling. On the ground. Everywhere *but* the toilet. The handprints on the wall told a horrible story. I could almost see each step of what had unfolded, from the act to the attempted cover-up and the eventual escape. The sink was even running at full blast, like the poopetrator had tried and failed to cleanse themselves of what they'd done, but no amount of water could wash this away. To paraphrase Macbeth, all Neptune's oceans could not wash the stain of what they'd done from their hands—and probably their pants and shoes.

I staggered backward, mouth open and fingers desperately squeezing my nose closed. My eyes fell to the center of the floor, where it looked like they had even tried to kick some of the evidence down a circular drain. I saw then that there were footprints leading out, and I finally stumbled backward out of the room.

I still had to pee, but violent flashes of the scene I'd just been exposed to were playing in my head like rapid-fire blasts of a strobe light. *The walls. The floor. The mysterious way the toilet was the only thing that remained unscathed.* I had so many questions, but I had to make it to a bathroom. I burst out of the faculty lounge walking as fast as I could. I distantly remembered passing a group of teachers who were heading to the lounge behind me with their lunches in tow. In the back of my mind, I hoped they wouldn't have to see the same thing I'd seen, but I knew they probably would.

I finally found a bathroom. By the time I was done, I knew my lunch would go uneaten, maybe my dinner too.

I was lost in my own thoughts when I stepped out of the restroom a couple of minutes later, and I almost didn't stop when I heard my name.

"Kira," said the voice.

I turned and saw Rich approaching down the hallway. Female students were freezing in their tracks like he trailed a wake of paralyzing fumes. Whispers followed, and when he stopped in front of me, I could already feel the rumors pounding within every student's chest, just begging to be released where they could spread like wildfire. Word of his interruption on the first day already had circulated the school, but I knew this would only make it worse.

"Maybe you should start wearing a name tag," I said. I was trying to sound casual, but my heart was still pounding from what I'd just seen in the faculty bathroom.

He squinted. "You okay?"

"What? Yeah. Why wouldn't I be? I'm fine. *Perfect.*"

He took me in with a slow, searching sweep of his eyes. "Well, I—"

"Hey!" a woman said in a hushed voice from behind me. She came and put her hand on my shoulder. I recognized her as Mrs. Bosch. I had a habit of thinking of the older teachers by their titles, while I thought of the younger teachers by their first names. Mrs. Bosch had been with the school over thirty years, which also meant she'd been around back when I was a student here. I still wasn't completely over the strangeness of that. In a lot of ways, it felt like I'd been allowed backstage at a concert I'd seen a hundred times. Except instead of half-naked rock stars and drugs, it was just a bunch of stale baked goods in the teachers' lounges and awkward team-building exercises.

Mrs. Bosch looked at Rich like he was a stray dog before positioning herself between us for a little privacy. "Are you feeling okay? I heard about . . ."

"I'm fine, why? What did you—" My eyes widened. I replayed the group of teachers I'd fast walked by on my way out of the restroom. I thought about what I'd left behind. The pieces clicked together in my brain and my stomach sank.

"People are talking about some 'violent pooper.' It's ridiculous, but I heard they saw you looking pretty distressed on your way out of the restroom, and—"

The sound of Rich's stifled laughter stabbed through me like knives. I looked past Mrs. Bosch and had no doubt Rich's ears were keen enough to pick up every whispered word.

"This is insane," I said quickly. "I'm not the violent pooper, okay? I had to pee, I went in there, and it was *already* like that. I came here to use a bathroom that wasn't desecrated, and that's all I know."

She squeezed my shoulder and gave me a tight-lipped, sympathetic smile. "Of course, sweetie. Just let me know if you need anything, okay? I have some antacids in my room if you need them next time."

I watched her walk away and then slowly looked back to Rich, who was looking at me with unhidden amusement.

"The violent pooper?" he asked. "Wow. That's quite the title. Do I need to meet with your PR rep next time I want to talk? Get a press badge or something?"

"I'm telling the truth," I said.

"I believe you. Mostly. Though seven years can change a person. And their digestive system."

"Rich," I said warningly.

He smiled. "I'm kidding, Kira. I believe you. And I'll swear on a Bible it wasn't you when the mobs come for justice, okay?"

"Yeah, you're a real saint. Is there a reason you keep showing up at my school at the worst possible times?"

"Yes, actually. I had a chat with your father a few days ago, and he gave me a great idea. It took a little digging, but I hear the theater department is pretty desperately in need of funding."

"No," I said immediately. "I see where this is going, and no."

"What? You're going to deprive your students of the chance to have a great show over a personal grudge?"

"If that's what it takes. I'm not letting this happen."

"I thought you might say that. So I also took the liberty of packaging my offer for the theater department with some renovations to the football fields, the tennis courts, the cafeteria, and the library. I just need every department to sign off on the donations, and we'll be golden. So you can probably see how it'd look if the theater department was the one thing standing between the school and all that funding."

I glared at him. "So this is your great idea? You'll get me to forgive you by being an unforgivable ass again?"

"I'm not sure I see the problem, Kira. I'm offering to give money to your department and your school. I never even said I'd be involved. Hell, I never said you'd have to *see* me to get a dime of it. Where's the part where this makes me an ass?"

"So you're saying you'll just give us all this money, no questions asked?"

A slow grin spread his lips, and I hated how good it looked on him. "Well, I didn't quite say that either."

♥ ♥ ♥

I called an emergency meeting with Iris and Miranda that night.

Iris had to work, and the only way I could get her ear was if Miranda and I rode in the back of her police cruiser while she was out on patrol. Iris was parked by a busy intersection in the grass. To her credit, she was actually watching the traffic with her radar gun aimed across the dash while we talked, even if we weren't technically supposed to be riding along with her.

"I don't like it," Iris said. "Anyone with half a brain can see what he's trying to accomplish from a mile away."

"I agree," Miranda said. "He's making a prostitute of you, Kira. Think about it."

I laughed. "Oh, come on. That is completely ridiculous."

"No, she's right," Iris said. "He's not asking you to *spread 'em and bed 'em* yet, but once he's pumped enough money into your program to get you feeling in his debt, he's going to expect it."

I shook my head. "It's not just my program he's giving money to."

"You're in denial," Miranda said. "You said he's going to personally oversee the way you use the budget for the theater program. Do you think someone like him actually cares what you do with a few thousand dollars?"

"Okay, fine. I admit it's suspicious, and I admit he's definitely trying to pull something. But can't you two have a little faith in me? Just because Rich is trying to insert himself into my life, it doesn't mean I'm going to start liking him."

Iris clicked her tongue and set down the radar gun. "It's not your *life* he's trying to insert himself into." She made a circle with her thumb and forefinger before sliding her index finger in and out, as if I didn't already get her point. "Besides, last time I checked, you don't have to like a guy to give him a blow job."

Miranda choked out a laugh. "Iris!"

Iris grinned. "I'm not talking from personal experience, obviously. I'm just saying. Hate and love are more similar than people realize. Spend all your energy thinking about someone, even if it's because you wish they'd choke on a hot dog, and you're bound to confuse your heart."

"That's horrible." I laughed. "I'm pretty sure people die from choking on hot dogs all the time. You can't joke about something like that."

"That's totally how you'll bite the dust." Iris chuckled. "But the hot dog will belong to Rich."

I heard horns blare outside just before a car blurred through the intersection.

"Shit!" Iris muttered before flicking on the sirens in her car. "I hope your seat belts are on."

"They're not. One seco—"

She slammed on the gas and sent me sliding into Miranda. I very gracefully rolled and scooted back to my seat once Iris straightened the car out. I clicked my seat belt into place and then looked to Miranda, who was glaring at me.

"My boobs aren't airbags," she said.

"No shit," I said, rubbing my elbow. "That felt like trying to break my fall with two single bubbles from a roll of Bubble Wrap."

Miranda sat up a little straighter and lowered her eyebrows even more. "Yeah, well, I bet jogging is really fun when those ridiculous things keep uppercutting you in the chin."

"It's called a sports bra."

She scoffed. "Do they make an industrial-strength variety?"

"Could you two shut up, please?" Iris asked through gritted teeth. Once the driver realized Iris was following, they both pulled to the shoulder.

"Stay in the car." Iris got out with a warning look to Miranda and me, as if we were kids in the back of our mom's minivan.

"I have to pee," I said quickly.

Iris sighed. "Seriously?"

I shrugged. "These seats are waterproof, right? Or you could just open my—"

"Get back in the car when you're done," Iris said. She pulled my door open and walked off. Miranda and I shared a silent look; then we both got out to follow Iris and eavesdrop.

The car she had followed looked fancy. *Very fancy.* When the driver's side door opened, it opened *up* instead of out and made a futuristic whooshing noise.

I'd mistaken Rich for his twin at the party last week, but this time there was no mistaking it. Cade King wore a button-down shirt with the sleeves rolled up, and his hair was in its trademark careless disarray. He took in the three of us and spread his arms wide like he was about to welcome us into a group hug.

"The solemn sisters!" he said, laughing. "What are you three doing out together? Fighting crime? You forgot the spandex."

"Tonight, it looks like you're crime. And I'd rather punch crime in the dick than fight it." Iris turned to us. "Get back in the car." There was an extra edge to her voice, and I had a good idea why. Cade and Iris had history.

For a minute, I honestly considered trying to take her gun away, but I knew Iris wasn't that hotheaded. Most likely, at least.

"Any chance you can let me off with a warning, officer? Or maybe just a light, sensual cavity search?" Cade said.

Iris pulled a pad from her belt and started writing something down. "Sure. It's two for one tonight. You can get a ticket *and* a warning. My friends and I aren't interested in you, your brothers, or any half-hearted apologies you may have planned."

If Cade was bothered by the venom in her words, he showed no sign of it. "Apologies? I hadn't planned on making any. And I wasn't talking to your friends. I was talking to you."

She pressed the ticket to his chest, but he let it fall to the ground when she pulled her hand away.

"That's it?" he asked.

"No," Miranda said. She started stomping toward Cade, but I took her arm and held her back as well as I could. Unfortunately, Miranda was stronger than she looked, and I was gradually getting dragged forward on my heels. "You guys can just *leave* West Valley while you're at it."

I stifled a laugh. "That's your best line?" I whispered to her.

Cade was smiling too. He took a few steps toward us. "You know, my little brother still has a thing for you. I can see why. You're feisty. Probably too feisty for him to handle, even."

"And you're an ass," Miranda spat.

"Girls," Iris said firmly, and I was impressed at how officerly she sounded. "In the cruiser. Now. Let me do my job."

I backed off, mainly because I didn't want Iris to start prodding me with her nightstick again.

Cade raised an eyebrow at Iris. "Is it time for the frisk? I promise, I'm definitely packing some heat. You'd better do a thorough pat down."

Iris gave us a final glare that sent us both reluctantly back to the car. In the end, Cade didn't get frisked, but judging from the mood Iris was in when she came back, he did get the last word.

Chapter 8
RICH

Principal Lockett insisted on giving me a personal escort through the school every time I showed up. He walked just a step in front of me, as if I needed a five-foot-five balding bodyguard to fight my way through stray students on their way to use the bathroom or get water.

"It's really quite admirable," he said. He was huffing for breath from our walk through the halls but didn't show any signs of wanting to slow his pace. "A man of your means still thinking of giving back."

"Ambition can get in the way of what's important. I'll be the first to admit it. I'm ready to start making things right, though."

He nodded sagely. "Very wise. I do wonder why you're paying such particular interest to the allocation of funds for the theater department. I'd think you might want to see the plans for what we're going to do with the athletics department or even the library."

An image of Kira flashed in my mind. I saw the look in her eyes— old, *old* anger with a hint of curiosity. It was glimpsing something behind all the hatred that had me so interested, I thought. Trap a man in the dark with no sign of light and he'd resign himself to his fate, but give him the faintest sign of the sun and he'd try to fight his way free until his last breath.

Coming home to West Valley made me realize how deeply I'd buried the regret over what happened all those years ago. It hadn't seemed like much at the time. A few words. A careless, cruel act of petty revenge. I'd been an idiot, and if she never forgave me for it, I couldn't even blame her. Still, it didn't mean I wasn't going to try.

"Perhaps it was an old hobby?" Principal Lockett prodded when I didn't respond. "A missed opportunity to feel the lights of the stage and the roar of the crowd." He wiggled his eyebrows and hissed in imitation. "I have to confess. I always thought I would've been a natural on the stage, but never quite had the stature to land a leading role. Maybe the two of us aren't so different, aside from the obvious points, at least."

"Maybe not," I said. "Thanks for walking me here." I patted him on the shoulder a little too hard apparently, because his knees buckled. "Sorry," I said, patting him again, more lightly this time.

Kira was sitting on the stage in the auditorium with a stack of papers on her lap and a mess of discarded folders to the side of her. She looked up when I came in and immediately jerked her head back down to her work.

"You can pretend I'm not here if you want, but I grew up with a brain-dead identical twin. I'm used to one-sided conversations."

"I have a lot of papers to grade, and this is my planning period," she said.

I looked around. "I don't see any teacher's assistants. Want a hand?"

She cocked an eyebrow. "From you? No. I'll pass."

I moved to the stage and hopped up to sit beside her. I took a peek at what she was grading, but she turned the papers to the side and scowled.

"I'll make you a deal," I said. "Ask me a random question from the quiz. If I get it right, you let me help. If I get it wrong, I'll leave."

"You'll leave West Valley?" she asked.

"Damn." I laughed. "No. The school. You really want me gone that badly?"

She watched me, but instead of answering, her eyes fell to the quiz. She was clearly searching for the most difficult question she could find. "How does Ophelia die in *Hamlet*?"

I looked up to the single stage light that burned bright overhead, searching my past for answers. I knew I had read *Hamlet* in high school, but the details were fuzzy. Thankfully, I'd always had a good memory—it was part of what made me so good at my job. "Got it," I said with a grin.

The look of fear on Kira's face was almost enough to make me laugh.

"Suicide."

Kira straightened. I could see in her eyes she thought she had me cornered. "Not detailed enough. How did—"

"She drowned herself." I did laugh then, because Kira didn't bother hiding an ounce of her annoyance. "Sorry. Good memory." I tapped my temple.

"Here," she said. Her voice was cold, and she was making an effort to keep her eyes down and away from mine. "You can grade these. This is the answer key." She shoved a small stack of papers at me and then set a single sheet down between us with the answers on it.

I took to the work quietly for a few minutes. Sitting beside her was oddly thrilling, even though nothing about my reunion with Kira had been going the way I'd expected. From that first day when I interrupted her class, to the party, and finally to catching her during her planning period, she had shut me down at every turn. Reality was slowly dawning on me.

Seeing her coldness was a slap in the face—a stark reminder that I had well and truly fucked up seven years ago. It took a special kind of grudge to grow stronger over time, but I was almost certain hers had festered and rotted like a wound. My coming back to West Valley was an explosion of foul memories for her.

"What will it take?" I asked.

"Six out of ten is a passing grade."

"No. For you to forgive me. Or at least talk to me."

She shook her head, eyes searching the empty seats. "You don't get it, do you? It's not about forgiving you. Forget what you did back then. I'm still alive and I'm doing fine. It's about the fact that I know what you're capable of, so I'd be an idiot to blindly trust that you're different now."

I let her words sink in and realized she had a point.

"Okay," I said slowly. "Then I'll prove it to you."

She sighed. "I don't want proof, Rich. I just want to get on with my life."

"Yeah, I get it, but I'm not really giving you a choice. We've invested too much money coming here for me to just disappear, and this isn't that big of a town. You're stuck with me, so you might as well give me a chance to redeem myself."

"God. You really don't give up, do you?"

"No, I don't. That's why I'm going to help coach your play."

She glared at me, then rolled her eyes. It was probably wishful thinking, but I thought she might be smiling a little. "It's direct," she said. "You don't coach a play. You direct it."

"Fine. I'll help direct your play."

"Let me guess. If I say no, you'll throw a bunch of money around until my life is ruined?"

"That's a really pessimistic way of looking at things."

"Is it wrong?"

"Not exactly, no. I'm just saying the more optimistic perspective is that cooperating means your school gets all the funding it could ever want."

I had a feeling I knew what she was thinking from the look in her eyes, and it stung. I was trying to make light of it, but I knew what I was doing was crossing every line I could. If I thought there was another way, I would've taken it, but she wasn't giving me many options.

"Admit it," I said when she didn't respond. "We had a good time together at the party. You might've thought I was my brother, but that was me and you talking. When you forgot to hate me, we got along."

"I don't hate you, Rich. I just don't want anything to do with you."

"Damn," I said. "Then winning you over is going to be a real challenge, isn't it?"

She gave me a sideways grin. The look on her face told me she wasn't being entirely honest. She was saying what she wanted to be the truth, but I suspected that inside she was battling with her emotions. "I can't decide if you're determined or just stupid."

I laughed. "If I get a vote, I'm going with determined."

She watched me, still wearing that grin of hers.

I felt a warm stirring sensation in my chest as I looked at her. In a sudden rush of realization, I knew I wanted more than her forgiveness. I wanted the smile she was holding back. I wanted her to look at me like she had when she thought I was my brother, without the reservation behind every expression. I wanted everything she had to offer, and my need for it bordered on greed.

"Then tell me," she said. "What happens when the determined man meets an immovable object?"

"The immovable object, huh?" I asked. I rocked sideways, bumping into her with my shoulder. I meant to give her only a slight shove, but she must've been caught completely off guard, because she toppled sideways and then nearly rolled off the stage.

I managed to catch her by the arm and straighten her back up. To my relief, she was smiling. "He turns his body into a battering ram, apparently," she said, laughing.

"Sorry." I'd never been one to blush, but my cheeks felt warm. *Since when was I clumsy too?* "It was supposed to be just a little nudge. Are you okay?"

"I'm fine. And apparently I'm not as immovable as I was making myself out to be. I guess I should be more worried about your unwanted advances if that's your strategy, though."

I felt a smile spread slowly across my lips. "No. Brute force wouldn't work with you. I think your case calls for a strategy of subtle, slow seduction over a long period of time. Carefully planned advances. Strategic compliments. Chocolate. Lots of chocolate."

"Bribery, then? I'll admit, chocolate might work. Just a little bit. But I'm proud to say I've never been seduced, and I don't plan to start anytime soon. You can help with the play, but that's it. Iris and Miranda would kill me if I agreed to anything more. Honestly, they'll probably give me hell even for this."

"Hmm." I stroked my chin. "I see. So you're saying it's not that you don't want to go on a date with me. It's just that you're worried about your friends finding out. I can work with that."

"No, no," she said, laughing. "That's not what I said."

"But it's what you meant."

She sighed. "I'm not hiding anything from my friends, Rich. And in all honesty, *yes*, I did have a good time talking to you at the party. But a date? When did this go from me forgiving you to me going on a date with you?"

"If we're going to direct this play together, I need to pick your brain. I have these tickets to a magician show and no one to go with. Maybe you could come with me, and we could talk after the show. Nobody has to call it a date. Think of it as a business meeting."

She stared at me like she was waiting for me to reveal the punch line of a joke. "Rich . . ."

"I get it," I said. "I wish I could just drop it too. But I can't, and I'm going to keep obsessing over this until you at least give me a shot. So we could make it pleasant, or you're going to have to see just how pathetic this can get if you keep making me beg."

Kira crossed her arms, but I thought I saw amusement in her eyes. "Richard King begging? I might actually enjoy that."

"Just something fun to do while we talk details. That's all it'd be."

"Just to be clear, I don't really have a choice, right?"

"You could choose to say no, but then I'll choose to keep thinking up ways to get you to talk to me. Your choice. Rip the Band-Aid off fast, or rip it off slow."

"I'll go to this thing with you, but it's not a date. You also have to let me bring Iris and Miranda."

I laughed. "Uh, no. I said I wanted it to be fun, not a reenactment of the Spanish Inquisition."

"Those are my terms. You want me to go, then it's all three of us."

I watched her for a few seconds, and my stomach sank. She was serious. Even as my frustration with her surged, I realized I was enjoying this—the push and pull. She didn't just roll over and give me what I wanted. She made me work for it, and I respected her for that. Kira was going to learn I was also just as stubborn, and I didn't like losing.

"I'm going to regret agreeing to this, aren't I?" I asked.

Chapter 9

KIRA

I waited with Miranda and Iris just inside a hangar on a private runway. Until a few minutes ago, I'd had no idea this place existed. A luxury airplane was parked in front of us, and the pilot was already warming the engines up.

"You said it was just going to be a magic show," Iris said. "You never said the magic show was Rich King whipping out his money dick and waving it around. I mean, look at that thing. It's ridiculous." She was glaring at me, and she had a right to. Iris and Miranda hadn't really bought my story about the unavoidable nature of Rich and his little scheme. I wasn't sure they'd believed me when I claimed I was going along with this only to get him off my back either. I could hardly blame them. I still wasn't sure I believed myself.

"Money dick?" I asked.

"Every guy has one. It's just that normal guys show off their money dick by picking up the tab for dinner. They buy you a drink. Maybe they pick you up in a nice car. It's the financial equivalent of an unsolicited dick pic. You turn around and *boom*. It's right there, in your face. They want to sneak straight past reason and protocol by blowing your ovaries out of your stomach in a single shot."

Miranda rolled her eyes. "You've put way too much thought into this."

Iris just gestured to the plane. "This is the money dick equivalent of getting texted a dick the size of a bodybuilder's forearm. Big, thick veins. Just bulging—"

"I get it," I said. "But I agree with Miranda. You're thinking too hard about this. Rich King has tons of money, and people with tons of money use private jets to get around. That's all this is. He probably didn't even think twice about it."

"Right." Iris crossed her arms. "I'm sure Rich is completely oblivious to the effect a private jet might have on the woman he's trying to seduce. Just like I'm sure you're not actually so naive that you think this is really supposed to be a platonic experience."

"I told you what I knew," I said through gritted teeth. I was looking around for Rich but saw only a nervous-looking guy a few years younger than us who was moving bags into the airplane. He wore a suit that didn't quite fit and kept glancing at us like he was expecting us to attack at any moment.

"She does have a point," Miranda said. "You have to realize this is a thinly veiled plan. Watch. Rich will do whatever he can to separate us as soon as he can. I'm sure he only agreed we could come because he had some kind of plan to get rid of us."

"Yep," Iris said. "Hired assassin. That's my bet."

A sleek black car pulled up on the runway and parked just in front of us. My stomach clenched when I saw *all three* King brothers get out.

"No," Miranda said. She took a step backward, but Nick moved toward her, arm outstretched.

"Hey, I was just—" Nick started.

Miranda held her hands up and stormed back toward the car we'd come together in. "I'll wait two minutes. Anyone who wants a ride back had better be in the car by then."

Iris looked at Cade, who was watching her with an amused little smile.

"Wipe that look off your face," she snapped.

Cade's grin widened. "Why? You're cute when you get riled up."

"I'll be in the car with Miranda," Iris said.

"Sorry," Rich said. "When my brothers heard all the West Valley girls were coming, I couldn't stop them."

"I'm sure," I said. "Just like I'm sure you had no idea your brothers coming along would scare my friends off. I can't just leave without them. Sorry. I need to go too."

"What if I send my brothers away?" Rich asked.

"Uh," Cade said, holding up a finger. "I object. I happen to fucking love magic, magic shows, magicians, and anything remotely related to magic. You're not sending me away unless you have something equally awesome for me to do."

"You can touch my dinosaur bones," Rich said. He suddenly looked very serious. "But if you break them, I will kill you."

"You're serious?" Cade asked. "I can?"

"Nick is going to supervise."

Nick sighed but nodded his head. "Probably a good idea. Last time Cade was alone with your dinosaur collection, he used a raptor femur like a baseball bat and broke a petrified dinosaur egg."

"You're the one who threw it to me," Cade said.

Nick shot Rich a guilty look. "He's manipulative, and to be fair, I read online that petrified eggs were supposed to be really hard."

"You can both be idiots, but at least with Nick there, I know the damage will be minimized."

"Fine, whatever. Deal," Cade said. He waved for Nick to get in the car with him, and seconds later, I was standing alone with Rich on the runway and the kid in the suit who had finished loading all the suitcases.

I shook my head. "Iris and Miranda are never going to forgive me if I don't go back to the car."

"Tell them I kidnapped you. Or maybe blackmail?"

"No. The more they hate you, the harder they'll be on me." I felt like collapsing in exhaustion at the sight of him standing there. He looked so poised. So perfect. He was an unstoppable force, and he wasn't going to quit until he got what he wanted from me. Little by little, his stubborn persistence was starting to charm me, no matter how hard I tried to fight it.

"But you'll come?" he asked.

I almost laughed at how excited he sounded. Moments ago, I'd seen every ounce of the powerful businessman he could be—how he could intimidate and command with a flicker of his features and the tone of his voice. But the idea of my coming to the magic show with him made all of that melt away. I nodded.

"I'll come. It's still not a date."

He reached for my hand, which I grudgingly let him take as he led me toward the small staircase leading inside the plane. "Jalen, take her coat."

"Just take it off her?" he asked shakily. "What if she—"

"I'm fine," I said, then paused. "Is he the pilot?"

"He's my personal assistant. Sort of."

"No 'sort of' about it," Jalen said with a wide smile. "I'm his personal assistant. *All the way.*"

Rich cringed. "You're making it sound weird now."

"Sorry. I just mean I help him with anything he needs. Anytime."

"We got it," Rich said. He put his hand on my back to urge me inside the plane and to a seat.

The seat was comfier than an airplane seat had any right to be. Then again, it looked more like we were in a five-star hotel lobby than an airplane. Most of the windows were covered by delicate curtains, the floor was padded with carpets, and the interior walls were accented with dark wood paneling. "If you're trying to impress me with your money, it's not working. Mostly, anyway," I said.

Rich sat in the chair beside mine, both of which swiveled. He twisted in his to sweep those calculating eyes of his over me. "I did say I was desperate, didn't I? There's no lame trick I won't resort to, and I have plenty of lame tricks."

I was about to respond when an older woman and a man boarded the plane. Rich shot up to his feet, jaw clenched.

"What are you two—" he started.

"Putting out a fire, it looks like," said the man. He turned to me, and I thought I saw something familiar in his face. "I'm Harper King. This is my wife, Edna. And this"—he gestured to the door—"is the door. Don't let it hit you on the way out."

I straightened. I was a lot of things, and stubborn was one of them. The fastest way to get me to want to do something was usually to tell me not to do it. "It's an airplane door. It doesn't close on its own. And I don't plan on leaving, so I wouldn't need to worry about it anyway."

Rich was watching me with wide, excited eyes. I could've laughed. I'd obviously chosen the right tactic by giving his parents some sass, not that I was trying to impress him.

"I want her off this plane. *Now*," Edna said. I had trouble figuring out who she was speaking to because her nose was tilted up so high.

Jalen looked to Rich. "Am I supposed to—"

"No," Rich said. "Thank you for visiting *my plane*. But Kira is just a friend. I'm still very much committed to Stella. Jalen, please help my parents down the stairs. They're getting up there in years, and I'd hate for them to fall."

"Rich . . ." Harper said. "This is a mistake."

"Jalen," Rich said again.

Jalen looked like he'd rather try to wrestle a pair of bulls than escort Rich's parents off the plane, but he put his arms out and started ushering them toward the stairs. "If you'll watch your heads," he muttered.

Once Rich's parents were gone and Jalen was up near the cockpit, I turned to Rich. "Stella? That's the girl you were with at the party, right? Is she your girlfriend?"

"What?" he asked. "Don't you follow the tabloids?"

"No. Believe it or not, I've done a pretty good job pretending you never existed until this past week."

"Stella is . . ." He paused, and I suspected he was putting a great deal of thought into the words he chose. "She's the reason you can stop suspecting I'm trying something devious with you."

"So she's your girlfriend?" I asked.

There was another long pause. "For about a month, so far."

I thought back to the party. It hadn't clicked, because I had thought I was looking at Cade when I first saw him with a woman at his side. It had been Rich, though, and the icy, princess-like woman at his side had been Stella. I was clearly doing a poor job of hating Rich, because a burst of jealousy spread through me. "That's wonderful. And does your girlfriend of about a month know just the two of us are going to a magic show together?"

"Yes. And you said it yourself. It's not a date, right?"

"Yes. I said something like that."

Chapter 10

RICH

We landed at a small private airport a few minutes from the restaurant. After a short drive, we arrived at the seaside restaurant with time to spare.

It was an older building on a rocky stretch of the coast. We were taken upstairs to an open rooftop full of seating. A live band played quiet jazz, and a few other couples were already drinking wine when we arrived. The view was incredible. To our right, the ocean stretched out wide, giving us a perfect shot of the waves and the miles of beachfront mansions. To our left, we could see the charming little historic city where people on beach cruiser bikes were almost more common than cars.

"This wasn't the kind of place I expected," Kira said after the waiter set down two glasses for us and a pitcher of cold water.

Kira looked incredible. I could tell she'd made a point of not dressing too fancy. She didn't want me to think she'd been anticipating our evening together, and she definitely didn't want me to think she was trying to impress me. But Kira probably could have rolled out of bed with her hair plastered to her cheek by drool and I'd still be impressed.

She was real, more real than the women I'd wasted my time with since leaving West Valley seven years ago. The fact that she was making such an effort to push me away told me as much. If she cared about my money or my fame more than who I was, she would've given in that first day outside her classroom. And if she'd given in, I think I would've lost interest immediately. I wondered how that would infuriate her—if she knew the fastest way to shake me off would've been for her to act like she wanted to date me. But that ship had sailed. I didn't know if there was anything she could do to make me lose interest now.

"I'm glad it's not what you expected," I said. "What were you thinking? A dingy, dark room with a guy in a cheap suit telling jokes?"

"Something like that." She looked around the patio, turning in her chair to look behind us. "I don't see a magician."

"Voilà," I said, spreading my hands. "He's very talented."

Kira smirked. "Funny. Seriously, though. Where is he?"

"He circulates around the tables. It's a casual kind of thing. Sometimes he barely does anything with you and your group. Other times he'll practically be glued to your table."

"Wait. You've been here before? This is only, what, an hour drive from West Valley?"

"Hour and a half, depending on traffic."

"Why come all the way out here before now?"

I shrugged. I had an answer, but it wasn't one I was about to share with her. "A man isn't allowed to get homesick?"

She narrowed her eyes. "This is an hour and a half from home."

"Maybe I didn't want to cause a stir."

"For some reason, I find that surprising."

"Oh? Do I strike you as an attention seeker?"

She leaned back in her chair and sipped her water, giving me a few moments of quiet to drink her in even more. She had matured, and she'd done it in all the right ways, and not only above the neck. Letting my eyes wander would be a recipe for disappointment, but I couldn't quite contain them. She looked good. *Damn good.* I wasn't sure if it was just knowing that she'd sooner knee me in the balls than let me put my hands on her, but the mere thought of stealing a kiss had me feeling like a hormonal teenager again.

"You strike me as someone who thinks the world is a competition," she said finally.

I felt my eyebrows pull together at that. In a few quick words, she'd managed to pluck something from the depths of my own personality that I immediately recognized as true, even though I'd never seen it in myself. "Damn." I laughed. "Let's say you're right. Is that a bad thing?"

"I am right, first of all." The shadow of a smile was pulling at her mouth, and the effect was mesmerizing. "Second of all, that depends. Can you turn it off?"

"Maybe not," I admitted. "I don't know. If you want the truth, I—"

"What else would I want?"

I laughed again. *Damn.* It had been so long since I'd spoken to someone who wasn't trying to kiss my ass. Trying to keep up with her made me feel like I was using a long-neglected corner of my brain. "Fair point. The answer is I don't know. Maybe it's the way I'm wired."

"Then maybe you can understand why I have no interest in accepting your half-assed apology. It's just a game to you. One more contest you want to win."

"No," I said, shaking my head. "That's not true. Maybe at first. Yes. I'll admit that much. I think I initially wanted to check a box off. The way things ended with you felt like a mistake, and fixing it would've been like housecleaning. Once I saw you again, it changed. Apologizing to you isn't just an item on my to-do list, Kira. It's—"

As if he were the magician of shitty timing, a man with his black sleeves rolled up his arms appeared at our table. He was in his thirties and had long hair pulled into a ponytail. "I dreamed about the two of you. Look," he said, pulling out an index card covered in writing. "I woke up last night and wrote all this down. I wasn't sure who it was about until I saw you two."

Kira was watching him skeptically. I couldn't blame her. In the past, the magician had come to my table and twisted the forks like they were putty and made our glasses seem to pop straight through the tablecloth. I wasn't sure where he was going with this act, but it felt cheesy.

"Does anything on here mean anything to you two?" he asked. He set the card down on the table between us.

I frowned at the numbers and letters on the card. At first glance, it all looked like nonsense. Then I noticed the numbers scribbled in bold black ink were my birthday. I grinned. "How'd you do that? This is my birthday." I tapped the date.

Kira was looking very intensely at the card as well. "That's the name of the band Iris and Miranda always said we'd start when we were kids. Lampshade Confessional Phone Booth." She saw the look I was giving her and smiled. "Don't give me that look. We were like twelve, and those were the kind of band names that were popular."

I laughed. "No. Lampshade Confessional Phone Booth is not the kind of band name that will be popular. Ever."

She gave me a sour smile but then looked up at the magician. "Seriously," she asked. "How did you do that?"

"I told you. I had a dream about the two of you." He shrugged. "Unfortunately, the real magic is the kind nobody else will believe, so I still have to do this to earn a living." He picked up a spoon from our table, ran his thumb and forefinger down its length, and set it back down. The handle was twisted in a neat curling pattern.

Kira looked at him with openmouthed astonishment. "You didn't tell me we were going to see real magic."

I laughed. "I doubt it's real."

The magician leaned back and raised his eyebrows. "Doubt isn't certainty, though, is it?" He walked off, leaving me to wonder if any of the other scribbles on the card had significance.

"Seriously," Kira said quietly. "I think that was a real-life wizard."

"He probably overheard us talking about some stuff and wrote it down when we weren't looking."

"You don't think you'd remember if I told you what we wanted to name our band when we were twelve? And I know you didn't tell me your birthday."

I sighed. "I actually feel a little bad I didn't let Cade come now. Seeing this probably would have been the highlight of his life."

The waiter came a little while later and took our orders. Kira and I occasionally dropped our eyes to the card and tried to figure out what any of the other random numbers and words meant but couldn't quite puzzle it out. I should have thanked the magician, though. The greatest magic trick had been that his stunt momentarily made Kira forget to have her guard up.

"So what happens after tonight?" Kira asked suddenly.

"Tomorrow."

"Smart-ass. I mean with you and me."

"Well, next you'll have to teach me how to help you direct your play."

"This is really your plan? Force me to be around you and hope that I'll eventually forget I hate you?"

"So you're saying it won't work?"

She shook her head slowly, then grinned. "I hope not."

"Hey, all evil plans aside, I really do think it'd be kind of fun to help you direct a play."

"Pardon me for having trouble imagining that's true."

"Seriously. I always thought if I'd chosen another line of work, maybe I would've done something where I got to work with kids. Teaching wouldn't have been so bad." I was a little surprised by my own admission. I realized what I was saying *was* true, even if I'd never seriously considered it.

"I think your students would get too distracted. Particularly the female ones."

"Oh?" I asked. "And why would that be?"

Kira's cheeks flushed red. "Because they'd wonder how such an ass managed to make it through an interview?" She let out a soft laugh and shook her head. "You know, I'm sorry. I take that back. Besides your utter bullheadedness in trying to force your way back into my life, you haven't been an ass. You've actually been pretty decent."

"I've been on my best behavior. It's only once you let your guard down that I'll allow my true colors to show."

"Oh, I'm sure. But now I'm supposed to believe your true colors involve dreams of teaching high school and helping direct low-budget plays?"

"Correction. Your play now has as big a budget as it needs. Smoke machines. Laser shows. Pyrotechnics. Whatever we need."

"It's a play, not a concert." She laughed. "Seriously, though, you think you would like teaching? Are you saying you don't enjoy what you do?"

I shrugged. Her question wasn't something I'd even begun to unpack myself. "It's not that, exactly. I think I enjoy the result of what I do, but not the process."

She tilted her head but nodded. "I think I know what you mean. That's how I feel with the, uh, *sweaters*," she mumbled.

I smiled. "The rodent sweaters."

"Those," she agreed. "Sometimes working on something so small makes me grind my teeth. I almost dread the process of putting it together, but once I'm done, I'm happy that I did it. I feel even happier when I see the pictures some customers will send of their pet wearing it."

"Yeah. That's what I mean. To do what I do, I have to step on a lot of toes. *A lot.* But in the end, I believe in what we do as a company. We take failing businesses out of the hands of people who can't run them properly. We streamline them and make them more effective. It's better for the customers and for the employees, but we also have to break the whole thing apart before we can put it back together. Being a teacher just seems like I'd be building people up instead of having to knock them down first all the time."

Kira looked thoughtful. "That's a good way of looking at it." She narrowed her eyes. "I need you to be honest. Is this the real you, or is this some conversation you scripted to make me like you?"

I sighed in mock relief. "So it worked?"

"A little." Her finger was running an idle circle on the table, tracing and retracing a line through the ring of water her glass had left. "In the end, I don't think it matters how I feel—how either of us feel. I made a promise to my friends, and that has to be more important than anything else."

The damn promise again. While I understood that it had made sense seven years ago, the fact that Kira and her friends still treated it like some sacred oath today bordered on ridiculous. But I knew saying so would be a mistake. "*Has* to be. It sounds more like you're trying to convince yourself than me."

She breathed out a soft laugh through her nose. "Is it that obvious?"

"Hey," I said, leaning in a little until I caught her eye. *God,* she was beautiful. She looked so vulnerable, but I knew there was a solid, unshakable core of strength in her. The combination was sexy as hell. She was soft enough to hold, but hard enough that she could stand on her own. "Despite what you may think about me, I'm not looking to rush you into a decision you'll regret. So take your time with it." I grinned a little mischievously. "Besides, I'm pretty sure the longer you delay the inevitable, the sweeter it's going to taste."

Her cheeks reddened again. "The inevitable, huh? And what exactly is so inevitable?"

"Us," I said simply.

Chapter 11

KIRA

Rich lived on the top of one of the biggest hills in West Valley. The house had belonged to some famous musician or other a few years back. By Rich's billionaire standards, it probably seemed modest. I guessed the garage held only four or six cars. It was probably five times the size of a normal house, but not so big you could definitely call it a mansion. But it took only one look to know it was bigger and more expensive than anything I'd be able to afford in my wildest dreams. It took only one look to know what kind of extreme wealth to expect on the inside.

I stepped out of my car and laughed softly at the thought. Rich and this house were similar in that way. What you saw was what you got. He looked like a guy who had been bringing the world to its knees for as long as he could remember. The kind of guy who could hardly contemplate the idea of failure because he was so accustomed to success. He looked like he had his life in perfect order. It was the kind of thing you'd see from a distance, maybe on TV or in a magazine, and you'd think there was no way—there was absolutely no way—anybody could actually be like that.

But I thought Rich might be exactly what he appeared. Or I had. His little scheme of forcing himself into my life wasn't supposed to work. My plan was to harden my feelings against him and endure it. I wanted to prove I never needed his apology, and more importantly, *I never needed him.*

I still didn't need him, of course, but I'd unfortunately glimpsed another side of Richard King. When Miranda and Iris had grilled me about my feelings for Rich, I'd felt like I was lying when I said I had no interest in him romantically. They'd made me promise to keep them completely up to date on everything he asked of me in his pseudoblackmail scheme. His latest request had brought me here. For reasons he chose to remain coy about, he supposedly couldn't come to the high school to "learn to be a codirector" and needed me to make a house call.

It was my own fault. Instead of actually talking at the magic show about how he could help direct the school play, I'd spent the entire time buried in a haze of hormones and dreamy eyes. The real magic had been how easily Rich had put me under his spell—how he'd changed his tactics so smoothly that I hadn't seen the next move coming. I'd been expecting a frontal assault, but he sneaked in through the back door and caught me off guard.

I grinned like a little kid at the thought. Apparently I lacked the maturity level to think of frontal assaults and back doors without getting perverted. Then again, I'd been having dark sexual thoughts far more often the last few days. I could play innocent and strong all I wanted, but my body knew exactly what it craved.

I knocked on the door and waited. It felt like my stomach was in my throat, but I did my best to calm my nerves. Even if my feelings were starting to get cloudy, it didn't have to matter. I was a big girl, and all I had to do was resist him like I'd resisted so many gallons of ice cream over the years. After all, what mattered at the end of the day wasn't if you *wanted* the ice cream; it was if you ate it. *Right?* Although I wasn't sure the analogy was a great comfort, considering I didn't count a few stolen spoonfuls at midnight as cheating when it came to ice cream.

When the door opened, I was surprised to see the ice queen herself. She stood proud and tall with a straight neck fit for a dancer and eyes that cut through me. She was beautiful in the most intimidating way, but I straightened my own back and tried to sound confident.

"I'm here to see Rich."

She arched an eyebrow, which she somehow managed without even wrinkling her smooth forehead. "That's a pity. I was hoping you'd come for me."

My lips compressed into a worried little pouch. Had I imagined it, or did she enunciate that strangely, like she was talking about an entirely different kind of coming?

What was she playing at? Was this some sort of rich-person-power-struggle game? Do women who are interested in the same guy have some kind of flirt-off to decide who gets him?

"With some convincing, maybe I would," I said. I swallowed hard, replayed what I'd just said, and made a mental note to strike that from my permanent memory banks if I ever had a chance.

She laughed. It was a tinkling, dignified sound. She put her long fingers on the small of my back and slid me into the house, letting the door close behind us. "Be careful with me," she said. "I've got a reputation for being persuasive, and you're tempting me to be very persuasive."

I forced my eyes not to drop from hers when she turned to face me. We were in the foyer, but I was too tangled in the strange, confusing game she was playing to notice anything else. I still had no idea what was going on, but an instinctual part of me didn't want to lose the game I may or may not have been playing, and I definitely didn't want to seem poor and uncultured.

Maybe the smartest course of action was to remain silent and wait for Rich to hear the commotion. Although I could hardly call the sultry, smoky sound of Stella's voice or my panicked breaths a commotion.

Stella tilted her chin down and took a step closer. She traced my jaw with her fingertip, considering me with those cold eyes. "Cocks are overrated. And men are dicks. All of them. *Especially Rich.*"

I nodded a little shakily. "People named Rich used to go by Dick, for short, after all."

The corner of her mouth twitched up into a grin. "You're saying Rich's dick is short? I'd always wondered, to tell the truth. If you believe his twin brother, their dicks are the size of fallen trees."

"Is a fallen tree any bigger than a standing tree?" I was desperate to change the subject. I was even starting to consider if I could outrun her, but her legs looked long, and I had a wild guess that whatever she did for exercise had her in better shape than my daily routine of not breaking two miles per hour except in the event of an absolute emergency, like getting to the microwave before the popcorn burned.

She laughed in that tinkling way again. "Well, not if it leaves behind a stump, I suppose."

"There is that. Maybe Cade was actually saying their dicks were the size of the stump of a fallen tree, not the—"

"Talking about my dick again?" asked Rich. "And get your hands off her, Stella. She's not for you."

Stella took an unhurried step back and made a tsk sound. "I don't think she's for you either."

"Kira is here to teach me to direct a play." Rich made the declaration like he was choosing to take up some obscure, quirky hobby.

"Codirect," I corrected. "And not by choice."

"I may have coerced her into coming, yes. But you would coerce someone who was drowning to get out of the water, wouldn't you?"

Stella tilted her head at him. "I can't imagine what point you're trying to make, but I can see you're trying to make one."

"That coercion isn't always bad."

"Except it usually is," I said. "And in this case, it's bad."

"Details!" Rich said loudly. "Come on. We've got a lot to learn and not a lot of time to learn it. Stella, you stay away. I saw the way you were looking at Kira, and you can't have her."

"Since when do I listen to you?" Stella asked. She trailed after us as I followed Rich deeper into the house.

"Not often. Starting with when I'd asked you to stay at your own place tonight."

Stella saw the look of utter confusion on my face and decided to take mercy. "Rich and I are pretending to be an item. It keeps our parents from meddling. I'm only interested in women. Especially ones who have a kind of sexy librarian thing going on." She reached to touch my shirt, but Rich casually swatted her hand away.

"What the hell is with people calling me a librarian lately?"

"A sexy librarian," Rich added, as if it mattered.

"Are librarians a fetish that nobody told me about?" I asked.

Stella planted her elbows on the kitchen island and leaned in toward me. "I could tell you about some of my fetishes, if—"

"Out," Rich said. He jabbed his finger toward the other room. "You had your fun. Now go."

Stella shrugged. "I was only teasing. I'm sorry if I made you uncomfortable, Kira. I forget how I must come across to people who don't know me."

"It's okay, really."

"Careful," Rich said. "She's like a chameleon. When one tactic doesn't work, she'll just try another. She wants to lull you into thinking she's kind and sweet now."

She stuck her tongue out at Rich, then winked at me. "He only thinks he understands me. Oh, and don't eat anything he offers to cook for you. He's a horrible cook."

"*Go,*" Rich barked.

She rolled her eyes and finally left.

"What are you smiling about?" Rich asked.

I put my hand over my mouth, as if I didn't quite believe him when he said I'd been smiling. Sure enough, I was. "Nothing."

Rich gestured for me to take a seat at one of the barstools in his kitchen. He moved around the island toward the refrigerator and grabbed two frosty glasses. He disappeared under the counter for a few seconds, clinked some heavy bottles together, and then emerged with a blender and some liquor in his hands. The bastard made eye contact with me while he unbuttoned the cuffs of his sleeves and rolled them up his forearms.

He absolutely knew what he was doing. It was the male equivalent of whipping out a little cleavage, and his forearm cleavage was unfortunately superb. Trying to pull my eyes off his tanned, muscular arms was as futile as trying to open those impenetrable plastic clamshell packages with your bare hands.

"Thirsty?" he asked.

I ripped my eyes off his arms and felt the blood rush to my cheeks. "I was just noticing your scar," I said. It was total bullshit, but he'd been enough of an ass to call me out on staring, so I didn't feel bad for fibbing. I scanned my eyes after the fact and noticed he did actually have a scar on the back of his hand like a little white smudge.

He chuckled. "Cocktails," he said. "I was asking if you were thirsty for cocktails."

If it was possible, I blushed even harder. "I knew what you meant." *I definitely hadn't known, and this was already shaping up to be a disaster of an evening.*

"The scar is a pretty lame story, actually."

"Richard King and lame in the same sentence? I'm intrigued."

I watched him mix the drinks with mild fascination. I'd never been a drinker. When most people said that, they meant they'd had their fun in high school here and there and now they only occasionally had wine with the girls or a beer after dinner. When I said I'd never been a drinker, I meant I'd literally never been drunk. My experience with alcohol was a sip of beer when my family toured a brewery on vacation several years ago, a sip of wine at my cousin's wedding, and that beer cheese dip you could get with pretzels sometimes.

My avoidance of alcohol had no moral explanation. It started out because I didn't like the taste, and then I just never saw a reason to start drinking, especially when I had enough money trouble as it was.

And yet here I was, watching Rich mix up some kind of neon-blue drink with ice, lemons, and a few additions of other mysterious substances.

"Are you going to tell me about the scar?" I asked.

"Sorry, I just—" He grabbed a metal cup, flipped some of the drink into it, and shook it over his shoulder a few times. "I've never been a good multitasker. One-track mind kind of thing." He sloshed a portion of the drink into each of the chilled glasses and pushed one toward me. "There. That's a Rich King special. I call it a slutty grandma."

I laughed. "I'm sorry. As tempting as that sounds, I'm not really a drinker."

"What? Why not?"

"Hey, I was the one asking questions. You were supposed to tell me about your scar." In the back of my mind, I knew I was screwing up. I'd come here with plans to be icy. Bone cold. The cold-eyed killer with a pair of rocks for ovaries. So far, I felt more like the melty-hearted teenager with a raging case of hormones and a brain that was being taken over by a vagina gone rogue. I didn't want to give him the wrong idea, and I didn't want to give myself any more bad ideas about Rich. Iris and Miranda would disown me if I decided I wanted to give Rich a second chance. Hell, *I'd* disown me.

But I was being pulled along by a kind of gravity when I was with him. The right words stuck in my throat and the only ones that would come dug me deeper and deeper into trouble. The worst part was that I was starting to enjoy the kind of trouble Rich brought.

I felt alive.

I wasn't just some small-town girl when Rich's eyes were on me. I wasn't the boring one of my group of friends in his eyes. I was something special. Something to be desired. Rich wanted *me*. Not just the idea of me. Not some version of me that might exist in the future or that existed in the past. He didn't want to hang me like a trophy on his shelf or parade me around to further his career. He wanted me. Plain and simple. Every last word of that was true, and I knew it as clear as day when I saw the way he looked at me.

"I'll make you a deal," he said. "Try a sip of my slutty grandma. Just give her a taste," he added, and he was clearly having too much fun with the name he'd given his drink. "You do that, and I'll tell you about my scar."

"Fine. I'll taste your slutty grandma," I said with a little grin. I wondered if he knew how much I felt like I was betraying everyone and everything with that little grin and the note of playfulness in my voice. Probably. I thought Richard King was the kind of man to know exactly what he was doing at all times.

I sipped the drink and was surprised it didn't have any of the off-putting alcohol taste that I expected. It was strong and fruity with a kind of kick in the aftertaste. "She's not bad," I admitted, even though I was more than tempted to take another sip. "Do I get to ask why you named a drink after your grandma?"

Rich choked out a surprised laugh. "Who says it's not named after a fictional grandma?"

"Well, I met your parents briefly, and I'm pretty sure neither of them are carrying the slut gene. So for you and your brothers to turn into such womanizers, it had to come from somewhere. Your grandma, maybe?"

"Womanizer?" Rich filled his voice with feigned disbelief. "I can't even manage to get a real smile out of the local sexy librarian. If I was a womanizer, somebody had better come take my card away and burn it."

"You forgot the part where you nearly ruined said sexy librarian's life and how she might have a good reason for holding back with you."

He frowned. "Come on. That's a little much, don't you think? It was some exposé you were writing, and I spoiled it. It was absolutely an asshole move, but ruining your life?"

I fixed him with steady eyes. I wasn't sure if it was the few sips of alcohol or the old, burning anger, but I didn't want to hold it all in anymore.

The whole mess between the King brothers and my group of friends was like a brief, fiery car crash. Miranda had been in Nick's friend zone for as long as any of us could remember, and Cade had been dating Iris for a few weeks. "You know I always had a huge crush on you back then," I said.

"Bullshit." Rich laughed. "You were the one girl in the school I knew I could never get. Just made me want you even more, though."

I shook my head. "If you wanted me, you had a funny way of showing it."

"You dated my brother. How was I supposed to interpret that?" Rich's sudden shift in tone told me everything I'd always wondered. I'd stung him deeper than I realized when I dated Nick, and he still hadn't forgotten.

"Maybe I just wanted you to notice me for once."

Rich laughed softly. "Somehow, I'm guessing you came to regret wanting my attention."

I sighed. No matter how I looked at it, agreeing to date Nick had been an immature and idiotic decision. I spent most of my high school career secretly swooning over Rich. I watched him work his way through the dating pool of eligible hot and popular girls week by week. I'd look at them holding hands or kissing in the hallways and feel an ugly jealousy swirling in my chest. Every touch and every kiss had felt like a personal attack.

"I still can't believe he told you about my story. I never understood why he did that," I said. In a lot of ways, I knew I should've felt angry with Nick for everything that happened. After all, if he hadn't told Rich, I never would've lost my scholarship. Not for the first time, I wondered whether the real reason what happened had hurt so long hadn't been the betrayal of trust, but *who* betrayed it.

I'd been writing an essay for a contest in the *Washington Post*. They were taking submissions, and the winner would win a free ride through college. Thanks to someone in their marketing department making a mistake, only our school and one other got any notification about the contest. In the end, about five kids entered. I knew my story could've won, but thanks to Rich, I never got to find out.

"He's my brother," Rich said. "It probably seemed like nothing to you, but being on the team was my life back then. That story might have been your ticket to a college scholarship, but it was probably going to be my ticket off the team and out of high school sports."

For someone who had made such a big deal of apologizing to me, I hadn't expected Rich to try to defend himself. Still, I'd never heard his side of the story. I'd only seen the hammer come down on myself and been left to assume about Rich's motivations.

"Well," I said. "If you weren't doing anything wrong, why were you so scared about me writing an exposé?"

"Because I had no idea what was in it. Those were my coaches. My teammates. My friends. Nick just said you had some dirt on the athletic department, and it might mean heads were going to roll. So, yeah, I told Coach."

"And your coach told the principal, and then I got threatened with expulsion if I didn't promise to delete the article."

Rich let out a long sigh through his nose. "Yeah. At the time, I just wanted you to hurt as bad as I did. It's shitty. Admitting it is even shittier. But that's what it was. When I found out you were with Nick—" He shook his head, and even seven years later, I could still see the ghost of those emotions flicker across his face. "I never even stopped to think how much it might fuck up for you. I just did it." He grabbed one of the liquor bottles on the counter and took a long pull directly from the bottle.

I pressed my lips together in a sad smile. "Yeah, well, it all worked out in the end. Didn't it? My dad was happy to pay for my classes. I guess it's the politician in him, but he never passed up opportunities to collect favors. Everyone had to owe him something. I honestly think it meant more than money to him. In my case, I know it did. When I wanted to leave West Valley after school to chase a job in another school district, he didn't let me forget that I still owed him too much to leave. Not money, of course, but I was his precious daughter. How would it look if I was so eager to leave behind my father, the mayor? What kind of family man can't keep his only child at home?" I laughed suddenly. "Jesus. Listen to me. I sound so bitter. Besides, it's not like you were the only bad guy here. I was the one who dated your brother to spite you."

Rich's forehead was scrunched together in concentration. His hand still gripped the bottle of liquor, but his knuckles were white, and I could see the tendons in his arm straining. "No." His voice was quiet, reserved. He shook his head again. "I never imagined what I did would hurt you so badly, but I meant to hurt you. I can't pretend I'm innocent, and I'm so fucking sorry for that. But sorry is just a word, and it's not enough."

He set the bottle down with a sudden, startling clank. He shook his arms around and rolled his head from side to side like a boxer about to step into the ring. "I think there's only one way to solve this. I need you to punch me as hard as you can. Right in the face."

I laughed. "What? No. I'm not going to punch you. Besides, it's not like that would even make me feel better."

"Punch me," he said. He took another long pull from one of the bottles and then shook off the burn with a groan. "Come on. Do it."

"You're serious?"

"Punch me in the face, or I'm going to kick you out and never speak to you again. I won't forgive you if you don't do it."

My eyebrows drew together. "Rich. Come on. This is ridiculous."

He tapped his jaw. "Right here. Just do it."

"I'm not doing it."

"Then I'm done talking to you."

I didn't plan on actually doing it, but before I knew what was happening, my fist was balled up and flying toward his face. It felt like I watched everything happen in slow motion, from my fist arcing through the air to Rich's widening, surprised eyes.

I connected with his eye, even though I'd been aiming for his jaw. He flinched back and then stared at me in openmouthed disbelief. "Are you crazy?" he asked.

"What?" I still had both my fists up like I was getting ready for nine rounds. I let them fall, feeling very, very silly. "You told me—"

"I was fucking with you. Jesus." He laughed, then touched his eye and winced. "And who the hell punches somebody in the eye?"

"I was aiming for you there," I said, putting my fingertips toward his jaw, but he flinched back and laughed again.

"Sorry," he said. "I just get gun shy around people who punch me in the eye without warning."

I crossed my arms and glared at him, but I couldn't help smiling a little. "Really? You practically demanding that I punch you wasn't warning enough?"

"Honestly, I didn't think you'd have the balls to do it."

"Who says you need balls to do something brave?" I asked. "Why do testicles get so much credit? What does a shriveled-up, hairy bag have to do with conquering your fears? It'd make just about as much sense as saying, *Damn, that took boobs.*"

Rich thought about that. "First of all, my balls are not shriveled. And manscaping should be an important part of every guy's routine. I'm not sure what kind of balls you've been playing with, but—"

"None," I said quickly.

His eyebrow shot up. "So you're either antiballs or a virgin? Is that what you're telling me?"

I grabbed the drink and took another sip, but I couldn't manage to peel my eyes from his. "I'm not telling you anything."

"Fine. Keep your secrets. If I press you too hard for them, you'll probably hit me again."

"Stop." I laughed. "I'm not violent. You're the one who begged me to do it."

He smiled. "If I knew begging was so effective with you, I would've tried it a long time ago."

"Oh? And what would you have begged for?"

He leaned closer. "A few minutes ago, it would've been forgiveness. Now I don't want your forgiveness. I don't think I deserve it. I just want to make it up to you."

I shook my head. "No. Look . . . what you did sucked. But honestly? I think I only agreed to date Nick out of some messed-up desire to get you back. I may not have realized it at the time, but I think that's what it was."

"Get me back? I hardly thought you noticed me."

I laughed. "You're serious? I was one step away from building a shrine to you in my closet. I hated that I was obsessed with you."

"Damn. Some womanizer I am. I spent most of high school thinking you thought you were too good for me. When I heard you were dating Nick, I lost it. I felt like shit after I went to Coach, but it was all like a blur."

I took another sip of the drink he'd made me. I noticed with a little shock of surprise that I was draining the last bit of liquid in the glass. *When had I even taken the second sip, let alone the dozens that must've followed?* "How do I know you're not just pretending you had a crush on me back then? Maybe this is a ploy to get me to forgive you. I mean, seriously, you had the entire town in the palm of your hand. Why would I believe you so much as noticed me?"

"I can think of one way to convince you I'm not full of shit."

"Oh? I'd love to see that."

I realized he'd crossed to my side of the counter without my noticing. I also realized he was standing dangerously close. So close I could've counted each of his thick eyelashes. Close enough that I could see the flecks of gold in his green eyes. I breathed in, and his scent overwhelmed me. It didn't smell like cologne or soap. It was his smell, and it was soft but absolutely intoxicating.

"Since we seem to have a hard time reading each other," he said. Each word sent a puff of his hot breath against my lips. *He was so close now.* "I'm about to kiss you. I didn't want any confusion this time. I'd also prefer if you didn't punch me again. That really hurt."

"And I'm about to let you," I whispered.

There was a world outside this moment, but none of it felt like it mattered. There'd be consequences and drama and maybe even tears, but trying to think about that was like worrying about the price of gas when I was eighty. It was so impossibly distant and so impossibly irrelevant.

Rich was here. His lips were parted and soft and so, *so* inviting. What else mattered?

He kissed me, or I kissed him. I didn't know who made the final plunge across those spare, electrified inches between our lips, and I didn't care.

I could taste the citrusy aftertaste of the cocktail on his lips and on his tongue. I felt like I'd been on a deserted island for years and somebody had just handed me an ice cream cone—except I was making out with the ice cream cone and not eating it, but that wasn't the point. The point was it had taken only one taste of him to know how starved I'd been for this moment. I was ready for the moment when his strong arms were going to pick me up and carry me off to a bedroom somewhere, but just as quickly as it began, it was over.

My lips were tingling all over, and my cheeks were red and alive from where his stubble had brushed against me.

He lifted me easily, and wrapping my legs around his waist felt frighteningly natural. I felt us teetering backward, but I couldn't make myself care about where we were going or why. My brain was too wrapped up in his kisses and following the burning path of nerves that trailed everywhere he touched me.

My back bumped against a wall, and his hard body pressed harder into mine. My hips slid down until I could feel the bulge of his arousal against me. Fallen tree or standing tree, it was big. I didn't need to investigate to know that.

Suddenly it all felt very, *very* real. I'd crossed over the line of getting caught up in the moment and then fallen headfirst down the hill of irreversible decisions. I was tumbling and tumbling deeper into him, and I couldn't find the will to even try to stop. I wanted this. Consequences be damned, I wanted Rich.

His hand found the hem of my shirt and slid up my stomach to find my bra. He gripped me there as his hips started slowly rocking into me. There was a music in his movements, like we were tangled in some silent dance, but we both instinctively knew the beat.

He tore his mouth from mine and kissed his way down my neck as his touch became more hungry. His hand found its way inside my bra. I barely felt the way my bra was digging into my back as he forced his hand under and cupped me there. A switch in my brain had flipped where every sensation that came from Rich was good—better than good. It was ecstasy.

And then it was gone.

I realized I was standing on my own again, back against the wall. The pleasant pressure of his manhood throbbing against me was gone, and all that was left of his kisses was the pulsing tingle on my lips. Rich stood inches away from me, eyes down and jaw flexed.

"Wow," I said.

"Sorry." He was biting his lip, and he did it in the way only hot guys could. There was nothing vulnerable about the gesture. It was predatory and full of dirty promise. "As much as I'd love to take this further, you're probably tipsy."

He was offering me an out. I could see it in his face. He was absolutely ready to dive back in. He *wanted* to dive back in, but he also knew we'd both been swept up in a moment. I felt my respect for him swell. He *was* a good guy. Yet I knew convincing myself that Rich wasn't the enemy was only part of the battle. One third of it, to be exact. Until Iris and Miranda believed it, letting this go on with Rich would be like dropping a nuclear warhead in the center of our friendship.

I closed my eyes and summoned up all the advice I'd ever been given about drugs, alcohol, and sex as a teenager. Just say no. *Just say no.* Knowing his touch was only one whispered word away was pure torture, but I grimaced and forced the right words out—the ones that wouldn't destroy my friendship.

"You're probably right," I said. I was proud of myself for agreeing with him. My vagina had been driving my brain like it had both hands on the wheel—if vaginas had hands, at least. I'd been ready to let it drive the whole thing over a cliff and watch it all burn down if it meant I got to have one more minute of Rich's hands on me, but distance was good. I was already seeing more clearly, and I knew it didn't matter how much we'd misunderstood each other in the past. What mattered was my friends. Miranda and Iris would never forgive me, and coming clean about the kiss was going to be bad enough as it was. At least now I could say we'd stopped it before it got out of hand.

"Damn. I was hoping you'd try to convince me you were sober." He was grinning, and his cheeks were flushed. I couldn't help letting my eyes wander down to those lips and feel a sense of wonderment that they'd been on mine only seconds ago. It was amazing how a few minutes of conversation and maybe a few too many sips of alcohol could change things.

"No. You're right. This isn't a good idea."

"So no codirector lessons for tonight, I take it?"

"Not until your slutty grandma is out of my system. No. Thank you for tonight, Rich."

"Yeah. Anytime."

I gave him one last lingering look before I grabbed my purse and headed for the door. I'd hardly known how I was going to survive Rich and his insistence on being involved in my life again before, but now I had absolutely no idea. This was hard enough when my feelings for him had been buried. Now that they were dug up and out in the open, it was going to be impossible, but I had to find a way.

Chapter 12
RICH

"No wonder you like her," Stella said.

She was wearing a long, flowing dress made from some silky white material, and she even wore a tiara with what I suspected were real diamonds studding almost every inch. A live band played pretentious classical music, and all the guests of the party looked appropriately bored. It was the way of these things. Being a true blue blood meant the world had lost its charm for you. The only appropriate expression to wear was one that said you'd been there, done that, and in fact, you'd had a more expensive, more distinguished version of *that*, several times.

Of course, Cade's expression said something more along the lines of *that looks expensive—I'd like to find a way to break it.* He was looking at a display of a brontosaurus skeleton that was nearly intact. In a museum, it would be too priceless to have anywhere but behind protective glass. At a party like this, it was the norm to have offensively valuable items out in the open. After all, is there a better way to say you're filthy rich than to have your priceless possessions one accident away from utter destruction?

The party was in New York, and I'd agreed to fly in to make it, because I had an unquenchable interest in anything dinosaur related.

It was a poorly kept secret that I'd never completely grown out of the phase most five-year-old boys pass through. Bones, history, videos, and even wild theories were all fair game. Big and heavy bones were even better. I grinned to myself, then said a quick prayer of thanks that Cade's claims of having a "twinepathic mental connection" that let him read my thoughts were bogus. He would've never let me live that thought down.

My parents were somewhere in the crowd. They came because this was an old-money party, and simply showing up proved you were invited, which reinforced your status as a member of the exclusive circle. Miss too many of these kinds of things and you'd risk someone's assuming you'd been exiled for some reason or another, and you could quickly find yourself on the outside looking in.

Stella nudged me. "I said I'm not surprised you like her. But I guess I'm supposed to have a one-sided conversation, because you're looking at that ridiculous thing like it's about to grow tits and sleep with you."

I pulled my eyes away from the brontosaurus. "Sorry. I just can't quite believe a private collector managed to get such an intact skeleton. Usually it's—"

Stella made a snoring sound and then smirked at me. "How undignified of me. I must have spontaneously fallen asleep when you started talking about your overgrown birds again."

"I'm just trying to figure out if that's actually a brontosaurus skull, or if they maybe substituted something like an apatosaurus skull. No one has ever reported finding an actual brontosaurus skull, so if—"

"Rich, please," Stella said. "I wanted to talk about your sexy librarian who is very much alive, not a pile of bones."

"There's nothing to talk about."

Stella rolled her eyes. "You won't even let me live vicariously through you a little bit?"

"Believe it or not, trying to convince Kira I'm not an asshole hasn't been smooth sailing. I also know you have a crush on her, so

I'm not about to feed you any information. I may be failing spectacularly with Kira, but I don't plan to let you take a swing at her either. She's mine."

"And what exactly do you plan to do about us and our little arrangement? I know something happened between you two last night. I heard you whistling after she left. *Whistling*, Rich. Will I at least get two weeks' notice before I'm fired from my role as your pretend girlfriend?"

"Nothing changes. Not yet, at least. If we call things off, my parents are going to start looking a hell of a lot closer at what I do. They already found out I was taking Kira to a magic show. The only thing stopping them from staging a full-blown intervention is you."

"I'm glad you're worried about yourself and not at all about my parents trying to force a dick in my mouth."

I choked out a laugh. "Somehow I think that's not their primary goal."

"Oh, trust me. If they knew I was gay, they'd stop at nothing to *convert* me. Whatever they thought would work."

I sighed. "I'll try to think of a way to get through this that doesn't end with you getting screwed."

"Actually, I wouldn't mind getting screwed, I just don't want my parents to find out, and I'd prefer it was by someone who shaves their legs."

"I'm sure Cade would shave his legs for you if you asked nicely."

She made a gagging sound but smiled nonetheless. "You King brothers are far too manly for my taste. I like the softer things in life. Like breasts."

"Well, at least we can agree on that much. But why does it even matter if your parents don't approve? You're a grown woman now. Can't you just live your life and tell them to get over it by now?"

Stella shrugged my question off, and it was clear she didn't want to give me a real answer.

Cade saved us the trouble of an awkward silence when he walked up and slung his arm around my shoulder. "I have an idea, and before you say no—"

"No," I said.

He groaned. "What if my idea was that we should find a totally sensible way to legally purchase one of them there dinosaur bones? Hmm? What then? Would you wish you'd let me finish my damn sentence?"

"And was that your idea?" I asked dryly.

"No. But you shouldn't just assume you know what people are going to say before they say it. It's dickish."

"You were going to say we should steal one of the bones, weren't you?"

"Not permanently. I thought it'd be hilarious to see if we could make it out of here with one. I'd put money on that one trying to tackle us if he saw." Cade nodded toward an elderly man with broad shoulders, a prominent belly, and a mustache that made him look like a walrus.

"I wish I didn't know you as well as I do, because then I could just laugh this off and assume you were kidding."

"Why would I joke about something like this?"

"Good luck with him," Stella said. "I'm going to get out of here before you two end up getting a cavity search from security."

"Cavity search?" Cade asked. "What kind of dinosaur bone could we fit up our asses?"

From the way Cade asked, I didn't think it was a hypothetical question.

"If you want to jam dinosaur bones up your ass," I said, "then you can count me out of the plan. If you actually wanted to see about buying them, then you could count me in."

"I wasn't thinking about my ass. I was thinking about yours."

"Why does that not surprise me?"

Cade pulled a face and did a not-so-subtle *oh shit, look at that* kind of bulge of his eyes.

106

I turned to follow his gaze and saw my parents approaching. Cade started slowly trying to back away, but I grabbed his elbow. "You're not weaseling out of this."

"Ass," he muttered.

"Are you two behaving for once?" my father asked.

"Of course," I said.

My mother stood a half step behind my father with her lips pursed like she'd been sucking on lemons. Sometimes I wondered what would actually satisfy the woman, but I thought it was a pointless question. Some people walked into a restaurant planning to be disappointed. Even if the service and the food were almost perfect, they'd ask for a manager and complain about the nearby group that was too rowdy or about the water spots on the silverware. That was my mother. She woke every morning with the unshakable belief that the world and everything in it was going to utterly fail to impress her, and she made sure she was never wrong.

"Would it kill you to run a comb through your hair, Cadwick?" asked my mother.

I covered a laugh with my hand. No matter how many times I heard my mother use Cade's real name, it cracked me up.

Cade straightened. "Cade," he said through clenched teeth.

"Honestly. I don't know what possessed you to start going by such a crude name. Cadwick was your grandfather's—"

"Hmm," I said. "Maybe he was tired of people assuming he was an eighteenth-century butler?"

"Or," Cade added, "maybe it was just that my name sounded like some deadly disease a sailor would come down with before shitting his guts out."

My father's lips trembled. I almost burst out laughing at the sight of it. Of all the things that could actually get a laugh out of my father, it was making fun of the name my mother had chosen for Cade. My father had named me, and my mother had named *Cadwick*. After

Cadwick, they'd agreed to compromise on Nick's name. That was the arrangement, and though my father would never admit it, I knew he thought Cadwick was just as ridiculous a name as we did.

"Your grandfather would be rolling over in his grave if he could hear you two," my mother said.

"Then maybe we should go have this conversation over his grave. I've always wanted to see a zombie," Cade said.

"Cadwick!" my mother said through tight lips.

"As good as it has been to catch up, Cade and I were just getting ready to retire for the night," I said.

"Cade and you?" asked my father. "Shouldn't you be *retiring* somewhere with your lovely girlfriend? I've given you a long leash with Stella, but people are starting to whisper. The two of you are never seen touching. You hardly speak to one another. And now there are rumors you've been spending an obscene amount of time following around this local girl."

My mother clicked her tongue. "Locals. It's *obscene*."

I held on to my patience with white knuckles. Obscene was one of their favorite buzzwords. Anything that might make people think we weren't as wealthy or prestigious was obscene. Chewing gum was obscene. Scratching your neck was obscene. Showing an interest in a local girl with no money to her name was probably the obscenity of all obscenities, in their eyes.

"My relationships are my business," I said. "You're my parents, and I show you as much respect as I think you deserve for that. I let Cade and Nick shower you with money. I let you follow us around the country like hungry puppies hoping for table scraps. I even let you *think* you have some kind of say in who I will date because it gets you off my fucking back."

My mother's head looked like it was retreating from her body—sliding ever backward until she'd given herself a few extra chins and her eyes were wide as saucers. My father was watching me with a tight jaw and clenched fists.

"But," I continued, "there's a point where I think it's good to give you two a reminder. You don't have *any* say in who I date or what I do with my life. You're spectators."

Cade was leaning in with an eager, amused look on his face. "This is fucking awesome," he whispered.

My father took a step closer to me, eyes intense. "Spectators? Maybe it's time to give *you* a reminder. You think your mother and I are some crusty, useless old bastards. I know you do. But all our 'frivolous' socializing means we have connections. Deep connections. Cross us, and I think you'll find yourself meeting unexpected difficulties at every turn."

I met his stare. "If you're going to blackmail me, why don't we make the terms crystal clear."

"Find a way to make it work with Stella, or you're going to find we have more than enough clout with the mayor and the federal government to delay the construction of your headquarters. We'll hamstring you as much as we see fit when it's finally done too. We'll make moving to West Valley the most costly mistake Sion Enterprises has ever endured. I guarantee it."

I laughed. "That sounds great. I'll be interested to see how long *Cadwick* and Nick continue funding your lifestyle when you start fucking with our company."

My mother was sneering. "We take their money because it's convenient, but we aren't fools. We've set aside plenty to get us comfortably by. We don't need you. Any of you."

Cade whistled. "Damn. This went from zero to a hundred really fast. So, just to be clear, does this mean I should cancel the check I was supposed to get to you guys for that west wing you wanted to add to the house?"

As much as I wanted to spit on their little threats and dismiss it all, I knew I wasn't just putting my own interests at risk. Calling off my relationship with Stella would put her directly back into her father's dating pool of eligible, rich bastards. I had the misfortune of knowing pretty much all of them, and I knew they'd be pawing endlessly at her, no matter how much she chose to disclose about her sexuality. I'd be selling her to the wolves for my own pride, but there was no reasonable endgame in this for us. Stella and I were never going to marry. We were only buying time.

Either way, I needed to give her a warning before I pressed the detonation button on this thing with my parents.

I gritted my teeth. "I'll think about your threat, and I'll talk to Stella. We'll see what she thinks."

Cade pursed his lips. "Very gentlemanly of you. Sorry, Mom and Dad, but I'm just kind of along for the ride on this one. Besides, odds are you two are going to die first—no offense—and I've got to pick allies with more . . . *vitality*."

I gave him an incredulous look. "Seriously? That's your argument? They're going to die first?"

"Statistically," he said. "I mean, they're—oh, they're gone."

He was right. My parents had stormed off. I blew out a long breath. *"Fuck,"* I said.

"Yeah. You kind of blew a gasket on them. What happened to you being the rational one?"

"It was a few dozen years of pent-up *fuck them*, I guess?"

He slapped my back. "It was good. Next time, though, give me some kind of signal so I can join in. We could've tag teamed it or something. Good twin, bad twin."

I grinned. "Well, now we get to see if Dad was full of shit, or if he's really as connected as he says."

"What, you're not willing to just shack up with Stella to shut them up?"

"Stella is a lesbian," I said.

"*Dude.* That's so politically incorrect. You can't just call somebody a lesbian because you don't like them."

I laughed. "No. She's actually a lesbian."

"Yeah, you're actually a dick, but it's not okay to just go around saying shit like that. Jesus."

"Stella prefers women over men."

Cade raised his eyebrows and threw up his hands. "I know what a lesbian is, dickweed. Oh, wait. You mean literally? If she's a lesbian . . ." Cade leaned in very close and scanned me from head to toe with his eyes. "Why is she dating you?" His eyes fell meaningfully to my crotch and then widened. "You *do* have a dick, right?"

Chapter 13

KIRA

I sat with my arms crossed and hoped I didn't look as much like a pouty teenager as I felt. I was in my classroom after school, and both Iris and Miranda had decided to get off work early to be my chaperones when they learned Rich was meeting me here.

"This is seriously ridiculous," I said.

Iris pulled out her nightstick and gave it a little twirl. She was getting better at that. "No. Ridiculous is putting your tongue down the throat of the enemy."

"My tongue isn't even that long," I said. I stuck it out. "The little connector thing on the bottom is super tight."

Miranda rolled her eyes. "Don't try to get out of this with your weird anatomy. What matters is you kissed him. *You kissed Rich.* Remind me about the special clause in our promise that said it was fine to make out with the King brothers as long as we came clean and said we regretted it a few hours later?"

"There wasn't one," I said.

"Exactly." Miranda paced around my classroom. She looked amazing, as usual. She was wearing some kind of outfit that looked like it was too many layers to be practical this time of year, but she'd also been blessed with the superhuman ability to never sweat or get the dreaded oily forehead syndrome. Miranda was basically a superhero, and if she wasn't my friend, I probably would've hated her on principle alone. It wasn't fair for one person to get so many of the good genes while the rest of us had to make do with second toes that were longer than our big toes and other little misfortunes.

"You proved you can't be trusted, and this is the consequence," Miranda said.

"What, you guys are just going to supervise every time I'm with Rich from now on?"

"If that's what it takes," Iris said. "I'll get a wire from the undercover guys and strap you up. We'll listen to everything. I'll even bug your phones."

"I have *one* phone. And I'm not wearing a wire. That's ridiculous."

Iris crossed her arms. "You're not in a position to decide what's ridiculous. *Traitor.*"

"I'm seriously sorry," I said. "I don't know how many different ways I can say it. I got carried away, and for a few minutes, he really didn't seem that bad. Besides, you guys are the ones who told me to go to the party in the first place." I closed my mouth before I dug the hole any deeper. I'd been about to ask if we really should be clinging to a promise we made when we were kids. It had been a long time since then, and Rich seemed like he'd changed.

Miranda scoffed. "Even if a woman tells her husband he can go to a strip club, I think it's assumed that she doesn't want him to sleep with any strippers."

"Seriously, though," Iris said. "Women who give their men permission to go to strip clubs are asking for trouble. I'm not going to let a dog loose in a sausage factory and then get mad when he ends up gobbling down an eight-incher."

"You would somehow manage to turn that sexual," Miranda said with a sigh, but there was a glint of amusement in her eyes.

"What was sexual about that?" Iris asked. "Was it just because I said eight inches? Would it be better if I used the metric system? What would that be, eighty . . . inchimeters?"

I pressed my palm to my forehead and laughed, but the sound of the door opening distracted all of us.

Rich took half a step in before he paused, eyes darting between Iris and Miranda. "Oh," he said, "I can wait outside until you two are finished."

"You can come right in, sleazeball," Iris said. "We're not going anywhere until you slime your way out of here." She sauntered over to Rich with exaggerated confidence and whipped out her nightstick. She prodded at his pockets and his chest, making him jump back and look at her like she was crazy. "Got any goodies in there? Maybe some drugs to soften our girl up again? A slutty grandma, even?"

Rich looked past her to me. "I take it you told them about the other night?"

I winced. "Kind of. Yeah."

"So," he said slowly, looking back between Iris and Miranda. "What happens now? You two tie me up and beat me until I agree to stay away from Kira?"

Miranda narrowed her eyes. "Tie you up and beat you? What is that, some kind of thinly veiled euphemism? You think you're going to turn this into a wild sex party?"

Rich laughed. "That's a stretch. No. Poor choice of words was all. I'm just trying to figure out if you expect me to have a conversation with Kira while Officer Iris is over here ready to whack me with that nightstick."

"What you do is your choice, *scumbag*," Iris said through her teeth.

I could've almost laughed. They were trying so hard to be intimidating that it was bordering on cringeworthy. "Guys, come on," I said.

Iris pointed her nightstick at me and bulged her eyes. "Coming to his rescue, are we? It's just like I thought."

Miranda leaned against a desk and gave me a long, searching look. "I think it's time you decide, Kira. Him or us. What's it going to be?"

"What?" I asked. I almost couldn't believe what I was hearing. I expected Iris and Miranda to be resistant—angry, even. But ultimatums?

She shrugged. "We made a promise. If that doesn't mean anything to you, I think we deserve to know about it."

"You agree with this, Iris?" I asked.

Iris hesitated, but she nodded. "It's time to choose. The dick or the chicks?"

Rich cleared his throat. "Kira. It's fine. I already fucked up once. I'm not about to talk you into screwing up your friendships on my behalf either."

"Dicks or the chicks, huh?" I asked. "I think the ones being dicks here *are* the chicks. I choose the one who isn't trying to manipulate and bully me. I choose him."

"Come on," Miranda said quietly. She stood and pulled on Iris's sleeve.

Iris was watching me in stunned silence. Miranda tugged at her, but she still wasn't moving. "You're serious?" she asked.

I couldn't look them in the eyes right now. I stared at my feet and let my thoughts churn. I'd spoken impulsively. I knew that. But as much as I tried to second-guess myself, I couldn't find a reason to change my mind. Whatever they might think about Rich, one thing was true: He wouldn't put me in a situation like they had. He wouldn't have ignored the fact that I'd changed and grown and that maybe I'd grown into somebody who could forgive a man for what he'd done seven years ago.

I was seeing it for the first time. My friends hadn't been paying enough attention to see me for who I was. Their lives had gotten busy, and it had become easier to remember who I'd been instead of learn who I was becoming. The ultimatum proved that.

I shook my head. "I'm serious. If you're going to make me choose, then I choose Rich."

"Come on," Miranda said coldly.

"Kira?" Iris asked.

"Iris, come on," Miranda said more loudly this time. "She made her choice. Let's go."

It felt like an eternity before the door finally closed and I was alone with Rich.

"Kira, I'm sorry," he said softly.

"Don't be. For once, I'm not going to lay the blame on you for this."

"I wouldn't fault you if you did."

"That's because you're a better person than I gave you credit for."

He laughed with more than a little mirth. "That depends on your definition of a good person. What matters more? What we do or what we wish we did?"

"Both?" I laughed.

"Then I'm a halfway good person and a halfway shitty person."

"Yeah, welcome to the club."

♥ ♥ ♥

I lived on the top floor of a two-story condo. The woman who lived below me was an elderly widow with a snake phobia. I didn't know much more than that about her, but I knew *all* about her snake fears. She'd wake me with a knock on the ceiling about once every week or so in the middle of the night. We'd communicate through my floor, which was far from ideal, because I could hardly ever figure out what she was saying. Usually, thinking a snake had broken into her home, she wanted me to come help her look.

Considering I wanted as much to do with snakes as I did with gonorrhea, it was far from an ideal way to be woken up in the middle of the night. I'd grab a kitchen knife—because I thought even a snake would be smart enough not to start a fight with somebody who was packing steel—and I'd sleepily make my way downstairs. Her house was always empty, and she always thanked me profusely for my help.

She'd woken me *twice* last night, so when I finally rolled out of bed to the sound of my alarm at six in the morning, I was so groggy I thought I'd need the jaws of life to get my eyelids open. My head was pounding, which was probably because I'd been crying before bed. I wasn't proud of it, and I'd done my best to hold it together in front of Rich, but at the end of the day, my best friends were pissed at me. I'd thrown a full-blown pity party, complete with the obligatory sappy movie, popcorn, and those puffy cheese balls I seemed to crave only when I was feeling down.

Someone knocked at the door while I was brushing my teeth. I took a look in the mirror at the haggard mess that was my face, decided I didn't care, and spit out the toothpaste. I headed down the stairs and opened the door.

"Dad," I said slowly. There was a specific voice inflection reserved for moments when a relative or friend shows up unexpectedly. It started out obviously surprised but made a quick recovery toward exaggerated excitement. For some reason, parents always seemed completely oblivious to it too.

I had to be ready for work in an hour and I was running on almost no sleep, but I also didn't want to hurt his feelings by acting like I wasn't happy to see him. Somehow, I managed to squeeze all of that into the word *Dad*.

Clueless as always, my dad grinned—like I'd just squealed and said how thrilled I was that he'd come. "Your mother couldn't make it, but it has been forever since we had a little father-daughter talk."

"Uh, yeah." I nodded. I was smiling, but inside, I was trying to figure out what I'd done wrong. Dads didn't just come to have a talk with you unless you'd done something horribly wrong or someone was dying. "Is everyone okay?"

"Oh, sure. Can I come in?"

"Y—yeah. Sorry, it's just a little bit of a mess up there."

"I wouldn't expect anything less. Trying to get you to clean your room was always harder than getting a tick off your Grandma Ray's back."

I gave him a quizzical look.

He laughed. "I always forget, she passed before you knew her. She would always lay facedown in this hammock of hers in the backyard. Of course, the forest behind her house was infested with ticks, so every time we went to visit, my mom would make your uncle and me get the ticks off. But Grandma Ray had a low pain tolerance and tried to buck free and swing at us any chance she got."

"Wait," I said, pausing halfway up the stairs. "That's a true story?"

"Unfortunately, yes."

I shivered a little. *Disturbing.* "So," I said while we climbed the stairs, "anything in particular bring you by?"

"Well, this is a little awkward, but yes." We got to the top of the stairs, and my dad plopped himself down on my couch. "People have been talking about you and Richard King."

"Okay," I said slowly. "People around here will talk if somebody wears a pair of socks that don't match."

"I'm just saying I've heard some rumors that the two of you are maybe—" He swirled his finger around and pulled his chin back, making some inscrutable expression.

"Maybe what?" I asked. My tone was a little sharper than I expected. *Surprisingly*, not getting enough sleep and having my dad mysteriously show up when I needed to be getting ready for work was testing my patience.

"Getting involved," he said carefully. "I've got no delicate way to put this, Peach. The man is a snake. I'd hate to see him hurt you."

I finally felt like I could relax. So that's what all this was about. Nobody was dying. I wasn't the suspect in a murder case. My father just wanted to be a typical dad and decide no guy was good enough for me.

"I can handle myself, Dad. It's not like we're going to run off and elope. If Rich isn't a good person, then I'll find out for myself by spending time with him. That's kind of how it works."

He frowned. "Listen. This isn't easy, but Rich has been canoodling with girls from all over town since he got here."

I felt a smile threatening to come. "Canoodling? I might need you to define that one for me."

"Canoodling. Picking the grapes out of season. Tugging on the anchor." He looked exasperated when I still wasn't seeming to understand.

"Maybe plain English would work better?"

"Sleeping with other girls, Kira. I don't know what he promised you, but I'm guessing he didn't let you know he was playing hide the sausage every chance he could get around town."

"Wow. Thanks, Dad. That's really helpful to know. But Rich and I aren't together anyway. He's welcome to hide his *sausage* wherever he wants."

My dad watched me with raised eyebrows for a few seconds. He sighed, slapped his thighs, and stood. "Well, that was pretty much what I came here for, Peach."

"Great. Thanks for the quality family time, Dad. I wish you'd come by more often to tell me about where people are putting their penises and how many blood-engorged ticks lived on Grandma Ray's back."

He glared. "Careful, Kira. I'm still your father, and I'm just trying to keep an eye out for my girl."

I nodded and smiled. "I know. I'm sorry, Dad. It was a long night, and everything has been kind of crazy. I'll think about everything you told me. Okay?"

He gave me a tight smile. "That's all I ask. Oh, and if he tries to touch you, tell me. I can bring the holy power of bureaucracy down on his fancy ass in a heartbeat. You remind him of that if he bothers you, you hear me?"

"I got it, Dad."

Once I closed the door, I leaned my back against it and sank down to sit. I raked my fingers through my hair. *What the hell was I doing?*

In a few weeks, I'd turned my back on my best friends and I'd let myself start falling for the only man in the world who was supposed to be off-limits for me. Now I had my dad telling me Rich was sleeping around this whole time. I thought I should feel mad or betrayed, but nothing he'd said rang true. Whatever I'd thought about Rich in the past, I knew I was a pretty decent judge of character. If Rich was still like that, I thought I'd have known. Besides, if any local girls had slept with Rich, I doubted they'd manage to keep it a secret.

No. I decided I didn't believe what my dad told me. Not at all. So the only questions were whether my own dad was lying to me on purpose or if somebody was feeding lies to him, and *why?*

Chapter 14
RICH

A bonfire that was unnecessarily large crackled and popped in my back-yard. Cade had managed to get himself in charge of managing the fire, which meant there were already three empty cans of lighter fluid nearby and about five times as much wood as the firepit was meant to hold. Nick was probably the only thing stopping Cade from accidentally burning down half of West Valley. When Cade wasn't looking, Nick was strategically moving logs around and dousing the flames to keep the whole ordeal under control.

I probably should have been paying more attention and helping, but I couldn't stop looking over my shoulder toward the house. I'd invited as many people as I could think of so it would seem less suspicious to invite Kira, but an hour had already passed, and she still hadn't shown up. The majority of the town, on the other hand, had shown. A relatively large group of the younger crowd was doing jumps off the dock and into the lake. More were in the house dancing and having drinks. My brothers and I had been out by the fire for most of the night, and we'd attracted a few wandering groups of women so far, but Stella's presence beside me kept the majority of the attention on my brothers.

"You look like a puppy waiting for its master to come home," Stella said from beside me. She was sitting straight-backed on an overturned log and, as usual, was dressed like royalty. Everyone else had opted for more casual clothes—myself included.

I turned back toward the fire. "Just trying to make sure people aren't breaking shit in the house."

"Right." She laughed. "Because you've always been so worried about your stuff."

"You did lock the dinosaur room, right?" Cade asked. He was already cracking the seal on his fourth can of lighter fluid.

"Of course I did."

"Then, yeah," Cade said. "He's full of shit. He's so hungry for some of that local poontang it's almost cute. At least it would be if it wasn't so pathetic."

"Come on," Nick said. He nudged a log that was hanging over the edge of the firepit back into the center. "Admit it. You've thought about what it would be like to give it another shot with Iris. I know you have."

Cade made an indignant raspberry sound. "If by another shot you mean one night of strictly uncomplicated sex? And maybe a little unlawful use of that nightstick of hers? Then sure, I've thought about it. But that?" he said, pointing the bottle of lighter fluid at me. "That is pathetic. That's . . . I'd almost call it—" He shuddered visibly and then laughed. "Fuck. I can't even say it."

"Love," whispered Stella.

"Stop. Both of you. Kira is fun to be around. Sure. But it's nothing serious like that."

"Right," Cade said. "It's so not serious that you got into it with Mom *and* Dad for the first time in your life. Your face was so red. It looked like somebody had your balls in a headlock."

"It's not a headlock if it's on the balls," Nick noted.

Cade turned to him while still spraying lighter fluid. "Uh, a headlock is a *technique*. It doesn't matter where you use it. I could put your legs in a headlock if I wanted."

"That's the dumbest thing you've ever said," Nick said. "That would be a leg lock. Or a ball lock. Or—"

"Headlock!" Cade shouted, tossing the bottle of lighter fluid aside and diving for Nick's legs. The two of them fell to the ground as a group of girls who had been drinking beers nearby cheered.

"Take off his shirt!" one of them yelled.

The suggestion was met with a chorus of whoo from the onlookers. *Whoo girls. They were the absolute worst.*

I got up and headed for the house.

"Goodbye, loyal boyfriend," Stella said lazily. I'd warned her about the threat my parents had made and about my intentions, which I still wasn't sure I fully understood. She'd claimed she'd figure it out, but I still felt guilty when I remembered the brief flicker of fear she'd shown at the idea of being at her dad's mercy again. Stella was strong, but the thought of her dad finding out she wasn't straight terrified her.

I stopped midstride when I saw Kira walking toward me from the house. She was wearing a gray cotton dress. The evening breeze was making the modest outfit look nearly obscene by pressing the fabric against her body—*and damn*, what a body it was. It wasn't my parents' kind of obscene either. It was the good kind. The kind that made the blood in your body flow to all the right places. I'd always had a weakness for women who didn't seem to know what they had. It was a rare quality, as most beautiful women I'd met seemed unable to think about much *except* what they had. They'd pout their full lips, let some of their impressive cleavage accidentally slide free, or wear only clothes that showcased their perfect asses.

I didn't fault them for being proud of what they had, but I could never get behind the self-obsession it brought out in the women I'd been with before. If Kira had any idea how hot she was, she hid it well, and it wasn't even fair how badly that made me want to show her.

"You came," I said.

She smiled and tucked some stray hairs behind her ear only to have them immediately blown back across her forehead. "Yeah, well, I didn't want to be rude or anything. But it looks like you invited the whole town, so I guess maybe I didn't need to worry about you missing me if I didn't come."

"Confession: I invited all of them because I wanted you to come. It's starting to feel like nobody wants us to be together, and I thought this might keep them from getting too suspicious."

"Well, bad news," she said. She nodded to the group of girls by the bonfire who had been watching a now-shirtless Cade try to pin Nick to the ground. They were all watching us and whispering. "I think the damage has already been done."

"Then what do you say we forget about what people will say? Just for tonight."

She bit her lip. "Who says I'd be interested in you, even if I didn't care what people said?"

I felt my hand moving up to touch the soft line of her jaw, and I knew I couldn't stop it even if I should. She felt so warm and inviting that I nearly kissed her right then. "The way you look at me says you're interested." I lowered my voice to a bare whisper. "Those little moans that slipped out of your lips the other night say you're more than inter-ested. You're *starving*."

She looked down and tried in vain to tuck her hair behind her ear again. "Does the way I look at you also say how mad I am at myself for that?"

"A little. But all the best relationships start with a little self-loathing."

She laughed. "Um, I'm going to need you to back that one up with some evidence."

"Romeo and Juliet. Their families hated each other. Ophelia's dad hated Hamlet . . . I could go on, but my knowledge of literary

124

relationships pretty much stops at tenth grade literature class. I had a good teacher that year."

Kira was watching me with an amused, crooked smile. For the first time since I'd come back to West Valley, I didn't think I saw any of the familiar reservation in her face. I wondered if I'd finally broken through all the old wounds and earned my chance at a fresh start with her. I let my hand fall away from her face, but I could still feel my fingertips tingling where I'd touched her.

"Fair points," she said. "But both of those women end up dead before the play is over. I'm not sure following in their footsteps would be the wisest choice."

"You're right. Juliet and Ophelia fought their feelings until it was too late. So I guess your only choice is to give in and admit it."

"Admit what, exactly?"

"That you are madly in love with me and you want me to carry you off to the woods so I can have my way with you."

Her lips crumpled as she tried to hold back a smile. "What about this? I'll admit I *maybe* was too hard on you. And I *maybe* have enjoyed spending time with you." She bit her lip again, and my eyes were drawn to her smooth, pink lips. "And I don't regret when you kissed me."

"Wait. You're the one who kissed me."

"No," she said. "You were definitely the one who made the first move."

"Nope. I'm far too chivalrous to kiss an inebriated virgin."

Kira laughed. "Virgin? I don't know what makes you so sure I'm a virgin."

"Hmm," I said, making a show of looking at her from head to toe. "It *is* hard to believe that a woman who looks as good as you could hold men away for this long, but I think I'm right."

"You're lucky you mixed a compliment in with all that."

"So? Am I right?" I watched her consider how she wanted to answer, from the way she bit her lip and nervously flicked her eyes up to meet mine to how she was idly rubbing her hand across her arm.

That was the moment I knew I had to put a stop to this. I'd come out to West Valley under flimsy pretenses. I'd shown up at her school with the weak excuse of wanting to clear the air between us. I'd even tried to write off my continued interest in Kira as a kind of passing distraction—like a hobby I'd eventually grow tired of. I'd known none of that was true, whether I wanted to admit it to myself or not.

Getting involved with me would make her life difficult. There'd be her father. My parents. Tabloids would slap her picture on them, and they'd snap a thousand pictures of her trying to enjoy the beach until they managed to get one that wasn't as flattering. It'd be blown up for everyone she ever knew to see. I didn't even know if I was capable of giving her the kind of love she deserved, because the adorable, sexy, and determined woman sitting beside me deserved a hell of a lot of love.

She finally decided on her answer, and the sound of her voice was enough to stir me from my thoughts. "What you are is an asshole for assuming I'm a virgin. And your reward for being an ass is that you don't get to know."

"That's probably fair."

The sound of glass breaking from inside the house drew my attention. I frowned up toward the second floor, where my collection was. "Hey, do you want to see something cool?" I asked. I knew exactly why I was asking, and I hated myself for it. I needed to find a way to cut things off with Kira before it got any harder for either of us. I desperately needed to. But it was too easy to convince myself I'd just enjoy her for a little bit longer. Just a few more minutes of pretending like nothing was wrong, and *then* I'd do the right thing.

She grinned. "If that's your pickup line, it needs some serious work."

"I promise, I'm not trying to get you to sleep with me. Not yet, at least. Actually, if anything, I'm pretty sure what I'm about to show you is going to have the complete opposite effect of making you want to sleep with me."

Chapter 15

KIRA

I stood behind Rich as he unlocked a door on the second floor of his house. Most of the partygoers were downstairs, where the music was loudest and the drinks were closest, and up here it felt like we had a slice of privacy.

I admired the way the muscles of his back were so clearly visible, even through his shirt. He was wearing a simple long-sleeved shirt and jeans. It wasn't really fair, but something about knowing a guy could afford anything he wanted made casual clothes seem so sexy to me. Then again, I'd seen Rich in a suit plenty of times, and there was a lot to love about that look as well.

Part of me felt like turning and running right then. It was amazing how quickly my thoughts could switch from defensive to offensive. One minute, I'd been so determined to keep him away. No matter how justified it felt to stop hating Rich, it was still hard to go from hating a man to fantasizing about what he looked like under his shirt so quickly. The more frightening part was my attraction to him wasn't just physical. The physical attraction had been there even when I hated Rich. Any woman with an ounce of the biological imperative to reproduce would be sexually attracted to the man. He was practically crack for the ovaries.

I was beyond curious to know what he was about to show me. Despite his jokes about killing my sex drive with whatever was in the room, I couldn't help wondering if he was about to reveal some kind of kinky sex dungeon. I hoped not. My idea of a wild night was eating my dessert before I had dinner. The thought of Rich and his penis getting anywhere near me was plenty of excitement for my brain, thank you very much. If he tried to add ropes and chains and whips to the equation, I'd probably have a nervous breakdown.

"Welcome to my little museum," he said as he opened the door.

My eyebrows drew together as I looked around the room. I suspected it was built to be the library in his mansion of a home. The ceilings were much higher than anywhere else, and the room was almost as large as a school gym. There were dinosaur bones everywhere. They were all carefully arranged by strings from the ceiling and put together in the shape of whatever monster they'd belonged to. There were volumes and volumes of books and a desk scattered with papers and folders full of more documents.

"Oh," I said quietly.

"Right?" Rich asked.

The childlike grin on his face made me smile. I couldn't help it. He looked exactly like a kid showing his friend a prized card collection.

"So you're into dinosaurs?" I asked. "I thought that whole thing about Cade touching your dinosaur bones at the airport was a weird inside joke."

His grin faltered a little. "I mean, it's not like I'm obsessed." He shrugged and looked at his feet. It was the first time I'd ever seen Richard King look self-conscious, and it was adorable. "It's more like a hobby, I guess."

I looked up at the bones of a pterodactyl dangling from the ceiling. "I think it's actually pretty cool. Most rich guys collect cars or something. This is unique."

He was smiling again, and some of the self-consciousness had already melted away. He led me deeper into the room, where stacks of what looked like dressers or maybe wooden filing cabinets were lined up against the wall. He pulled one of the thin drawers out, and I saw it was actually a glass display case full of tiny bones. "I've got some insects, too, if you want to see," he said.

I wasn't sure if laughing would offend him, so I just smiled and nodded. For the next hour, I listened to Rich talk about dinosaurs, prehistoric times, common misconceptions about which dinosaurs actually coexisted, and even a brief rant on what most movies got wrong. If I'd been asked to list the million most exciting conversation topics I could think of an hour ago, I was pretty sure dinosaurs wouldn't have cracked the list. But Rich was mesmerizing to watch. For a little while, he didn't seem so far out of reach. I could forget all the reasons I should have been about as compatible with him as oil is with water. He was just a man talking about something he loved, and when everything was stripped away, I could see the real Richard King,

Somewhere between the topic of feathers versus scales and why raptors would've likely been great pets, I'd started to fall for him, and it didn't feel like one of those times when you accidentally kick a stair on the way up and have to catch yourself. It was more like trying to walk down a waterslide while wearing an inflatable rubber suit. I was falling, sliding, slipping—whatever you wanted to call it—and I was on a one-way collision course with Rich.

"Yeah," Rich said. He had his hand on one of the leg bones of a massive dinosaur. "It's pretty cool."

I laughed. "Calling it cool might be a stretch."

He looked so suddenly and genuinely hurt that I laughed even harder.

"I was teasing you," I said. "It probably sounds dumb, but I liked seeing that you care about all this stuff. It made you feel a little more human and less like somebody built you in a lab to seduce women."

He wiggled his eyebrows and rubbed the dinosaur bone again. "You're saying my dinosaur room *is* seducing you?"

I chewed on my bottom lip. "Maybe a little. All these hard bones start making a girl's mind get all euphemistic, I guess." I pressed my hand to my mouth. "Wow. I didn't actually mean anything by that. It just sounded funny in my head, and then it sounded really dirty when I heard it out loud."

"Dirty sounds good from you."

The big room suddenly felt very small, and I was aware of how close we were standing. I could hear the thudding of the music from downstairs coming up through the floor and even the sound of splashing from the lake if I strained my ears. It was like reality had seeped back into the room through the cracks and crevices. For the hundredth time, I thought of Iris and Miranda. They'd pushed me to say something rash back in my classroom when they asked me to choose between them and Rich. Thinking of them made my stomach clench, and all the free easiness I'd felt moments ago seemed to wither up and die.

"Maybe we should get back out to the party," I said. "It's getting a little stuffy in here."

Rich watched me for a few seconds, disappointment clear in his features. "Yeah, sure. Come on."

Nick and Cade were standing outside the door to Rich's dinosaur room when we opened the door. They nearly fell inside because they'd been leaning on the door.

"What the fuck?" asked Rich.

Cade straightened and brushed off his shirt. "Sorry. We were just trying to figure out if you actually managed to get a woman to sleep with you in your dinosaur room. Nick said it was impossible. I thought maybe if you came through with the right number of sexy dinosaur jokes, you could pull it off."

"Sorry," Nick said. "But dinosaurs don't seem like the most ripe topic for jokes."

"Uh," Cade said. "Then tell me why dinosaurs have sex underwater?"

"They didn't?" Nick said.

Cade sighed through his nose in frustration. "Just say *why.*"

"Why?" Nick asked in a monotone.

"You try keeping a thousand pounds of pussy wet."

Rich and Nick groaned in unison. I was still coming to terms with the idea that the two of them had actually been listening from the door, but I still couldn't help grinning a little.

"One more," Cade said. "Why can't you hear a pterodactyl using the bathroom?" When nobody seemed to want to indulge him by asking why, Cade answered anyway. "Because the *p* is silent."

"Is this why you were laughing like a lunatic at your phone earlier?" Nick asked. "Seriously? Dinosaur jokes?"

Cade shrugged. "I *dino* what to tell ya. I guess your sense of humor isn't developed enough to appreciate them."

"Please stop," Nick said.

"Wait," I said, holding up my hands. "You two were listening in?" I asked. I knew I hadn't actually done much of the talking in the room with Rich, but I still felt indignant. Besides, what if I'd let something happen between Rich and me?

"Barely," Nick said. "Cade was breathing louder than a bulldog taking a nap."

"What?" Cade rounded on Nick. "That's the dumbest thing I've ever heard come out of your mouth."

"This is coming from the man who thinks you can put somebody's balls in a headlock," Nick said.

"If you want a repeat of the beatdown you just got, I'll be happy to give you a refresher."

"Do you two mind?" Rich asked.

Cade looked at me. "Wait. Before you two frolic off into the moonlight. You've gotta tell me. Would his moves have worked if he didn't show you he was a dinosaur nerd?"

"Rich didn't try any *moves*," I said impatiently. I already felt confused enough about the whole thing without having to explain it to the peanut gallery outside. "We were just talking."

Rich rubbed the back of his head and grimaced. "Actually, I did try a couple moves. Apparently, they didn't work as well as I thought."

Cade and Nick burst out laughing.

I felt another, bigger wave of guilt roll through me. Here I was, standing with not just Rich, but all three of the King brothers. Meanwhile, Iris and Miranda were probably at home trying to imagine what kind of traitor things I was up to tonight. At least I hadn't taken Rich's silent invitation to kiss again in the dinosaur room. It had been written as clear as day in his eyes, but this time I'd managed to resist.

It felt like I needed to lie down or maybe take a cold shower. I couldn't get my thoughts straight lately, and the two people I normally would've gone to for advice hated me right now.

"You okay?" Rich asked. He put his hand on my back, and even the innocent touch sent trickles of warmth through me.

"She looks like she needs CPR," said Cade.

Nick frowned at him. "Usually, people who are standing up and conscious don't need CPR."

Cade shrugged. "Just trying to be a wingman."

"More like a wing nut." Nick laughed.

Cade's hand shot out and popped Nick between the legs. Nick hunched over in silent pain.

"Call me a wing nut again," Cade whispered with a wild grin.

"Anyway," Rich said, urging me away from the two of them and toward the stairs.

"They don't seem to get along," I said. I was desperate to talk about anything but Rich and me. I really did enjoy being with him, but every time the silence stretched out long enough for me to feel where gravity was trying to take us, I wanted to run.

"Cade and Nick are always fighting, but they are also always together. It's kind of like an old married couple, but with more testosterone and penis jokes."

"Charming." I laughed.

"Yeah. Cade is smarter than he lets on, but he's also dumber than he seems."

I laughed again. "I'm not sure that actually makes sense. I think a statement like that needs an example."

"Okay. Easy. I can give you a few. I once caught Cade trying to find his phone by looking under the couch with the flashlight app *on his phone*. I also saw him learn half of a chemistry textbook in a few hours because he was determined to blow up a mailbox using only what we had in the cabinets at home. He once told me everybody uses the toilet wrong, because if you sit backward, you have a built-in table."

"Yeah . . . but wouldn't you need to take your pants completely off first?"

"Like I said. A smart idiot. Do I need to go on?"

I was smiling hard enough that my face hurt. "Need to? No. But I'm highly entertained. I think I want more."

"Maybe the best example would be when he got locked in the backyard of our house when we were kids. He tried the gate and couldn't get out, but the house was locked. He couldn't climb it, and he didn't have his phone. By the time we found him, he'd made his way onto the roof of the house by jumping about three feet from a tree branch to the roof. He was actually trying to go down the chimney. Cade wasn't as amused as we were when he realized the gate wasn't locked—he'd just been pulling instead of pushing."

I laughed. "Okay, so I believe you that he's dumb, but I'm not exactly getting the whole smart thing."

"Well, it's just that the same person who got into all those idiotic situations is the one who has played a huge part in getting Sion to where it is. When it comes to negotiation and people, he's pretty much a genius. He could probably talk a vegan into eating a Philly cheesesteak."

"And what about Nick?" I asked. "He never struck me as stupid. I feel like I remembered him being pretty much awesome at everything in school when it came to academics."

"Yeah. Nick has probably never tried anything he wasn't immediately good at. That's also his problem. Most people learn to bust their ass, because they find something they want to master and *have* to work hard to do it. Nick never had to learn to work hard, because everything was so easy. I think he likes being around Cade because keeping him from offing himself is probably a challenge, even for Nick. Everything is so easy for Nick that he always ends up seeming bored. I thought Sion would be enough of a challenge for him, but he's like a human computer. Give him a problem, and he spits out a solution. It's honestly scary, sometimes."

"And what about you? Cade has the superpower of being a capable idiot. Nick is a bored genius. Wait, let me guess. Your power is seduction. I mean, come on. You've obviously used the dinosaur room to seduce scores of women before me. My ovaries were practically banging together like maracas by the time you were done."

Rich chuckled. "I'm pretty sure that's not how ovaries work. Are you sure they weren't trying to help each other commit suicide? Like a biological reflex to sterilize yourself before you pass on my weird obsession with dinosaurs to your offspring?"

"In all seriousness . . ." I smiled, then licked my lips. *Damn it.* I could feel it already, even before the words came. I was sinking back toward that inevitable pull he had over me. It was like trying to walk up a slide when I was a kid. I could take a few steps, but no matter how hard I tried, I'd always come flopping back down to the bottom before I made my way off the slide. Only this time, there was a gorgeous billionaire waiting at the bottom for me. I wasn't even sure why I was trying to resist. What was at the top of my metaphorical slide, anyway?

I'd climb my way out of my feelings for Rich, and I'd be right back in my boring life of ice cream and Netflix.

"In all seriousness," he prodded with a slow smile of his own.

"I might share Cade's superpower, because the dinosaur room may have actually worked on me. *A little.*"

His fingertips were on my face again. The look in his eyes was the same as before we'd kissed in his apartment. "You wanted to know my superpower? It's making the difficult choices."

I frowned. "What do you mean?"

His smile looked sad now. "I mean being with me will only cause you trouble. I've been thinking about this, but I wasn't sure I'd be able to do the right thing this time. I have to, though."

"The right thing? I don't understand. What's the right thing here?"

"Everything I've been doing was just selfishness. I'm sorry I didn't see it sooner, but this won't work. I can't tear you away from your friends, Kira." He leaned forward, and I felt the warm press of his lips on my forehead. It was gone as soon as it came. A platonic peck on the forehead. He still wore that sad smile. "Forget about all the codirector stuff. I'll fund the programs. Tell Miranda and Iris that you told me to go fuck myself. I think it had better be something dramatic to convince them you're not a traitor anymore. I'll back whatever you say up."

"Rich . . ." Wasn't this exactly what I wanted? Hadn't I been telling myself since the moment he showed up in West Valley that all my problems would be solved if Rich would just butt out of my life? Yet even then, I think I'd known I was lying to myself on some level. I secretly felt a thrill from his attention. I'd known I could never have him, so secretly wanting it had been harmless. I'd been able to pretend those dark thoughts hadn't been churning just beneath the surface all along. I clenched my hands at my side until my fingernails dug painfully into my palms. I wanted to make a fool of myself begging him not to just throw me away because he thought it was for my own good. I wanted to get on my knees if I had to and beg. Instead, I only stood there, mouth open and forehead creased as I tried and failed to find the words to tell him how I felt.

He gave me one last lingering look. "Goodbye, Kira."

And I watched him go, even as it felt like I was screaming on the inside. I felt like I was in one of those dreams where no matter how hard I tried to make my voice work, nothing happened. All I could do was watch him walk away and realize for the first time that I didn't want him to go.

Except it was too late now, wasn't it?

Chapter 16
RICH

"Stop moping," Stella said.

She had tagged along with me on a trip to New York. I was meeting with a collector who claimed to have a pristine raptor talon he was willing to part with for the right offer. We had landed a few hours ago but had to kill another hour before the meeting. We were in a local pizza shop downtown. Nick and Cade, who should've had better things to do, insisted on coming. The two of them were currently fawning over the pizza shop's collection of classic arcade games. Cade, for some inexplicable reason, looked to be explaining a scheme to Nick detailing how they could actually reuse the same quarter over and over in those old machines. It looked like it involved gum and a piece of floss, and it also looked like it would never work.

"I'm not moping," I said.

"You're moping." She took a bite of her salad and then leaned back, wiping her mouth with a napkin. "Do you really think you're able to be low profile in anything you do? The entire town of West Valley knows what happened at the party. They saw the sad goodbye. The tears in her eyes. They saw you walk away. Very dramatic. So yes, you're moping. You broke up with your little distraction, and now you're feeling sorry for yourself. I'm just trying to figure out why you broke up with her."

"Because her friends hated her for being interested in me. Because her father was ready to work with my parents to fuck our lives over if I didn't call it off. Because taking things further with her would've meant screwing you over. Because I was an ass to her back in high school, and I'd probably end up breaking her heart again. Do I need to continue?"

Stella rolled her eyes. "Weak."

I glared. "What?"

"Weak. I said you're weak. Really? People threatened you, so you got scared and backed off? You thought you might be a meanie head, so you ran?" She scoffed. "Maybe our relationship *could* work out after all, because you obviously don't have any balls."

I couldn't help grinning at that, but the humor was fleeting. "I'm trying to protect her. I'm not *running*. I'm walking away, because staying would be bad for her."

She looked unimpressed. "If that's what you have to tell yourself."

"It's the truth," I snapped. "I do what has to be done." I thrust my arm toward Cade and Nick, who were laughing like idiots when Cade's scheme seemed to actually work. "Not everybody can coast through their lives doing what they feel like at every opportunity. Some people have to do what's hard, even if it feels like shit."

"Is that what you think? You're the self-sacrificing martyr? Or maybe you're just afraid to let yourself be happy for once. Maybe you think you deserve to be miserable."

"That's bullshit." My answer came immediately, but the words felt hollow. Even as I denied it, I could feel Stella's accusation sinking deeper into my thoughts and taking root. "If Kira thought I was wrong, she would've stopped me from leaving anyway."

Stella grinned. "Somebody doesn't look as confident as they did a few seconds ago when they were saying they did the right thing."

"Shut up," I said. "At least now you don't have to worry about telling your father the truth yet. It looks like our farce of a relationship will live to fight another day."

"Silver linings." She sighed.

Chapter 17

KIRA

I walked into Bradley's with a stereo I'd borrowed from school over my head. It wasn't technically a boom box, but I hoped my friends would get the reference anyway. The CD player also didn't work, so I had to awkwardly wait in my car until a half-decent apology song came on the radio and then rush in with the thing held up high.

Everybody stopped talking and turned to look at me as I came walking in slowly, eyes locked on the table where Iris and Miranda were watching with wide-eyed horror.

I could hear tables breaking into excited whispers as I passed. It was peak breakfast time, and Bradley's was absolutely packed. Everyone knew the drama between my trio of friends and the King brothers already, including the "breakup" that had happened last night between Rich and me. Considering I never thought we were officially dating, I thought calling it a breakup was a bit dramatic.

Iris regained her composure first. She put her hand on her holster and looked to Miranda. "I think I could shoot it out of her hands if she keeps moving at that speed. Then again, I might miss and hit her. Either way, I think we could call it a win."

I set the stereo down on the table. "Can I sit?"

Miranda pressed the power button, and once the music was off, I could hear the ocean-like whoosh of dozens of whispered conversations all around us. "You may," she said coldly.

I sat down. The whispers quieted, and nobody was trying very hard to act like they weren't watching. I ignored all of them. I felt like the village idiot. Not only had I thrown away my friendship for a guy, but I'd managed to lose the guy too. To top it off, everyone in West Valley seemed to know exactly what had happened.

"You turning yourself in, or do you want to do this the hard way?" Iris asked. She pulled out her handcuffs and twirled them on her finger.

I worked my lips to the side, not sure if I was supposed to smile or not. "I confess that I was an ass. And I'm sorry I broke the promise. But I'm coming back with my head hanging low, ready to accept my punishment if you two will just please talk to me again."

Iris wiggled her eyebrows. "I'm over it. It's not fun trying to kick a girl when she's down anyway, and you're so, *so* far down it's honestly pathetic. It's kind of like *The Scarlet Letter*, except yours would be an *L*, because you look like a total loser in front of the whole town. And at least Hester Prynne got laid to earn that *A*. Wait, did she actually get laid in the book, or did everyone just assume she did?"

I nodded. "She was guilty."

"Yeah, so, whatever," Iris said offhandedly. "You transgressed, child. You strayed from the path, but you know what? I just can't quit you, Kira Summerland. You're my crack. My sexy librarian."

I laughed. "Thank you. I think. And thanks for putting it so delicately. I have been feeling pretty self-conscious, so it's good to know it's every bit as embarrassing as I imagined."

Iris looked to Miranda. "We forgive her, right?"

Miranda crossed her arms and wouldn't raise her eyes to meet mine.

"Miranda, come on," Iris urged. "Rich put her through enough on his own, didn't he? Do we really need to pile on?"

"Yeah, fine. I guess it's silly to keep putting so much focus on the promise after all this time anyway. To be completely honest, it had started to feel more like a joke at some point. But when they came back, it was like some kind of switch flipped. I mean, I'm still not going near any of the Kings with a ten-foot pole, but getting pissed at you for making your own choices? Yeah. I let it get out of control, and I'm sorry."

Iris nodded. "The best friendships are the ones that are full of past drama and infighting. I mean, how else do you know it's good if you never test it, right?"

"Thank you for trying to make me feel better," I said. "But I promise I wasn't intentionally trying to test our friendship. It means more to me than anything."

"Well," Miranda said. "I owe you an apology anyway. Asking you to choose between Rich and us was way over the line. Especially in front of him. You had every right to tell us to go fuck ourselves."

I smirked. "I don't think those were the words I used."

"Of course not," Iris said. "You were all polite. *Actually, I think I'd prefer to pick the one who isn't being a big meanie, thanks.*"

I laughed. "I don't sound anything like that." I took a deep breath and braced myself for what I was about to say. "But I have to admit something."

"Oh jeez," Iris said.

"I have feelings for Rich. He broke things off with me, but"—I swallowed hard—"I wasn't happy about it."

Miranda raised her eyebrows. "What are you saying, exactly?"

"I'm saying that I can't come here and pretend I'm some changed woman and the idea of being with Rich is behind me. I have trouble thinking about anything *but* him. He's on my mind constantly."

"Especially in the shower with that detachable showerhead of yours, I bet," Iris whispered.

I glared but couldn't help smiling. Miranda was grinning, too, which was a relief to see. I knew it was weird for both of them, but I sensed that they were slowly coming to terms with the idea that I had feelings for Rich, even if Miranda was coming along more slowly than Iris.

"I've never masturbated in my life," I said. "Thank you very much."

Iris nearly spit out her coffee. "Oh, obviously. Because that dildo you forgot to put away when we visited your dorm in college was just for clubbing home invaders, right?"

I sat up a little straighter. I'd forgotten about that particular experience. "The point is that I have feelings for him. Okay? It probably doesn't matter now, because he decided I'm better off without him."

Miranda's foot was shaking a little aggressively, and she looked like she was fighting not to say something.

"What?" I asked.

She stared at the ceiling a few seconds before finally blowing out a sigh. "I can't believe I'm going to actually encourage you here, but are you really going to let *him* decide what's best for *you*?"

"Wait," I said. "Is that question the same as you giving me your blessing to date him?"

"It's me saying that you shouldn't let some rich asshole decide how you live your life. If you want him, take him."

"For clarification," Iris said quietly, "you probably shouldn't take that advice literally. Because, you know . . ."

"As much as I appreciate the advice, I'm pretty sure it isn't going to matter. He made himself pretty clear last night."

"Come on," Miranda said. She seemed to be focusing so hard on winning the argument that she was forgetting she was trying to reignite a relationship that had very nearly ended our friendship just a few days ago. "The guy mauls you one night, and then he shows you his dinosaur bones the next. I think we can pretty safely say he wants you. He just thinks he's being noble by turning you down. You go to him and you say *fuck that*."

"You could also say *fuck me*," Iris suggested.

I slumped down on the table and let my forehead bang painfully against the wood. "I don't know what I'm going to do. Maybe I'll just clear out the ice cream aisle at the grocery store and watch some movies tonight."

"Not by yourself, you won't," Iris said.

♥ ♥ ♥

Cade and Stella were sitting in my tiny condo. Surreal didn't begin to describe it. One moment, I'd been moping around the house with a stomach that was not happy with the quantity of ice cream I'd forced into it last night, and the next, *them*. They looked so out of place on my dingy little couch.

Cade had somehow decided to open the drawer by the couch and discovered several of my works in progress. There were sweaters for everything from ferrets to gerbils, and I wasn't sure I'd ever seen anyone look as amazed as he did. He was picking each one up, holding it in front of his eyes, smiling, and then carefully setting it down in front of him on the coffee table.

"We actually didn't come here to admire your tiny-sweater collection," Stella said. "Though it's a very nice collection."

"It's more like a hobby," I muttered. "Extra pocket money."

"Right, well . . . I'll get straight to the point." Stella sighed as if she knew she'd regret what she was going to say. "Rich needs you. He'll never admit it, and I'm sure he'd be content to go on punishing himself by avoiding you, but he needs you. You brought out a better side of him."

Cade nodded. "He wasn't as cranky when you two were, *you know. Coupling.*"

"We never—" I started, then stopped myself. What we did or didn't do wasn't their business. Then again, I was painfully desperate to find my way back into Rich's life. Stella's words felt like a thread of hope, and I knew I'd grasp it, no matter how unlikely it was to work.

"Never did the deed?" Cade finished. "Rich really didn't have much of an effect on you, did he? Poor guy."

I shook my head. "It would've been easy if he didn't. None of this has been easy."

"In all seriousness," Cade said. "Would you be able to make these for men with small penises? I promised Rich I'd knit his cock a sweater a few weeks ago, but it looks like you could save me the trouble. I'm thinking something that'd fit maybe two inches? Actually, we better make it one and a half. No point trying to boost his ego and giving him something that'll be way too big."

I looked at Stella for help.

She just shrugged and shook her head. "Sometimes it's easier to just pretend you didn't hear him."

"Uh, I can hear you," Cade said.

She turned to look icily at him. "If only your brain worked as well as your ears."

He scrunched up his face. "Last time I checked, the only reason ears work is because they're connected to the brain. So, yeah, don't feel so smart now, do you?"

"When I'm forced to talk to you? No. I don't feel smart at all."

He sniffed victoriously and resumed searching through the sweaters.

"I'm not sure what you want me to do," I said. "Even if I did want things to work between Rich and me, it's not like I can just go knock on his door and beg him to take me back."

"You could," Stella said slowly. "But I have a plan that's a little more elegant. If you're interested, that is."

Chapter 18

RICH

I waited in front of the restaurant where I was supposed to meet Stella, Cade, and Nick. As usual, they were all late. By now, I should've learned to save myself the trouble and show up to any arrangement at least ten minutes late, but the thought alone made me clench my teeth with stress.

The night was pleasantly warm. I leaned against one of the support poles beneath the restaurant's pavilion and watched groups arriving for dinner. Most of the guests were couples, but one large business party did pass by. Gradually, my thoughts wandered to Kira, even though I'd been trying to train myself not to think of her.

Tough decisions. That was what I did best. I'd always been good at bottling things up. I took a kind of pride in it. I felt like the shield for my brothers. I absorbed the harsh truths of what we did to make Sion successful and let them live guilt-free. I took all the negativity and shoved it deep down where I didn't have to think about it.

Doing the same with Kira had been like a reflex. I'd thought about the problems it would cause for us to be together. I knew my parents well enough to know they wouldn't stop at sabotaging my business to prove their point. They'd come down on Kira too. I'd be putting everyone I cared about at risk, and for what? *Love?* Did I even know what the fuck love was?

I knew I couldn't stop thinking about Kira. I wasn't hiding behind the idea that I needed her forgiveness anymore. That wasn't what drove me to chase her all this time. I was chasing the way I felt around her. Success and money had jaded me, but not around her. She looked straight through the bullshit with me. She let me feel like a person instead of an idea.

Gradually watching yourself melt into some unrecognizable *average* was an inevitability of celebrity status. You stopped getting the chance to make first impressions. Your every action was not only up for interpretation, but it was also subjected to "expert" analysis. People would speak from a place of imagined authority about you and shape the way others saw you. It was maddening if you thought too hard about it.

When people think they know you before they meet you, you're always living in the shadow of someone else's ideal. I'd lost track of the number of women who'd loved "me" before they met me. Nothing I did could convince them otherwise. Relationships felt empty. I couldn't connect with somebody who was more interested in who they wanted me to be than who I was.

But that was not Kira.

Kira had given me the choice to screw things up if I wanted to but also the chance to make them good. And just when they were finally going well, I'd let reflexes and fear kick in. I'd fucked everything up.

I leaned my head back and closed my eyes. I willed all those thoughts down deep where they could join the rest of my regrets. What was done was done.

"Hey," a woman said in my ear.

I jolted upright and opened my eyes. "Kira?" I asked.

She gave a little shrug and a shy smile. "Surprise?"

"What are you doing here?" I looked around quickly, noting how many people were around and how many of them were probably already planning to spread a new rumor at the first opportunity.

"Stella and Cade helped set this up. I'm sorry. I felt bad tricking you, but they thought this was the best way."

My hand was on her cheek before I realized it had moved. I pulled it back and frowned, but Kira gripped me by the wrist and pulled it back, leaning into my touch.

One gesture. One surge of warmth from her skin. That was all it took.

I pulled her into a tight hug and threaded my fingers through her hair. "I'm glad you came."

"Good." She laughed into my chest. "Because I didn't have anything fancy enough for this place and I had to buy this skirt. I guess I can take the tags off now."

"Well, are you hungry?"

Dinner was good, and the fact that we managed to go nearly half an hour without talking about "the breakup that wasn't" or anything more serious than how we preferred our steak cooked was even better. Talking to her was easy. It was comfortable, like sinking down into an old, well-worn chair. Even though I knew bigger questions were looming, I was able to relax.

The waiter took our dinner plates away, and we ordered dessert. The restaurant was busy, but the dining room had a kind of cozy design that muffled the noise of so many conversations. Our own little booth was in the corner as well, which meant there wasn't much to look at except Kira.

"You know," she said. "Despite all the crap I gave you about forcing your way into helping with the play, the kids are devastated that you're not going to be part of it now."

I grinned. "You told them I was going to help?"

"It might have slipped out. I regretted it, though, because it was all the girls talked about for the past few weeks. You'd think I told them their dogs had died when I said you weren't going to be helping after all."

"So you're saying you need my help?"

"*Need* is a strong word. I'm saying your help would be appreciated by the students."

"I've got to be honest. I'm more worried about what their hot teacher would appreciate."

Kira licked her lips, but her eyes didn't leave mine. "My guess is that she'd appreciate it if people didn't try to decide what was best for her without her input."

My stomach clenched. There it was. We'd done our best to dance around the topic of what I'd done after the party, but I knew we couldn't avoid it forever. She needed to know, and I needed to decide. Was I still trying to put an end to us, or was it back on?

"That's fair," I said slowly. "I'm not going to lie. I've thought about the choice I made. A lot. I've wondered if it was the right one."

"You know, not long after we started sort of . . ." She trailed off and made a circular gesture.

"Started sort of what?" I asked.

She sighed. "You know."

I chuckled. "When you decided to stop hating me and gave me a shot? Or do you mean when you unleashed your sexual desires and nearly mauled me at my place?"

Kira finally laughed again. "That's both an unflattering and inaccurate description."

"If my memory serves, you pretty much rammed me into the wall and started grinding on me, so . . ."

"Rich!" she half whispered and half laughed. "Not so loud."

"So you don't deny it."

"No. I do. I'm just more worried about your delusional memory landing in someone's ear where it can become gossip." She lowered her voice and leaned forward. "I will give you that it was mutual, but that's as far as I'll go."

"Mutual. Hmm. That's one way to describe it."

"You're getting away from the point. I need to know where we stand. I need to know I'm not just going to get tossed aside without warning if I open myself up to you again."

"I didn't toss you aside. I was trying to protect you."

"From what? Because from where I'm standing, it felt like the only one hurting me was you. I was perfectly happy until you made me feel like an idiot for starting to have feelings for you."

"Come on. You only *started* to have feelings for me? I think that ship had sailed and docked around the time your tongue was down my throat."

She glared at me.

"Okay," I said. My smile faded. I knew I needed to take this conversation seriously, but I also felt a mounting certainty that I'd been the one to screw up. I'd told myself I was doing the smart thing by breaking it off with Kira, but the more I thought about it, the more I realized I'd made the coward's choice. If I committed to a public relationship with Kira, my parents would disown me. Admittedly, that wouldn't be a huge loss on the surface, but deep down, I'd always hoped to find some resolution with them. If I hadn't, I would've walked away from them a long time ago. Stella would suffer the consequences and so would my company. Worse, I'd be propelling Kira into the national spotlight, and I wasn't sure she fully understood the perils of celebrity status.

I was about to speak when the waiter set our dessert down. It was a huge bowl full of ice cream, fruit, and chocolate. He took a minute to explain, as was the custom in expensive restaurants, why each ingredient was better and fancier than we might realize. The fruits were a wild variety that had just been picked in the restaurant's private garden that morning, the ice cream was handmade from an exclusive type of cow that had been meticulously bred for a century to give the best, sweetest milk for desserts.

We waited patiently while he rattled off everything there was to know about the dessert, but I barely heard any of it.

He left, and neither of us touched our spoons.

"Kira," I said. "I was an idiot. Being with you isn't going to be easy. There are people who are going to try to stop us, but I don't care. And you're right. I shouldn't have tried to make the decision for you."

"I agree," she said. There was the shadow of a smile on her lips.

"Wait, with which part?"

"You *were* an idiot."

I laughed. "Fair enough. But what about the rest?"

"I think I'm supposed to hold my cards close here," she said, "but I was never good at card games. I don't care about my pride. I just don't want it to end. These few weeks have been amazing. Even with all the stuff going on in the background, I don't think I've ever felt happier. So, yes. A big, *big* yes."

"I'm happy that your answer is a *yes*, but I don't recall asking a yes or no question."

Kira pointed her spoon at me, presumably meaning some kind of threat. "I don't think being an ass is your best strategy right now."

"No? If you were in my shoes, what would be your next move?"

She took a bite of the dessert and paused just long enough to savor it. The fact that she could still pause at a moment like this to enjoy some good food made me like her even more. "That depends," she said finally. "If I'm going to tell you what your next move should be, I think I need to know your intentions."

"Getting you into my bed. Naked, preferably."

She choked on the sip of water she was taking.

It was good to see I could still make her blush.

"Well," she said slowly, "if that was your goal, I'd say you should tackle the biggest obstacle first."

I sighed. "Is this where you tell me I need a time machine? Or maybe a way to wipe your memory?"

"No. The biggest obstacle is that we're in a restaurant right now and your bed is at least thirty minutes away. I'm also fully clothed, and the bra I'm wearing has a strap that's a little tricky." If it was possible, her blush deepened.

My eyebrows crept upward. Kira had the most adorably dirty mind for someone who came across as innocent as she did. I still suspected she was a virgin, but there was such a vulgar streak to her that it was almost hard to believe. I felt the last shreds of my reservations evaporate into thin air.

Screw consequences. Screw my parents. Screw anything bad that might come from following my feelings. Actually, better yet. *Screw Kira.* That sounded like a better plan.

"We could call for a helicopter," I said. "Also, I've got bolt cutters in the garage at my place. I don't care if your bra is made of Kevlar. It's coming off."

Chapter 19

KIRA

I'd thought Rich was kidding about the helicopter. Apparently, when you have billions of dollars, it's actually not that hard to arrange for a helicopter to pick you up on short notice. Less than ten minutes after my vagina stole control of my brain from me, I was ducking into a helicopter in the empty parking lot behind the restaurant.

The ride was incredible. I got to see West Valley like I'd never seen it before. Unsurprisingly, Overlook Point had never done the town justice with its measly view. *This* was the way to appreciate all the natural beauty of the place I'd called home all my life.

I was unfortunately too distracted for most of the ride to give it the attention it deserved.

I don't know what I expected, but nothing had gone the way I imagined. The last time I'd spoken to Rich, he looked like he had made up his mind. He and I were over, and that was final.

At dinner, I'd seen an entirely different look in his eyes. It had barely been twenty-four hours since the party, but Rich didn't look anywhere near sure about ending things. I hadn't mentally prepared for that. Before I knew it, I felt like I was sitting in the back seat as my lower half ran my mouth and essentially *asked* him to take me back to his place and sleep with me.

Oops.

Considering I still wasn't sure I would know which end of the penis went where, it was a bold move. Foolishly bold, for certain. It was also too late to back out.

I should have felt terrified. For all I knew, I'd be a bumbling, clumsy mess. My dress would get stuck on my chin, and I'd be left flopping around blind and half-naked in front of Rich. Despite what I'd said to Miranda and Iris, I knew from my brief explorations with masturbation that I was incapable of enjoying myself in a quiet, dignified manner. As soon as the heat started flowing, I turned into a version of myself that I wasn't proud of.

By the time we landed in Rich's backyard, my fists were in tight balls around the hem of my dress, and I was starting to wonder if I'd be able to seize the controls of the helicopter from the pilot and fly away. Couldn't my stupid, horny mind have said something more practical? Maybe I could've told him the biggest obstacle was that I never slept with guys on Thursdays, and we'd have to wait until Friday? Technically it would've been true, since I never slept with guys on *any* day of the week, but who was keeping track?

A day would've been enough time to do some internet research on how to be good in bed, right? And why had I never thought to research that before now? Was I an idiot?

We hopped out of the noisy helicopter, leaving the sound-canceling headphones in our seats. Rich waved to the pilot once we were on his back patio, and within seconds, the roar of the engine was just a distant, faint sound.

We were alone, and the quiet was terrifying.

"You okay?" he asked.

"Oh, absolutely," I said. I was talking too fast, I realized, but I wasn't sure I could stop myself. "I'm completely okay. Sex isn't a big deal to me, actually. I have sex all the time."

The corners of Rich's eyes crinkled in amusement. "Is that right? With your right hand, or your left?"

"Excuse me?" I laughed at the sound of my own outraged voice a second later. *God.* I wished I could get it together.

"I was asking which hand you usually masturbated with."

I could see from the look on his face that he was messing with me, but I was too overwhelmed to take it in stride. My mouth gaped, and I couldn't seem to think of an appropriate response.

"I was hoping you'd laugh," he said softly. "You looked nervous."

I swallowed and nodded a little too fast. "A little. Yeah."

He took me wordlessly by the hand and led me inside his house. Soft music seemed to come from everywhere. It wasn't cheesy *I'm about to get some action* music. It was just a nice, pleasant kind of ambience.

"Does that just play all the time?" I asked. My eyes searched the ceiling for speakers, but I couldn't spot any.

"When the doors are opened," he said. "So I guess if anyone ever decides to rob my house, they'll get a mellow soundtrack to work by." He must've seen the look on my face, because he tilted his head to the side and continued. "It gets a little lonely in here when it's completely quiet."

"I always imagined you as the type who would enjoy solitude."

"Being in the spotlight is a strange kind of lonely. It feels like the whole world is looking over your shoulder, but they only want to watch the entertaining parts." His eyebrows pulled together in thought. "Did you ever jump from a hot tub to a swimming pool when you were a kid?"

"Uh," I said slowly. "Yeah, actually. Miranda's parents had a hot tub, and sometimes we'd just go back and forth. Are we still talking about loneliness?"

"Well, do you remember how some days the pool wouldn't feel cold, but if you came from the hot tub, it was like ice?"

"Yeah. And the hot tub felt like it was going to melt your skin off after the pool."

"Right. Being a celebrity is kind of the same. If I go out to eat or to some event, I'm absolutely suffocated by attention. Then you get home, and the silence feels so intense by comparison."

I studied his face. I could see something more buried in the sharp lines of his features now. I thought I understood how hard it must be. He wasn't just some golden child who had everything go his way from birth. He was talented and gifted and lucky in so many ways, but his life wasn't perfect. Nobody's was. For once, I thought I understood that Richard King was no exception.

I put my fingers on the lapel of his coat and ran them down it. A rush of adrenaline spiked through me, because I felt like I wasn't in the driver's seat of my mind, but I knew exactly where I was headed. I wanted to make him feel better. I wanted to take away some of that loneliness, because I felt it too. Maybe not for the same reasons, but I always felt like I was different, and my differences created barriers between me and even my closest friends.

"Well," I said quietly. "You're not alone tonight, at least."

He cupped my face and locked his eyes on mine. I thought my knees might give out from the intensity of the moment—his touch so soft against my jaw while his eyes bored straight into me. "I regret a lot of things." His words brushed against my forehead. They were warm and still carried a faint scent of the fruits we'd had in our dessert. "I don't intend for tonight to be one of them."

A chill prickled across the nape of my neck. "Then I only have one question."

His eyes roamed my face with a casual, unhurried reverence that was making it hard to think. He was absorbing every detail of me—I was sure of it. "Ask it."

"Would your biggest regret be if you didn't show me your dinosaur bones again? Or were you talking about something else?"

His lips twitched up at the corners, but his eyes still carried that unstoppable heat and purpose. "There will be plenty of time for that. *After*."

"After what?" I asked, even though his tone gave me no doubt that I knew exactly what he was talking about.

Instead of responding, he scooped me up and carried me up the stairs, taking two steps at a time. I giggled, even though I'd never been the giggling type. "Don't drop me," I said.

"Don't worry. If you get injured, I've watched enough medical TV shows to be your doctor."

"I'd rather not need a doctor, thank you very much."

"Oh, but I'm pretty sure you'd enjoy your visit." He kicked open the door to his bedroom.

It was a beautiful space. The decorations were sparse, but they weren't needed because of the sweeping view the far wall gave of the backyard, the river, and the twinkling lights beyond it.

"What would your treatment be if I broke my leg?" I asked.

He tossed me on the bed like I weighed nothing more than a throw pillow. I landed with another unexpected giggle, except this time, the laughter faded faster. A pulsing, burning heat was building in my stomach, and trying to take my mind from the inevitable was useless. He was going to take me, and it was going to be *sublime*.

"Broken leg?" he asked. He started loosening his tie while he thought, stripping off his clothes with that same slow, deliberate pace. "I'd prescribe bed rest."

"And would I be resting in this bed alone, Doctor?" I asked.

"Unfortunately, no." He took off his jacket and dropped it to the floor. "You would need constant supervision."

I grinned. "I guess it's too bad you didn't drop me, then."

He started down the buttons of his shirt, giving me tantalizing inch by tantalizing inch. I was surprised for a minute to see his chest wasn't hairless but immediately decided the amount of hair he had on his body was perfect, which shouldn't have been a surprise. I was so used to muscular, fit men obsessively shaving themselves clean as babies, but the fact that Rich wouldn't be so vain made me like him even more. Besides, I thought it might require some rare form of brain damage to have any problem with Rich's body—hair or no hair.

His shirt was on the floor now, and he seemed to tower over me. His broad, sculpted shoulders and arms flexed and shifted as he pulled his belt free and dropped it to join the rest.

"My professional diagnosis is that you're overheated," Rich said. "No broken bones, but you're going to need to lose the clothes."

"Call me crazy, but your professional diagnosis doesn't carry much weight with me."

"No?" He knelt down and picked up his shirt. "Should I just put this back on and call it a night, then?"

I could've laughed at how fast I got my own shirt off. Any thoughts of being self-conscious or worrying what he might think of me were drowned by the fear of messing this up. I was joking with him, but it was only to distract myself from the numbing barrage of doubts and fears bouncing around in my brain. I was about to sleep with a guy for the first time, and he was probably going to know it the moment things got serious. Forget the shit storm this would probably cause in West Valley and even in the media. That would all come tomorrow. I was fairly sure of it.

No matter how hard I tried, I couldn't think past tonight. I didn't *want* to think past tonight, even if I was so nervous I thought I might forget to breathe.

"Drop that shirt," I said.

He let it fall back to the ground. I expected him to continue his little striptease, but apparently, he couldn't hold himself back anymore. He crawled onto the bed, giving me a delicious anatomy lesson in all the places a man's torso could be covered in rippling, flexing muscles.

My head was on his pillow, and his eyes were only inches from mine. My rapidly rising and falling chest was so close to his that I could feel my breasts press into him each time I inhaled.

"Either you drugged me, or I'm experiencing some kind of hotness-induced paralysis right now," I said.

Rich was apparently past laughing. He was just looking down at me in that searching, absorbed way of his. When he licked his lips, I felt myself lurching upward against my will. The idea of my tongue gliding across his full lips was enough to make me want to scream with anticipation.

"That sounds like a ploy to get me to undress you," he said. "But all you had to do was ask."

"I wasn't kidding when I said this bra clasp was tricky. Good luck."

Rich scoffed. He pulled me up to a sitting position and wrapped his arms around me as he reached for the clasp of my bra. The position put my face right in his chest, where I could breathe in how amazing he smelled. I'd always rolled my eyes a little at women who gushed over the idea of being held by a strong man. I never understood the appeal until now.

Rich wasn't even technically holding me, and after a few seconds, he was cursing and tugging in frustration at the clasp. "You weren't kidding."

His voice rumbled through his chest and into my skin. I chewed my lip, thanking my bra for the first time in my life for being a cheap piece of crap. It was now a miracle worker because it meant I had an excuse to sit and be wrapped in Rich's arms, even for a little longer.

"Fuck it," he said. He yanked his arms apart and tore my bra in a single, abrupt motion.

I gasped in surprise and put my hands up to cover myself as my bra slid down to my waist. Rich shook his head, peeling my hands away.

"Don't cover yourself. Not in front of me. I've waited way too fuck-ing long for this, and I won't have you being self-conscious. You're too perfect for that."

"If you say so," I whispered. I barely heard him. The words coming out of his mouth didn't matter as much as the way he said them and the glint of hunger in his eyes. Words could be chosen carefully and crafted for a purpose, but I didn't think the way he was looking at me could be faked. The way he sounded was real, and I never felt sexier or more wanted than I did in that moment. If I'd still felt reservations before that moment, they were gone now. All that remained was desire. Liquid, hot, and irresistible desire.

"I do. And it's true," he said. He pulled my hand up and kissed my palm with a wicked grin. "Besides, if you keep using these to cover yourself, I'll have to restrain you."

"I'll behave," I said.

He kissed my neck softly while his hands explored me. His voice was soft—almost tender. "I know this is probably your first time. You don't need to be scared about it. It's not something you can mess up, okay? It's not about the result, it's about the experience."

"Who said it was my first time?" I asked.

"The fact that you're trembling. The way I can see desire and reservation battling just behind your eyes." He kissed me again, this time just above my clavicle. It sent shockwaves of heat spearing through me. "All you have to do is enjoy yourself. That's what I want, and if you are having a good time, I will too. Understand?"

He had told me exactly what I needed to hear, even though I hadn't realized I needed to hear it. "What if I only last a minute?"

He laughed. "It's just guys who have to worry about that." His fingertip followed a slow, tingling path down from my collarbone to my breast. He bent to kiss my nipple, swirling his tongue in one warm sweep around it before pulling away with a satisfied smile. "Let me take the lead. Just relax." He gave me a shove in the chest that was just forceful enough to catch me by surprise and send me flopping back to the bed.

He took my skirt in both hands and tugged it down. I laughed a little when my whole body slid a few inches down the bed and off the pillow from the force of his tug.

"There's a zipper," I said. "In the back."

Without a word, Rich flipped me over and yanked the zipper down. He tugged on my skirt again. This time, it slid free.

I was topless, in my panties, and the lights weren't even off. In a moment of awkward panic, I wondered how weird I'd look if I clapped twice just in case he happened to have sound-activated lights. Thankfully, I resisted the urge. I would survive.

I never knew why it was so hard to believe there was something in me to be desired—that to some man or some pair of eyes I might actually be perfect. I wondered if it was just the fresh new-relationship chemicals that were blinding him to the obvious. When my arms were straight, my left elbow looked like a winking smiley face. My knees were knobby. My hips never seemed womanly enough, and when I saw pictures of myself, it always looked like my smile was crooked. And those were just my insecurities when I was wearing clothes.

But nothing in Rich's body language said he was finding faults in me. He still held my skirt like some kind of war trophy as he straddled me and looked me over. "I could get addicted to you," he said.

I rolled over and bit my lip. "You say that now . . ."

He bent down and kissed me on the lips. It was a soft, reassuring kind of kiss, and I loved that he could sense that I needed reassurance. "You're right. And in about an hour, I'll be saying I *am* addicted to you."

"Addictions are something you wish you could quit. I'd rather be your hobby. At least people like their hobbies."

"Would you settle for an obsession?"

"Obsessions can be nice."

He kissed me again, then straightened and shimmied out of his pants and underwear. The next thing I knew, his face was between my legs. "Not that I'm assuming you're a virgin, but if you were, I'd want your first experience to be a good one."

I smirked. "Not that you're assuming." My heart was pounding relentlessly. As if my goal was to torture myself, I was running through how insane it was that the guy I'd had a crush on, hated, and gone back to having a full-blown, grown-up crush on, was looking up at me from between my legs. His hands were still roaming me like he already owned me, and I knew it was going to be only a minute before I'd give him the part of myself I'd never given anyone before.

"Are you listening?" he asked.

I realized he'd been speaking, but my thoughts were firing off too quickly for me to take it all in. "Yes," I said.

"Liar. I said I was going to show you why some women think foreplay is the best part of sex. And then I'm going to show you why sex is the best part of sex."

"O—okay. And I just lie here?"

"That's exactly right." He pressed his lips against me. It was through the fabric of my panties, but it was the single hottest moment of my life. My entire body reacted to the touch. Sparks of fire went off in my belly, making my blood itself feel like it was running hot. My back arched upward, and my lips parted. I held back a premature gasp of pleasure, but only barely.

If it felt this good through my panties, how was I going to handle what came next?

"I knew you would taste delicious."

"Is that just something you say because it sounds hot, or do I really—"

"You really do," he said with a soft chuckle. "Now stop talking and let me enjoy this."

I wrinkled my nose at him but did as I was told. I plopped my head back on the pillow and bit down a nervous squeal when he slid my panties down.

There was no turning back now. Well, I guess I could've still turned back. It's just that now I'd be completely naked while turning back, versus partially clothed, which didn't seem like a very important distinction to make.

I braced myself for the moment when he'd put his mouth on me and shivered in surprise when his lips touched my inner thigh. He used his hands to push my legs open a little wider, giving him access to every inch of skin he could want. Kiss by kiss, he came closer to my waiting heat.

I was already rocking my body into his kisses when the soft warmth of his lips found my pussy.

It was too much. I'd held back the sounds of my enjoyment so far, but there was only so much I could take. The first of my moans spilled out of me like a whisper, but I knew they were going to get louder.

The slight, nearly imperceptible hitch in his kisses told me he'd heard it, and the increased intensity a second later told me he'd liked it too.

It didn't take long to figure out that Rich was like a vampire for my pleasure. Any indication of enjoyment I gave out seemed to flow straight into him as energy. His kisses grew heavier and more sensual every time I moaned or squirmed in his grip. His breaths grew heavier and his movements more desperate.

It was a frantic race to a finish line I could sense but not see—a test to find out how high we could climb before one of us would fall.

I dug my fingertips through his hair, squeezing hard enough that it probably hurt, but I couldn't stop myself. His tongue slid across my most sensitive places, exploring me with a familiarity and thirst that was as carnal as it was intimate.

"I'm ready," I breathed.

"I don't remember putting you in charge," he said from between my legs. The bastard didn't even move far enough away from me to stop his lips from moving against me with each syllable. Every word teased me deeper.

"Tough shit." I laughed. It was a desperate kind of laugh. I needed to come or I'd burst. It was almost too much. *Too good.*

He gave me one parting kiss between my legs before he kissed an agonizingly slow, meandering path up my body. He took an extra-long detour around my breasts, and when he finally reached my chin, he kissed his way up my jawline and paused at my ear. "You're lucky I'm so desperate to get inside you, Kira. Otherwise, I'd make you play by the rules."

Each word slid into my ear and seemed to take on a life of its own, curling across my body like wisps of hot smoke. I suspected I was supposed to have something witty to say. Something so devilishly sexy that it would make him laugh and want to sleep with me all at the same time. So of course, I delivered on all counts.

"Okay," I whispered back.

He *did* laugh. "Okay, then." A determination and focus colored his eyes, and he reached down between us with one hand. I felt the silky head of his cock against me. I was wet. *God,* I was so wet it was almost embarrassing, but something told me it would only turn Rich on more. If my excitement was his fuel, then what more pure form could it take, after all?

He pushed his hips forward slightly, and in a single, eye-opening moment, I understood what the fuss was all about. Years of lying to myself about how I didn't actually *need* a man went up in smoke. I understood it wasn't just about the sensation—that wonderful friction and the fullness I felt with him inside me. There was a connection words couldn't describe. We'd both stripped away all our clothes and our barriers. We wore our feelings for each other on our sleeves in the most plain, inarguable way possible.

It was pure. It was beautiful. And I wondered how I'd ever think about anything except chasing this moment and all the moments like it for the rest of my life.

I tightened my thighs around him, pulling him closer to me and causing him to bury himself even deeper. My back arched, and my mouth was agape. Distantly, I realized I was gasping and moaning for him, but it felt like the sounds were coming from too far away to be from me, like I was slowly floating away from my body to a place where nothing negative could touch me.

Just like when he was between my legs with his mouth, he seemed to feed on my pleasure. The intensity of his thrusts and the tightness of his grip on my hips and breasts and shoulders increased with a gradual inevitability like a piece of music climbing toward a crescendo. Except there weren't enough notes or instruments complex enough to carry music to such heights. We climbed and climbed together, his body becoming slick and hot against mine as we made love and as we *fucked*.

I dug my fingernails into his back and my heels into his ass like I was worried someone would try to pull us apart.

He had a way of reading me, of pushing me to the brink of climax and then pulling back or changing his movements just enough to keep me from falling over the edge. Each time he diverted me from the inevitable, the building pressure inside me grew.

It was ecstasy and torment all wrapped into one.

Finally, even he couldn't stop it from happening. He gripped me by the cheeks and kissed me like I'd never been kissed. All the while his hips kept pumping against me. My walls tightened involuntarily, gripping him until the friction felt unbearably good.

Rich slid himself out of me, and I felt something surprisingly warm spread across my belly and sink between my legs. *He came too.* I don't know why the thought struck me with the remote surprise it did, but I guess I'd secretly been afraid he was only pretending I was doing a good job.

Even after he slid out of me, the waves of white-hot bliss didn't stop. I gasped into his mouth and lay trembling against his lips while my body unleashed what felt like a lifetime supply of chemicals into my system. There couldn't have been any drug that compared—no natural high could have come close. I thought back to what Rich had said about getting addicted and knew if he was, it would make two of us.

Chapter 20
RICH

Kira wore one of my button-downs, which was big enough to fit her like a long-sleeved dress. She sat at my kitchen table a little after midnight with a cup of hot chocolate, and I couldn't get enough of the way she kept grinning at me over the rim of her cup.

"What?" she asked.

"It's nothing." I leaned against the kitchen counter and took a gulp of water. I felt surprisingly drained after our little encounter. *And thirsty.* "You've got the afterglow. Flushed cheeks. Smiley." I shrugged. "It's a good look on you. That's all."

"What you're saying is you like how I look after you've had your way with me?"

"Actually, I liked how you looked before, during, and after."

Kira's smile hinted at amusement. "I hope this doesn't come off like I'm fishing for compliments, but I'm genuinely curious. What is a guy like you doing with a girl like me?"

"A guy like me? You mean someone with money?"

"There is that part. I mean, what if I was just some kind of gold digger? How would you even know? Isn't that why rich guys usually end up dating rich women?"

"Are you saying you're only interested in my money?" My tone was loaded with sarcasm. Kira might not have thought so, but I knew her. The real her. I had no fear that she was chasing the zeroes in my bank account, but I also enjoying teasing her.

"I mean, I'm a teacher. We're kind of notorious for being poor. It would make sense if I was making a move on you for your money, wouldn't it?"

"Refresh my memory. When was the last time you made a move? From my recollection, I've been the one with all the moves."

She smirked. "You're right. There was the infamous dinosaur room. The helicopter. Dumping me and then sleeping with me the night after. You're absolutely loaded with top-notch moves. I'm surprised you're not already married."

I raised an eyebrow at her. "And with a mouth like that, I'm surprised you don't get into more trouble."

"Trouble . . . is that what you call last night? Because I'll happily keep talking if it's going to lead to more of that."

"Last night is what you get if you behave."

Kira nodded seriously and made a lip-zipping motion.

I walked over to her and hugged her from behind. I put my lips to her ear and whispered. "I should tell you, though. The reward for good behavior is taking you to my bed. The punishment for bad behavior is bending you over and slapping your ass so hard you'll feel it the next day. And I have to admit, the idea of slapping your ass kind of leads me straight back to fucking you again."

Kira bit her lip. "When did you get to be so dirty?"

"I've just been on my best behavior before now. Besides, this is the good part. We need to enjoy it while it lasts."

"What do you mean?"

"I mean there's no such thing as good or easy. Not from my experience. My parents wanted me with Stella. Your friends didn't want you talking to me, let alone sleeping with me. There's too much tension out there for this to just go off without a hitch, trust me."

"Life doesn't have to be like a movie. There's not always some secret blowup looming in the distance. Besides, Miranda and Iris have come around on the whole *us* thing. So relax a little." She reached up and ran her fingers across my cheek.

My skin prickled. I was still leaning by her ear, and the casual but sensual gesture was one of the first she'd initiated. It said more to me than last night or any of the words we'd spoken. I knew my own feelings for her were rapidly spiraling from intense to out of control, but at least the quick caress she gave told me I might not be alone in the plunge.

I kissed her neck and then straightened back up.

I wished I could agree with her about not needing to worry. "Miranda and Iris are probably fine, but not my parents. They've spent their lives getting what they want. Have you ever seen how a toddler reacts when you take away their favorite toy?"

"Other than the disturbing mental image, I'm not sure I should be too worried about your parents crying and throwing tantrums."

"Toddlers use all the tools they have available to lash out when they don't get what they want. That's what my parents will do, except they have more than crying and shitting their pants to use as weapons. They have money and connections. Get what I'm saying?"

Kira finally looked like she was taking the issue seriously. Her expression had fallen, and she was frowning at the table. "What kind of stuff are you talking about, exactly? Are you thinking they might, *you know* . . ."

I raised my eyebrows expectantly.

"Make us sleep with the fishes," she whispered.

I couldn't help laughing. "No. They're old money, not the Mafia. They'll come at your bank account, not your life."

"Oh," Kira sighed with relief. "Why didn't you say so? They can have it. Last time I looked, it was in the negatives. See, banks do this really great thing where they punish you for being poor by making you poorer. The electric company billed me two days early, which over-drafted me, so they charged me an overdraft fee. Then they billed me a maintenance fee for not having enough money when the month rolled over."

"I can help you with that, if you want."

Kira stiffened. In an instant, her body language had completely changed. She'd gone from casual and relaxed to stiff. "No. I'm fine. They made credit cards and debt for a reason."

"Kira. I appreciate that you want to—"

"Rich." Her voice was firm. "It's important to me that I do it myself, okay? I have a real job now. I make decent money. I just haven't quite had long enough for it to catch me up on everything. But I'll be fine." She paused, and when she spoke again her voice was soft and sincere. "I appreciate the offer, though."

I waved her off. "No, I get it. I'd be the same way. But to answer your question, my parents can do more than come after your finances." I pulled one of the other chairs at the kitchen table out and sat on it backward. "They probably know half the judges, police chiefs, politicians, and anybody else you can think of who is remotely important. And if they don't know them directly, they have a good friend who does, or a friend of a friend."

"You're saying they could tow my car if they wanted?"

I chuckled. "I'm saying they could get you fired. Get you brought up on bullshit charges for something you never did. Get you fined. Make it so your taxes were never received by the IRS . . . I could go on."

She looked a little queasy. "No, actually, that's good."

I frowned. "Sorry, Kira. I'm not trying to freak you out just for the hell of it. Before yesterday, I didn't think my parents actually had the balls to do anything like this. I still have a hard time believing it. I just want you to know what the risks are. I probably should've made it clearer yesterday, but—"

"You don't have to apologize. Kind of ironic, isn't it?"

I laughed. "Actually, it's far from irony. If there has been one constant since I've come back to West Valley, it's that you don't want my apologies."

"Except this time, it's because I don't think you should have to. I'm a big girl, Rich. I can make my own decisions. I always admired people who stood up for what they believed in, even when it seemed like the world was against them."

"It's not the world, though. Just two crusty, grouchy old people with a lot of money and too much time on their hands."

"Yeah, well, I'll feel a lot more cool for doing it if we stick with my phrasing, so you lose the vote."

♥ ♥ ♥

I met my brothers at the construction site of our new headquarters just after sunrise. I still had the taste of Kira's last kiss on my lips. We'd stopped for danishes. She'd gone with raspberry, and I'd picked blueberry. I didn't even remember what we'd talked about, just that we'd talked, and it had come easy. It always seemed to with her. We shared a wavelength, and we could jump from seemingly unrelated topic to seemingly unrelated topic without needing to always explain why.

But if I was going to avoid running my company into the ground, I needed to stop thinking about her, at least for a little while.

There was a surprising amount of work to be done on a construction site of this size. During the earlier stages, we'd delegated the task to a team of contractors, but they had left a lot to be desired. Shortcuts were being taken, and corners were being cut. That had never been how my brothers and I ran our company, and it wasn't how I wanted our headquarters to be built.

So coming to the site and making sure things were being done the right way had become our full-time jobs lately, but today, there were no cars in the parking lot. I double-checked my watch, even though I knew exactly what time it was.

My brothers were already waiting for me in the parking lot when I got out of my car.

"Where is everyone?" I asked.

Cade winced. "You're not going to like this."

Nick shook his head. "That's an understatement. Rich doesn't like when waiters clean up his bread crumbs in front of him, because it makes him feel like a barbarian. This? Rich is going to hate this."

"Can we get to the part where you tell me?" I snapped.

Cade pointed toward the main entrance, where Mayor Summerland was leaning against the door. I pushed past my brothers and headed straight for him, even though I was already fairly sure I knew what was happening.

"Where are all the construction workers?" I asked.

"I think you know where they are," he said. The mayor wore such a smug expression on his face that it took all my willpower not to punch it off him. I needed to remember that I was also looking at Kira's father. It was hard to believe, but I could see the similarities in their features if I looked hard enough. Thankfully, Kira wore them much, much better.

"Humor me," I said.

"West Valley is a small town, Mr. King. And you? You're quite the big fish for such a little pond. You don't think word is going to travel if you rush out of a dinner date with my daughter and fly back to your place in the middle of the night? Then you drop her off at work this morning?"

"We had to work on the details of the school play. Remind me. When did this become your business?" I barely controlled my anger. I couldn't seem to unclench my teeth, but it was better than hitting the mayor. Not only would that likely complicate things with Kira, but I also felt pretty certain it wouldn't make any of my problems go away.

"And those details were between my daughter's legs, I suppose?"

I took two fistfuls of the mayor's shirt and lifted him up to press him against the door. "Careful," I said.

To his credit, he looked down at me with calm eyes. "You sure this is the route you want to take?"

I held him there with fists so tight my fingers were digging into my palms. Not only was he threatening me, but he'd been keeping tabs on me. And from the way he'd talked about Kira, I didn't sense any kind of fatherly love. This was a man who was using his daughter as an excuse to be a piece of shit, not because he cared.

I finally let him slide back down, but I knew I wasn't far from losing my temper again. "You're going to tell me this all goes away if I break things off with Kira. Is that right?"

"No, not exactly. I'm going to tell you that you will break things off with Kira, *and* you will propose to Stella."

I hadn't realized Cade and Nick had caught up to us until I heard Cade suck in a breath between his teeth. "That's not going to go over well," Cade whispered.

"Agreed," Nick said.

"How much are they paying you?" I asked Mayor Summerland.

"I have no idea what you're talking about. This was my idea."

"Right. Because you have so much personally invested in Stella and me getting engaged."

The mayor conceded his lie with a small tilt of the head and a shrug. "It doesn't really matter, does it? The facts are clear. You do what we want, or your headquarters is going to fail every inspection and commit every code violation in the book. It'll be years before this is anything but a hunk of expensive materials. Correct me if I'm wrong, but you boys and your company invested quite a bit in this little stunt, right?"

Cade whistled. "Damn, Mayor Summerland. You should grow a pointy little mustache so you can twirl it after you say diabolical shit like that. Seriously. It's all that's missing."

"A top hat would be good, too," Nick added. "It would cover the fact that he's starting to go bald."

"Well, what is it going to be?" asked the mayor. "Do you boys want to test my patience, or have you realized there's only one smart way out of this?"

"Me?" I asked. "I'm going to go find your daughter. I'll tell her how much I enjoyed last night, and then I'll take her out again tonight. Maybe we'll start off at the town fair and work our way back to my place."

Nick cleared his throat. "I'm not sure if that's tacky or not, considering the circumstances."

"I approve," Cade said. "Personally, I think Rich should've added a little more detail. You know, tell him how his daughter likes it rough or something."

Mayor Summerland was watching us with a clenched jaw. It was good to see I'd finally broken through his cocky indifference. I didn't care if I'd crossed any lines. The man was lucky I had enough restraint to stop myself from releasing with my fists the anger that was boiling inside me.

"I'll let them know you've made your decision, then," the mayor said. He walked into our building, and I heard the sound of the doors locking.

"Did he just lock us out of our own building?" Cade asked.

"Yeah," Nick said, "but the south wall isn't even finished being built yet. If we really wanted in, we could just walk around to the back of the building."

I shook my head. "I can't do what he wants." I looked between my brothers and wondered if they would resent me for this. The company was ours. It was our asses on the line and our money. I had the power to undo all the damage that was coming, but I knew I wasn't going to do what they wanted.

"I don't want you to," Cade said. "I wish he'd told me not to do something too. I can't even have justice sex to spite that dickless dweeb."

"Justice sex," Nick mused. "I'm fairly sure there's no such thing."

Cade looked at him like he was an idiot. "There are all kinds of sex. I wouldn't expect you and your inactive dick to understand that, though."

"Is this really the most important conversation we should be having right now?" I asked.

"Inactive dick?" Nick said. "Just because a woman is willing to have sex with you, it doesn't mean you should. I have higher standards than you. That's all."

Cade laughed. "Okay. First of all. I've turned down plenty of women. Second of all, I happen to be very selective about who I will spend my time with. And third, let's not kid ourselves. 'High standards' is just code for you having such a hard-core crush on Miranda that you're not willing to date anyone else."

"And you're over Iris, I guess?" Nick asked.

I opened my mouth to try again to get them back on a more important topic, but I knew better. When the two of them got into arguments, there was no separating them until they'd hashed it out.

"Um," Cade said, "obviously. She's a small-town police officer. I mean, come on. I can't think of two less sexy words than that."

"Are you being serious? Small-town police officer. That's four words, you idiot."

"They are compound words. Now who is the idiot? When you say them in a pair, it only counts as one word."

Nick threw his hands up in frustration. "Forget the words. I'm just saying if you didn't still want to get back with Iris, you wouldn't have been so eager to come here."

"You three could argue about all of this somewhere else," came a muffled voice from behind the door of the headquarters. It was Mayor

Summerland. "I was just waiting for you all to leave, and then I was going to go to my car."

"Fuck you," shouted Cade. He slammed his fist into the door three times to emphasize his point.

I let out a long sigh. I never understood how I always seemed to wind up surrounded by so many idiots.

"As I was saying," Nick continued. "You jumped on the idea of coming to West Valley. Wild guess. You wanted to get back with Iris."

"Listen," Cade said. "I'm not pathetic like the two of you. I don't want a relationship. I don't want to lay in bed and talk about our favorite colors and that time we almost drowned at the beach when we were kids. Would I be happy to make Officer Iris have the orgasm of her life? Sure. Am I going to lose sleep thinking about it? Hell no. So don't try to drag me into your pathetic little lovesick world."

Nick shook his head in disgust. "I wonder if you actually believe half the things that come out of your own mouth."

"You two are welcome to keep this up," I said. "But I'm going to go find Kira."

"And bring the wrath of Dickless down on us," Cade shouted as he banged on the door again before putting his mouth against it and shouting. "Good. I say you sneak into his house and have a good, dirty fuck right on his bed. With Kira," Cade added.

"I know I'm going to bring shit down on our heads," I said. "But I care about Kira. It's that simple. I wish it didn't mean consequences for all of us, but I don't think it would matter what he threatened me with. It's not going to change the way I feel."

"Barf," Cade said, but he was smirking. *"Go to her,"* he whispered.

"Yeah, get out of here. I think Cade and I are going to stay put for a little. I'm actually feeling a nap coming on."

Mayor Summerland finally decided to speak again. "I heard you say there was a way out the back. I'm not an idiot."

"Good," Cade said through the door. "Then we're going to stand here and watch you awkwardly scurry back through the weeds to your car. And that's *if* you can find your way through the building in the dark."

Nick was smiling wide. He nudged Cade and gave him an approving nod.

I was almost sad that I didn't stay to watch the awkward retreat of the mayor. *Almost.*

Chapter 21

KIRA

West Valley was "famous" for the summer fair we put on every year. In other words, everybody in town looked forward to it and nobody five miles outside West Valley had any clue about it. I was excited all the same, especially because Rich had agreed to spend the evening with me.

I met him near the main street, where tents were already set up for people to show off their favorite home cooking, crafts, and talents or just sit around in the shade and watch everybody enjoy themselves. Music played from everywhere and merged into a kind of nameless buzz of thumping bass and plucked chords.

It had always amazed me how a certain smell could practically zap me back to the past. Someone was making funnel cakes, and with one sniff, I was seven again. I could almost feel the grips of my mom's and my dad's hands in mine. I could remember how I'd pitched a fit because they made me wait until after lunch to come to the fair, since they didn't want me to fill up on junk food. Even back then, I hadn't been close to them. Not really.

The smell passed, and the memory floated away with it.

Seeing Rich was its own kind of strange. I kept expecting to get used to it, and yet every time I saw him, there was a giddy rush of disbelief. I'd play back snapshot memories of what we'd done together, of words he'd said. I'd scrutinize them like a detective trying to find what I was missing. *There had to be a catch, right?* But no matter how hard I looked, I found myself falling only deeper for him. I'd remember the way his eyes would crinkle and his lips would twitch if he thought I'd said something cute. Or the way he seemed so casual and calm, but if I ever stumbled or did something clumsy, he was immediately there to catch me.

The truth was right there in my head, and if I doubted it, all I had to do was see the way he looked at me. Richard King was the most unattainable guy I'd ever known. And I was starting to think he loved me. I was starting to think I loved *him*.

"You okay?" Rich asked. "You're looking a little devious down there."

"Down there? Come on. You're not that much taller than me."

Rich put his hand on top of my head like kids used to when they'd compare height in elementary school. He put his chest up close to me and then slid his hand across the gap between us. It caught him right in the middle of his chest, probably a full foot or more below the top of his head. "If you say so," he said.

I grabbed his hand and pushed it up a few inches. "I did a lot of walking this morning. My body has compressed some. That's my normal height. Right there."

Rich laughed. "Your body has *compressed*. What do you think you're made of, clay?"

"It's true. Your spine compresses throughout the day. Look it up."

He pulled me in for a one-armed hug and kissed the top of my head. "I'll trust you."

I knew it was silly, but heat surged through me. It was pathetic how easily he could melt me. The simple gesture and his words felt like they meant so much more than it would seem on the surface.

I smiled like an idiot as we walked, replaying the moment a few times so it'd still be crystal clear whenever I wanted to pull it back up again.

Rich had a way of making what I would've called dress clothes look casual. He wore the white button-down shirt, dark-blue pants, and dress shoes like it was the most natural thing in the world. I was wearing a simple summer dress that I'd snagged secondhand.

Even though he'd just been joking with me, I thought I saw something dark in his eyes as we walked through the outer edges of the fair.

"Is everything okay?" I asked.

"Yeah. It's fine."

"Hey," I said, taking his wrist and making him turn to face me. I lowered my voice, even though I probably didn't need to with all the music and commotion of the crowds. "I don't know if what happened last night was just par for the course to you, but it was a big deal to me. So you'd better spill those beans you're holding, or I'm going to get offended really quickly."

He chuckled. "Of course, even your threats are adorable. You know, most women would threaten that they were going to get pissed. Your threat is that you're going to get offended?"

"Well, yes. I will if you keep things from me."

He bent down and kissed me. It was between a peck and the kind of kiss you savor. It left me leaning up and forward as he pulled away, hungry for more but also knowing we were playing a dangerous game kissing like that out in the open. I put my finger to my lip and smiled. "That's your strategy? Just kiss me to shut me up?"

"No. I kissed you because it's hard not to. And apparently the whole town already knows about us, so there's no point in being sneaky."

"What? Did somebody say something to you?"

"Your dad, actually."

"Wait, *what*? My dad?" I hadn't expected that. Aside from the awkward conversation in my condo, my dad hadn't shown much interest in what I'd been doing for years now. If I wasn't needed for a public appearance before an election, I wasn't on his radar. It could've come from my mom, but I doubted that too. She and I had never been close, even though we got along well enough on holidays. My parents honestly felt more like friends that I'd grown apart from than family. My mom had been mostly detached for as long as I could remember, and my dad had been using me to advance his career since I was born.

Rich shrugged. "He kind of went evil supervillain on my brothers and me. I'm fairly sure my parents put him up to it. Probably padded his pockets with cash. I wanted you to hear it from me, but I was hoping to wait until tonight to tell you. This all looked fun, and I wanted one more night with you before we had to have all this looming over both our heads."

"Wait, all what? And what do you mean *evil supervillain?*"

Rich told me an abbreviated version of the conversation he'd had with my dad. A minute later, I was wondering if everything he told me would ever fully sink in.

"I wish I could say I didn't believe you," I said.

"For what it's worth, I'm sure my parents offered him a ridiculous amount of money. Nothing is worth more than their reputation."

I closed my eyes. I tried to imagine what my mom would say if she knew. The part that made me feel sick to my stomach was that she probably wouldn't actually care.

Deep inside, something shifted, and I knew the strained, imperfect relationship I had with my parents was never going to be the same again.

"Why don't we just enjoy the fair for now," I said. "From the sounds of it, the best way to give my parents and yours the metaphorical middle finger would be to have fun together, right?"

"Yeah," he said, "although I have to admit it has been a confusing road to this moment. But right now, I couldn't care less about any of them. Your father is going to do what he can to sabotage our company.

My parents will probably try something else if they think we're not planning on stopping. But I don't really care. They can only take things away from me. Stuff. Money. Nothing they do could take you away."

"Well," I said. "I hear hit men aren't that expensive. Technically, if they were really determined—"

Rich let his smile spread in that slow way of his. Most things he did were slow, but not in a lazy, frustrating kind of way. He moved to a pace that was a step behind the normal, like he lived his life to a different, more mellow beat than the rest of us. With him, something as simple as reaching to scratch his forehead could be captivating. "My parents are crazy but not hit man crazy."

"Silver linings," I said. "But what about poison?"

"Hmm. It's possible. I guess I'll just have to stay at your side from now on. You'll need to let me taste everything you eat, just to be sure."

The tone in his voice brought me straight back to last night when he was playing doctor. My mind flashed with vivid images of his hands tight against my skin, of my body wrapped around him as I gasped into his bare shoulder. Or had I *bit* his shoulder? I honestly couldn't even say for sure.

"That sounds totally reasonable," I said. "We'd better go start enjoying ourselves. I know Iris and Miranda are here somewhere. If they spot us, I'm pretty sure they'll do their best to put a stop to our fun."

Rich took my hand and led me down the gently sloping main street toward the more congested area of the fair. People were dancing to live music, but more of them were sitting wherever they could fit, with paper containers full of greasy fried foods or desserts.

"Iris and Miranda still don't approve?" he asked.

"It's complicated. I think they get it on the surface. I mean, the way I feel is the way I feel, right? It's just hard to rewire your brain after seven years of . . ." I trailed off. It didn't sound quite appropriate to say *hating you and your brothers' guts like it was a hobby* or *wishing you'd all come down with rare, incurable diseases.*

Rich squinted at me. "It's funny to think, all this time I imagined you would've purged me from your mind. Instead, it sounds like you were the leader of my own personal hate cult."

"Hey. Don't flatter yourself. We hated your brothers too. And I was hardly the leader. More like a cocaptain."

"Well, well, well," said Iris.

"Jesus!" I said, jumping and turning to face her. I hadn't even seen her coming.

Miranda was beside Iris, and the two of them wore looks that said I had been exactly right about how this was going to go.

"Holding hands?" Iris asked. She wasn't wearing her uniform, but for some reason, she was actually carrying her nightstick. She lifted it and prodded our hands. "Interesting. Isn't it, Miranda?"

Miranda rolled her eyes. "Sorry," she said to Rich and me. "Iris found the craft beer section and got a little too involved in tasting the best of Norway. She was also hiding the nightstick inside her shirt or I would've made her leave it at home. I tried to take it away, and she gave me this." Miranda held up her arm to show a decent-size red mark on her wrist.

Iris shrugged. "You tried to assault an officer of the law. You faced the consequences. In my book, that's justice."

Miranda looked at me like she wished I could save her. I grinned. I had missed my friends. Thankfully, one thing we'd had a lot of years to practice was getting in big, knock-down drag-out fights and then making up. If anything, we always seemed to come out feeling closer in the end.

"It's okay," Rich said. "I should warn you. My brothers are here too. I know the two of you—"

Miranda held up her hand and nodded. "Enough said." She tugged on Iris's sleeve. "Come on, Officer. We've got to get out of here. Bedtime is early tonight."

"Bedtime?" Iris asked. "I am the law, Miranda. Nobody tells me when to go to bed."

I could still hear Iris pleading her case as Miranda dragged her back up the street. Apparently, Iris had drunk enough that her nightstick skills were failing her, because when she tried to beat her way out of captivity, Miranda easily caught her wrist and took the nightstick from her.

Rich stuck his hand out toward me and wiggled his eyebrows once Miranda and Iris were gone.

I stared down at his hand in confusion for a few seconds, then realized he wanted a low five for some reason. I slapped my hand down on his.

He laughed. "Thanks, but no. I was asking you to dance." He nodded toward the shop front where a few local guys were doing a cover of some eighties band I recognized vaguely but couldn't name.

"Oh no. I shouldn't."

"Kira. Come on. Everybody knows already. You said it yourself. We should have fun while we still can."

"No, I mean for the sake of everybody with eyes, I really shouldn't dance. I might scar someone for life. You know how they wanted you to think people were killing themselves in *Bird Box* because of demons? It was actually just images of me dancing everywhere."

"Okay, now you're just being ridiculous. It can't be that bad. Come on," he said.

I could see that he wasn't going to give up easily, and the music *was* catchy. Besides, it had been years since I'd even tried to dance. Maybe I'd grown out of my awkwardness. I summoned up the courage to take his hand and let him drag me into the group of a dozen or so people who were dancing. Most of the people sitting around with their food were watching the dancers, which ratcheted up my nerves a few levels.

The music was relatively fast, and Rich fell straight into what looked like the perfect moves for the song. Nothing flashy, but he clearly had a natural sort of rhythm and grace. I smiled awkwardly and tried to do a more girly version of what he was doing.

I tried a kind of hip-swaying, finger-snapping movement. It seemed like I wasn't moving my feet quite as much as everyone else, so I tried mixing in a few little kicks to the side. I let my head get into it, too, tilting it to the right or left as I snapped. I had a sneaking suspicion that the end result was something between Carlton's dance from *The Fresh Prince of Bel-Air* and Elaine's from *Seinfeld*. I laughed anyway. It felt good to dance for once and not care what people thought.

But within seconds, Rich looked like he wasn't feeling well. He muttered an apology and walked away from where everyone was dancing. I followed after him. I tried to remember if he'd eaten something already and could've possibly developed some sort of food poisoning.

"Your face is all red. Are you okay?" I asked.

Rich sank down to sit on the front steps of a store and covered his face. For a split second, I thought he was crying, but then I realized he was laughing hysterically.

At first, I felt outraged. I balled up my fists and glared, but my anger lasted only a second before I found myself laughing with him. I replayed my dance as well as I could in my mind, trying to imagine how it would've looked from his perspective.

"Was it that bad?" I asked when his laughter had quieted down.

He moved his hands away, and his eyes were actually glistening. His whole face was a shade of red like he'd spent too much time in the sun. "No," he said through twitching lips. "It was amazing. You have a really unique style."

He held a straight face for approximately three seconds before he sank into another fit of laughter.

I couldn't do anything but watch him and smile at how amused he was. I didn't enjoy making a fool of myself, but I liked seeing Rich laugh so hard. Even when he was joking around, he could seem so serious. This was yet another side of him I hadn't ever experienced, and I found myself liking it.

"What's so funny?" asked Nick.

Nick leaned on the railing in front of us while Cade stood directly in front of Rich. Cade was eating peanuts, shells and all. Nick had a slice of cheese on a paper plate.

"Nothing," Rich said. He looked like he had finally calmed himself down all the way. "What the hell?" he asked suddenly. He pointed to Cade. "You know you're supposed to take the shells off, right?"

"What?" asked Cade. He bit straight into another peanut, gnawing his way through the shell and then chewing up the contents before speaking again. "Are they poisonous or something?"

"No, but they have the texture of tree bark," Nick said. "You've been eating the shells? Are you really that dense?"

"Yeah, and cheese is just a loaf of old milk," Cade shot back. "So bon appétit, asshole."

Nick looked at his cheese with a slightly disturbed expression and then set it down on one of the steps. "It looked like Kira was having some kind of episode or mental breakdown, so we thought we'd better come check on you two," Nick said.

I glared.

Nick reeled backward like I'd balled up my fists to punch him.

"I was dancing, not having a mental breakdown," I said.

Cade burst out laughing. "This guy," he said, looking at Nick. "I'm supposed to be the one who is dumb enough to say something like that out loud. You're supposed to be smarter than that, Nicky boy."

"Shut up," Nick said. He cleared his throat. "So, other than costing us millions of dollars, what are you two up to?"

"Well," Rich said, "we're waiting for people to stop harassing us so we can enjoy the fair."

Cade nodded sagely. "Yeah. People suck. It's like you just want some space to breathe, and they're always there, just taking up space. You know?"

Nick took Cade by the arm and tugged at him. "He's talking about us, dumb ass."

"Oh. *Oh.*" Cade waggled a finger at me and winked. "I got you. You two want some alone time. Don't forget to wrap it up. Actually, wait. *Do* forget. I would love to see the look on Mom and Dad's face if you got her pregnant. Can you imagine? Mom would want you to name it Rosenthal. Or maybe Gretchen."

"Cade," Rich said.

"Got it. I'm gone. Oh, one last thing. You might want to start giving that personal assistant of yours more to do. I heard he ended up in some drunken orgy last night. Nobody has seen or heard from him since."

Rich grimaced. "It's fine. Jalen was a lost cause anyway. And I haven't needed him since we've been out here."

"Yeah, because you've been chasing Kira so much that you hardly spend any time doing actual work," Cade said.

"And I've still been doing four times as much work as you. What does that say about you?"

"That I'm efficient and you're slow?"

Rich sighed. He pulled out his phone and checked a notification. I thought I saw his expression darken even more.

"Everything okay?" I asked.

"Yeah. It's fine. Hey, is that fried ice cream?"

I nodded, and even though I suspected he was changing the subject on purpose, I decided he was right about one thing. We should enjoy the time we had while we had it, because there was no telling what was coming next.

Chapter 22

RICH

We had two great days together. It was more than I'd expected. Mayor Summerland made his threats in the morning, and I spent the afternoon and most of the evening wandering the fair with Kira. Then we used the pool at my place and watched a movie on the back wall of my house with the projector. We had both felt daring, so we watched *Jaws* while floating on an inflatable duck together. It was highly romantic, ridiculous, and honestly a little terrifying.

Yesterday had been normal in the best possible way. It was a Monday, so Kira was at work for most of the day. It was the first chance I'd had to really dig into what kind of obstacles the mayor and my parents were putting in our way. My lawyer had texted me when I was at the fair with Kira about a "big problem." In a very uncharacteristic fashion, I'd put off getting back to him until I dropped Kira off at work. I didn't want anything spoiling my mood when I was with her.

After a long meeting with our team of lawyers and experts, I learned the obstacles were significant. Worse, it wasn't one of those problems you could fix by throwing enough money its way. We either had to find a resolution with my parents and the mayor, or we were looking at six months of delay, minimum.

We did have options. The headquarters was a luxury. It was outfitted with amenities that would keep our employees happy and our clients impressed. But it was just our expansion into the East Coast. We could run a bare-bones operation out of a garage if we had to. It would be a lot harder like that to draw the best talent to our company, but it was possible.

The headquarters was more of a problem because it was costing us money. We had projects on hold, employee relocations planned, materials being custom-built and stored until we were ready, and dozens of construction contracts lined up. A delay this big could throw a massive, expensive wrench in the middle of everything.

It should've had me on the verge of a mental breakdown. A month ago, it would have. I probably wouldn't have put my phone down for days until I was done chewing through every last available option.

So why did I feel so calm about it all? It had to be Kira. For so long, work had been my life. Nothing had ever been able to compete. Until now, apparently.

Whether I was calm or pissed, I still had my brothers to think about. I also had to think about our employees. People might have taken me for a hard-ass who didn't care about things like that, but I knew the guilt would eat me up if I neglected them. So I made a few calls, and two hours later, I was touring a mostly vacant business park in West Valley. I didn't get where I was by rolling over and taking it when somebody put an obstacle in my way. If my parents wanted to halt construction on our headquarters, I'd show them the building itself was nothing but a convenience. Our new employees could work out of these offices. They were a step up from garages, at least.

After finishing my business at the office park, I met Stella at my place. I felt bad when I realized I hadn't even been making an attempt at selling our "relationship" lately. A quick internet search brought up countless pictures of Kira and me. Some showed us at the restaurant and getting into the helicopter, and others showed us holding hands at the fair. As usual, the headlines were entertainingly bad.

Billionaire's New Baby Mama: Knocking Up the Schoolteacher. Billionaire Power Couple Splits, or Was It a Raunchy Affair? Richard King Enjoys Southern Hospitality a Little Too Much.

It all made me want to roll my eyes. Silly or not, the fact of the matter was that the ruse Stella and I had been putting on was over, and I needed to at least apologize for my part of what had happened.

Stella was uncharacteristically fidgety. She sat across from me on the couch, and she kept picking at the nail polish on her thumb while her leg shook violently.

"Has your father started asking questions?" I asked.

"No. I almost wish he would. Just to get it out of the way."

"You still don't think telling him would be a good idea?"

She laughed. "That depends. Do good ideas usually lead to you getting disowned?"

"No. Not usually."

"Then, no. Rich, I do appreciate that you gave me this long to get off the dating carousel, and I don't blame you for going after Kira. So all this," she said, gesturing to her face. "It's not because I'm upset with you. I'm mostly pissed at myself for being too chicken to come clean to my dad, and because I know what comes next."

"Any chance you're wrong about how he'd react?"

She made a dismissive sound. "Our parents are pretty much the same. The thing my dad wants most in the world is for his legacy to be preserved. Second to that, he wants his reputation to be more impressive. I can help both of those by marrying someone in the right family. Take a guess what my coming out and getting in a relationship with a woman would do to his legacy and his reputation."

"Yeah. I can see what you're saying. Well, hey," I said suddenly, "I've recently been disowned. It's not so bad."

She snorted in a very unladylike way. "Yet. All they've done is fire a warning shot. I'm sure there's more to come. Do you have any plan to get them off your back, or are you just hoping to weather the storm?"

"I have a plan, but it'd require a pretty big favor from you. And it's going to require some good luck on my part. *And* I'm almost positive it's not going to get my parents off my back, but it's going to feel so goddamn satisfying that it'll be worth it anyway."

Stella looked uneasy. "Usually, I can hardly believe you and Cade are brothers. Right now, though . . . I can see the family resemblance."

I grinned. "You're right. This plan is probably straight out of Cade's playbook. So, want to hear the details?"

"I'm sure I'll regret this, but yes, I do."

♥ ♥ ♥

Kira didn't ask me to, but I stopped by her school to help her and the students work on the play. It was probably a mark of how far I'd fallen for her that I'd already memorized her schedule and the class times. For once, I was okay with admitting that I cared about her.

No. I was short selling it. The way I felt wasn't just caring about her. It was much more.

Principal Lockett had managed to catch wind that I was on campus before I even made it ten steps past the lady who worked the front desk. He intercepted me as I entered the school courtyard.

"Mr. King," he said. His voice was lacking the usual bubbly, chipper energy I'd come to associate with the man. He even stepped partway in front of me to make me stop walking.

"What's going on?" I asked. "Is it a bad time for me to visit her?"

"Well, yes."

"Is she okay?"

"She is."

"Tell me what the fuck is going on," I snapped. I pushed past him and started walking toward her room.

"Mr. King, if you'll just—" I heard his footsteps trailing as he tried to catch up with me.

I knew I'd just asked him to tell me, but my feet didn't seem willing to listen to my brain's orders to stop. I half ran to Kira's room, and when I yanked the door open, I saw a woman I didn't recognize. Her name was written in dry-erase marker on the board, and the students looked bored out of their minds with worksheets in front of them. "A substitute?" I asked.

"Can I help you?" asked the woman.

The students spotted me, and the room broke out in excited whispers.

"Quiet! Please!" the woman shouted as she slapped her palms down on the podium. It managed to dim the sound but not extinguish it.

Principal Lockett finally caught up with me and gently pulled my arm to get me back out in the hall. I let the door close behind us.

"Where is Kira?" My voice was level, but I felt a barely contained rage threatening to boil over inside.

"I didn't have a choice, Mr. King. I truly didn't. They said it was her or me, and—"

I started walking away. I didn't need to hear any more to know exactly what had happened.

"Mr. King!" Principal Lockett called. "I really am sorry. And if there's anything I can do to help—anything at all—just ask."

Chapter 23
KIRA

The biggest downside of not being a drinker was how pathetic my self-destructive moments were. Instead of passing out with a bottle of wine in a drunken blaze of glory, I buried myself in ice cream and daytime TV. Infomercials were my drug, especially the ones where they cut things. The Slap Chop might as well have been porn. I'd bought one once, but then I realized you needed to finely chop vegetables, meat, nuts, and other small objects only if you cooked. So I ended up with a pile of chopped onions and no idea what to do with them. Still, I occasionally whipped that bad boy out and Slap Chopped away my frustrations.

I'd already eaten enough that I had to untie the drawstring on my sweatpants to make room for my swelling stomach. It was an official ice cream baby.

Once again, Rich King had led to the destruction of my well-laid plans. Only this time, it hadn't been because of any cruelty on his part. I'd been complicit too. After his warnings of what his parents might resort to, I hadn't fully believed him. At least not until Principal Lockett had pulled me into his office after first period and let me know he was going to have to fire me. I didn't even blame him. The tears he was obviously trying to hold back told me it wasn't his choice.

I didn't call anyone. I grabbed the essentials out of my classroom—the few things that were mine—and carried them out. I was able to get my things during planning period, which meant I didn't have to face any of my students. As much as part of me wanted to tell them I was being unjustly fired, I also suspected Principal Lockett had been browbeaten into doing it.

So I stayed quiet. Since Rich had dropped me off that morning, my car wasn't in the parking lot. Thankfully, I lived only about five miles from the school, so I'd taken the long walk home and used the time to think about what I was going to do.

The culmination of my grand plans was apparently double-chocolate ice cream with Oreos and a private in-home screening of *Look Who's Talking*, because if talking babies and John Travolta couldn't cheer me up, what could? Genius struck halfway through the movie, driving me to get out the Slap Chop and dice my Oreos into smithereens so I could sprinkle them on my ice cream.

It was as good as it sounded in my head.

Rich showed up a little after three. He knocked so hard I thought he was going to break the door down. I half expected him to yell at me for not calling him and telling him what had happened, but as soon as I opened the door, all he did was wrap me in a tight hug. After a few seconds, he started running his hand through my hair. It was hard to feel bad in those arms of his. I closed my eyes and breathed him in, letting him rock me slowly in the doorway at the bottom of the stairs to my condo. I also sucked in my stomach, just a little. He didn't need to know I was carrying a dairy child that didn't belong to him.

He'd never actually seen my tiny little home. I wasn't sure I wanted him to either. What would it look like compared with all the palatial places where he'd probably lived?

"We're going to fix all of this," Rich said quietly.

"How?" I asked.

"I have a really stupid plan. But it's the good kind of stupid."

I pulled away from him to frown up at him. He looked excited but a little crazy.

"Should I be scared?"

"Probably," he said. Rich dropped to one knee.

I watched it all happen in a daze, like when the bullets start to fly in an action movie. Time slows down, and all sound is reduced to a whooshing kind of roar. Except there were no bullets flying. There was just the most drop-dead gorgeous man I'd ever met falling to one knee and reaching for something. As if some kind of commentary was required for a moment this shocking, my stomach let out a deafening gurgle of surprise.

I'd seen enough movies to know one of two things was about to happen. He was about to draw a concealed weapon and light me up in slo-mo, or he was going to propose.

Neither made enough sense. A murder-suicide *would* qualify as a stupid plan, so it had that going for it, but Rich wasn't that crazy.

A proposal, though? To call our relationship rocky since Rich came back to West Valley would be an understatement. We'd not dated, broken up from not dating, slept together, had some fun. Then, of course, my father turned evil supervillain and nearly sabotaged Rich's company and got me fired from my job. It hardly seemed like the kind of stability cue that normally pushed a guy to pull a ring.

But sure enough, Rich took a tiny black box out of his back pocket and held it up to me. He frowned a little and then smiled. "I actually can't remember from the movies if I'm supposed to flip the box open or if you do."

"I think you do," I said very, very quietly. Quiet was all I could manage when it felt like someone was squeezing my throat closed.

He pulled the top of the box back, and I saw the ring. I'd never been much of a jewelry person, so the fact that it wasn't weighed down by some massive diamond the size of my knuckle was a perk. It was elegant instead, with a sleek twirling band studded with a few smaller diamonds and then set with a single modest diamond in the center.

"Will you marry me?" he asked.

"Rich," I stammered, spreading my hands. "Isn't this sudden?" I hated saying anything right away but yes, but I had to know more. It all felt like it had happened so fast. *Too fast.*

"It is," he admitted, and from the look on his face, he had been expecting me to ask questions. He didn't seem bothered by it, at least. "Feel free to tell me I'm a lunatic. But it feels right." He shook his head, and the look on his face was so earnest and open that it melted my heart. "I love you, Kira. I really do. I don't need another week, another month, or another year to be sure of that. And I didn't want anything to have a chance to come between us before I could do this. It's crazy, and people will probably think we're idiots for doing it, but I want to do it anyway. So . . ."

My head was spinning. I'd heard of people getting married after being together only a few weeks, and I'd always thought they had lost their minds. I'd made sarcastic comments about how long those marriages were likely to last, then laughed because I knew I was so much more refined than those people.

Except . . .

Why did I feel like I was being pulled toward him? I was desperately searching for a reason to say no, because it felt like I was supposed to, given the circumstances. I thought of what Iris and Miranda would think—of what my parents would think. Worse, I thought of what the town would think. Everyone would assume I was some expert gold digger who had worked her way into Rich's wallet and orchestrated the proposal.

Those should have been halfway decent reasons to say no. *Should have.* Except there was one glaring, blazing obvious reason to say yes.

I loved him too.

I loved him.

Teenage me might have thrown a haymaker at me right about now if she could hear my thoughts. Thankfully, teenage me was about as weak and scrawny as I am today, so it probably wouldn't have done much damage. I wasn't supposed to love Rich King. Not then, not now, not ever. He was the enemy. He was so obnoxiously perfect that part of you couldn't stand hating him for it. But he was a good guy. He was sweet and kind. He was funny when he wanted to be but serious when he had no other choice. Teenage me was going to have to get over it.

I licked my lips. "Is it a bad sign if I feel like I'm going to say yes even though it's a stupid decision?"

Rich thought about that. "Wouldn't it be boring if it seemed like an obvious choice?"

"I can't tell if you're manipulating me or making sense."

He grinned. "It's your choice. You can say no, and I'll be absolutely fine. I'll pick up the shattered remains of my heart and toss them in a bush on my way back to the car. I'll probably even be able to drive home within the broken, rotting husk that will be left of my body."

I shook my head and gave him a sour smile. "Okay, now I know you're manipulating me. Poorly too."

"Also, no pressure, but if I'd known this was going to be a debate, I'd have worn a kneepad. Do you mind if I—"

"Go ahead," I said.

Rich shifted his weight and got on his other knee. He rolled his neck, grunted a little, and then nodded. "I'm good now."

Just say it. I balled my fists and tried to swallow, but my throat felt so dry. I *wanted* to say it. Rich was like Morpheus from *The Matrix*, except not taking the ring was like taking the blue pill. I could leave the ring with Rich, and the next time I blinked, I'd be back in my old, boring life. I wouldn't be worried about how Harper and Edna King were going to destroy my life or how messed up it was that they were using my own father as a puppet to do it. I'd be back to worrying about my old, stupid problems.

Or I could take the ring. *The red pill.* If I took the ring, I'd see how deep the rabbit hole went. I'd be stepping through a terrifying door, but I'd be doing it with Rich.

I closed my eyes and took a deep breath. That was it. It didn't matter which future seemed more or less frightening. What mattered was which choice let me keep Rich.

"Yes," I said. The word came out with a rush of air, like I put every last bit my lungs could hold into saying it. I felt light-headed and giddy all at once.

"Yes . . ." he said slowly. "I want to be excited, but I also asked you if you'd marry me at least"—he held up his wrist and acted like he was doing intensive mental math as he checked his watch—"four hours ago. So are you saying yes to—"

"Yes. I'll marry you," I said. I cupped his face and kissed him.

When I pulled back from the kiss, the only emotion left was excitement. Yes, getting engaged this quickly was borderline crazy, but I didn't care anymore. Besides, it wasn't like the wedding was going to be tomorrow. Engagements usually lasted a year, and I'd have plenty of time to wrap my head around all of this later.

"You're supposed to let me put the ring on you," he said when I went in to kiss him again.

"Oh, right." I let him take my hand and slide the ring on my finger. I looked down at it and bit my lip. I'd never been the type to want a caveman to bash me over the head and carry me back to his cave, but I had to admit part of me liked being claimed like this. His ring was on my finger, and now everyone would know I was taken. *I was his.*

"There's just one more thing," Rich said as he stood and winced. He shook out his leg and stretched his back.

I laughed at his little show of being sore. He had been kneeling for only five minutes at the most. Probably, at least. I guess I didn't really know how long it had been. "You don't think that was enough of a surprise for today?" I asked.

"Maybe you should sit down for this part," he said.

I frowned. "What? Why don't I like the sound of this already?"

"Because it's going to sound like a really dumb, bad idea at first. But I need you to hear me out." He took me by the shoulders and guided me to the steps leading up to my condo and sat me down. "I thought of a way to maybe get my parents off our backs."

"Okay," I said. I searched his face for some clue of what was coming, and all I could find was hesitation. Whatever he was about to say, he really thought I wasn't going to like it. Not a good sign.

"So, the one thing my parents care about more than anything is their reputation. That's what all of this is about in the first place. Stella's family is well respected, so if I married her, it would boost my parents' reputation. You and your family, well—"

"I get it. We're like street urchins to them. It doesn't offend me. Don't worry. I know you don't see it that way."

He nodded and squeezed my knee. "Right, because I've never wanted to bend a street urchin over the nightstand and—"

"Rich," I said with a smirk. "Are you focusing right now?"

He looked like he was about to make a case for himself but then shook his head and continued. "The point is that my parents don't just want to stop us from being together. They want to stop anyone from finding out that we are together. Right now it's rumors and pictures. That's good enough for the public, but in their social circle, it won't carry enough weight yet. Soon, the rumors will be too widespread to deny, even in their world. So my parents are going to be desperate to split us up before it reaches that point."

"Oh my God, Rich." I covered my mouth. "Are you trying to say we should hire hit men?"

"What is it with you and hit men?" Rich laughed. "No. I'm saying we should make sure nobody has any doubt we're together. We make it known before they have a chance to stop us, and *maybe* that will convince them there's no use in wasting time and energy keeping us apart. The damage will already be done."

"What if it just pisses them off and makes them want to sabotage us even more out of spite?"

"That's a possibility. But I think this is our best shot. The other option is we just hunker down, let them keep lobbing nasty shit our way, and hope they eventually get bored."

"You're right. That doesn't sound appealing. So where does your dumb plan come in?"

Rich took a breath, and his eyes flickered across my face. I'd never seen him look so nervous.

"We make it look like I got engaged to Stella. We put a decoy ring on her, make announcements to the press. Plan the wedding. The whole deal. Except it's *our* wedding we'll be planning. When the day comes, everyone will be watching, and it's not going to be Stella who comes down the aisle. It'll be too late for anyone to stop us by the time they realize."

I stared at him. "You're right. That is a dumb plan."

Rich's shoulders slumped. "I thought you might say that."

"But," I said, "I must be dumb, too, because I think we should try it."

Chapter 24

RICH

Looking my parents in the eye was surprisingly difficult. Part of me wanted to laugh in their faces, and the other part wanted to shout at them. Instead, I kept my expression neutral and sat beside Stella.

They'd reacted to the news that Stella and I would be engaged just as I'd imagined.

My father wore a smug look on his face. He kept spreading his hands as he spoke, like he was trying to be humble in victory and wanted us to be old pals again.

"It really is for the best, son," he said for the tenth time in the five minutes we'd been sitting there. "Your mother and I are sorry things had to get ugly, but you're a businessman yourself. You understand doing what has to be done."

"Of course," I said. It was hard not to laugh, because he was more right than he realized. I absolutely understood. It was why I was sitting next to Stella and pretending we were engaged. It was why I was willing to go through any of this circus act. Because it wasn't the easiest choice, but it was the one that needed to be made.

My mother waved her hand in our direction. "At least look like you're in love. Hold her hand, for God's sake."

I took Stella's hand stiffly in mine. "How's that?" I asked through clenched teeth.

"And would it kill you to kiss her? I swear I haven't seen the two of you so much as hug each other, let alone kiss. She's going to be your wife. You might as well start acting like it."

"I've actually had a bit of a sore throat," I said quickly. I could feel Stella tensing beside me. "Don't worry, though. You'll see quite the kiss at the wedding. I'm sure it'll make you want to jump right out of your seat."

My mother looked unimpressed. "And remind me: Why is it that you're pushing to have this wedding happen so quickly? It's unseemly. One month? How do you expect everyone to clear their schedules on such short notice?"

"It's what we're doing. If people can't make it, then they can't make it. We're not worried about that."

My mother clicked her tongue in disapproval. "People will talk, you know. They'll think you got her pregnant. Did you?"

"No," I said.

My father leaned forward with a conspiratorial smirk on his face. "There will be plenty of time for that on the honeymoon, right, son?"

I cringed. This was the same man who was willing to do anything in his power to stop me from being with the woman I cared about. He'd sabotage my company, her life, and anything else he could think of to get his way. And he really thought I'd be able to chum it up with him again?

I made myself smile. "Well, we've got to go. Like you said, the wedding is coming up quick, and we've got a lot of planning to do." I slid my hand out of Stella's and stood. "Come on, dear," I said with a sarcastic twist of my lips that only Stella could see.

She glared as she stood. "Of course, *honey*. I'll be right there."

Cade and Nick were waiting for me inside the entrance of our soon-to-be headquarters. As soon as we'd announced the engagement between Stella and me, my parents had agreed to get Mayor Summerland to start undoing the damage he'd done.

We had a month to get our legal team working their asses off and go overtime on the construction of our West Valley headquarters. By the time the wedding happened, our parents would find their own series of legal roadblocks if they tried to come after us again.

"It's coming along," Nick said. He plucked a strip of blue tape from his belt and put it on the wall where someone's tool had left a black streak on the paint. "I'm not sure I believe it'll be done before this wedding of yours, but it's getting there."

Cade, who had been deep in thought, grunted. "Does it even matter? You heard the lawyers. They showed their cards when they put a stop to the construction before. We've got ourselves covered now. I doubt you even need to have the wedding. We beat them already."

"It still matters," I said. "If they think there's any chance they can stop the truth about Kira and me from getting deep in their social circles, they'll still try anything. The wedding makes it all final."

"Seems kind of cold," Nick said. "Was Kira really okay with you just using marriage and a wedding as some kind of strategic move?"

"She's okay with it because we want to get married. The fact that our wedding will possibly shut Mom and Dad up is just a bonus."

Nick squinted. "Is it, though?"

"Yes." My voice was firm, and it pissed me off that he was challenging me on the issue. "I explained everything to Kira, and she's on board. So frankly, it doesn't matter if you agree with it or not."

Nick held up his palms in surrender. "I get it. I was just curious." He walked over to me and squeezed my shoulder. "And seriously, I'm happy for you. It's kind of insane that you proposed to Kira after like . . . four days, but I'm happy for you."

"It has been longer than four days. And thank you."

"I wish I could say I was happy," Cade said. "But it's hard to congratulate a man who puts his dick in handcuffs. Oh, wait," Cade looked to Nick. "Are they not handcuffs anymore if you put them on your dick? *Didn't think of that, did you, Mr. Headlock?*"

Nick put his palm to his forehead. "The worst thing about you is that your twisted logic can actually make sense sometimes."

Cade puffed up victoriously. He was as sore a winner as he was a loser. "That's right. You can write me a formal apology or you can kiss my ring. It's your choice."

"You're not wearing a ring—not that I'd kiss it if you were."

"Like I said. It's your choice."

"Marriage isn't handcuffing yourself," I said. "Before I met Kira, maybe I would've agreed. But I want to marry her because, well—" I groaned. "You know what? I'm not about to say anything remotely sappy in front of you two. I know you'll never let me live it down."

Cade threaded his fingers together and begged. "Please. Don't dangle it in front of me like that and then take it away. Besides, if you don't tell me what you were going to say, I'm going to imagine something ten times sappier and make fun of you for it."

"I was just going to say that I know I love her, so it doesn't feel crazy. I always wondered how people knew. I thought it was bullshit when they'd say you just do. But that's how it is. I just know. I know I love her."

Cade held a serious expression for a few seconds, then acted like he was violently throwing up in the corner.

Nick patted my shoulder again. "I'm happy for you. He is, too, beneath the thick layers of idiot he communicates through."

"Super happy," Cade agreed. He wiped imaginary vomit from his mouth with the back of his hand. "Pussy," he added with a smirk.

"Just watch," I said. "It'll get you too one of these days."

"Fuck. I hope not."

"Me too," Nick agreed. "For the sake of the poor woman Cade might actually fall in love with."

Chapter 25

KIRA

Iris and Miranda sat around my kitchen table. We couldn't meet at Bradley's, because Rich and I had to avoid being seen together in public. Rich was there, too, but he'd had to use an Uber and dress low-key with sunglasses and a hat to avoid being spotted. For once, my friends weren't being obnoxious to him. I think the whole spontaneous engagement thing must've at least told them Rich and I were too serious to dissuade with snarky comments and glares. If they were going to have to live with it, they'd might as well make it comfortable.

We each had magazines full of wedding colors, gowns, and decoration ideas.

"I always thought cream and violet was gorgeous," Miranda said. "Classy, but not stale."

"What about red and silver?" Iris asked. "It's got a kind of badass *I'll smile and be sweet, but if you cross the line, I'll absolutely judo chop your throat* kind of vibe."

"What do you think, Rich?"

Rich jolted, like he had been sleeping with his eyes open. "I think whatever colors you pick will be great."

I sighed. "That's such a guy answer."

"Okay," he said. He snatched one of the magazines with color swatches and started flipping through the pages with an extremely serious look on his face. He finally shook his head in defeat. "I'm sorry. I just want you to be happy. To me, as long as they make our marriage official, I'm good with whatever decorations you pick."

"Such a guy," Iris and Miranda said at the same time.

Rich raised his eyebrows. "Guilty as charged."

"So, Richard King," Iris said. She leaned forward and narrowed her eyes. It seemed like she wasn't capable of speaking to Rich without turning it into an interrogation straight out of a low-budget TV cop drama. "You don't care about the details of the wedding ceremony. All you care about is getting this show on the road as fast as possible. *Curious*, isn't it? It's almost like you have something to hide."

"There's nothing curious about it. I love her."

He said it so simply that the words hit me with a new kind of shock. I'd heard him say he loved me before now, but his matter-of-fact tone made it sink in deeper than anything yet. I had to admit I was still secretly terrified that Rich *was* using the marriage as a tool and not because it was what he really wanted.

But his plain statement of love convinced me where nothing else had. He was telling the truth. Potentially getting his parents off our backs was just a fortunate side effect of the proposal. This *was* about love.

I squeezed his hand under the table. Rich looked back at me and gave me a little conspiratorial wink.

"So," Miranda said, "do you really think your parents have no idea?"

"Yeah," Rich said. "It helps that they're so used to getting what they want. I don't think it ever really occurred to them that blackballing us wasn't going to work. So when it seemed like their plan had succeeded, they were more than ready to believe it."

"And what happens if they go berserk at the wedding?" Iris asked.

"People will get a show?" I suggested.

Miranda and Rich grinned, but Iris was glaring at me. Iris was overprotective to a fault. She may have backed off exiling me for my interest in Rich, but she had apparently made some kind of internal vow to make sure he didn't hurt me ever again.

"You're okay with that?" Iris asked. "It's supposed to be your dream day. *Your wedding.* You want two old farts throwing a tantrum in the middle of the ceremony?"

"I'm okay with it," I said. "I think a wedding that goes off without a hitch is kind of boring. I actually always thought it would be cool to have a wedding where somebody objects when the pastor asks if anyone has any reason the bride and groom shouldn't wed. It just seems . . . romantic."

Rich chuckled. "I don't know if that's what I'd call it."

Iris was glaring at me with her arms crossed. "I'm bringing my Taser. *And* my nightstick. Make sure I'm sitting near them, okay? If they get out of line, I'm dropping them like a banana with one of those nasty gray spots."

"Like a—what? Why does your mind go to such weird places?" I asked.

"What—do you expect me to eat a diseased banana?"

Rich was looking at Iris a little strangely. "You know, I can kind of see how you and Cade dated. I'm actually surprised you two aren't still together."

"Yeah?" Iris said stiffly. "Well, I'm not surprised. He can go screw himself for all I care."

"And what about you?" Rich asked Miranda. "Why do you hate Nick so much? I never really understood. You two were such good friends, and then suddenly it was like world war three."

Miranda took her coffee in both hands and looked down without a word.

Rich waited a few seconds and then turned to me. "Maybe it'd be better if I just gave you girls some time to look at this stuff on your own."

I gave him a quick kiss and leaned in to his ear. "They'll come around. I promise," I whispered.

Chapter 26

RICH

Kira had tried to convince me it was too risky to invite her to the wedding rehearsal, but I wasn't hearing it. I wanted her to be there. I wasn't willing to compromise her wedding experience any more than we had to for this little scheme of ours. In an ideal world, we wouldn't have to compromise at all, but those just weren't the cards we were dealt.

Everyone was there. My parents and a small army of extended family. The media—though we'd managed to ensure they were stuck outside the gates to the property where the rehearsal was taking place. Even Iris and Miranda had come. Kira had said if I was going to insist on her coming, her friends should be here too or it'd look too suspicious. At least this way, it looked like I'd been relatively indiscriminate in my invitations. There would still be whispers, but a pending engagement and wedding were enough to keep them at bay.

Stella was glued to my side. As usual, we avoided physical contact in a way that probably looked entirely unnatural from a distance. Many old-money marriages were bordering on arranged marriage, though, so a loveless pairing wasn't unheard of. Otherwise, we likely would've seemed more suspicious.

"My father is here," Stella said quietly.

I scanned the room and found him without much difficulty. It took all my willpower to wave and smile casually instead of recoiling from the intense stare he was directing at us.

Her father was tall, thin, and imposing, with white hair and glacial eyes. I'd seen him in person only a couple of times, but it was a fresh reminder of why Stella was so afraid to come clean to him about her sexuality.

"You're not planning on telling him tonight, are you?" I asked.

"I already told him," she said.

My chest tightened like an invisible fist had taken me around the ribs. I stared at her in disbelief. "What? Why would you do that? Why now?"

"Because, asshole, this isn't just about you. You may be ready to burn every bridge in the world with your parents, but I'm allowed to choose how my parents learn about this, aren't I?"

I gritted my teeth. She was right, of course, but I didn't like the surprise discovery. Especially not right now. "You didn't think I might want to know about this so I could plan for it?"

She regarded me icily. "I could've said the same about Kira. I don't remember being warned before you started showing up with her in public like you didn't care if anyone would notice or start to ask questions."

I closed my eyes and forced a calm to come over me that I didn't feel. "You're right. You're a bitch, but you're right."

She favored me with a faint grin. "That's fair. And to ease your mind, he's not going to tell anyone. *Probably.*"

"What? Why isn't he going to tell anyone?"

"Because he took the news better than I expected. It turns out there's a girl connected to much more money and respect than even you and your family. My father always wished he had a son to pair with her, but there are rumors she's not interested in men anyway. *So . . .*"

I smiled. "That's good, Stella. That's really good."

She finally smiled back. "I know. She and I might have nothing at all in common, but for once, I won't feel like I'm going against my parents' wishes. Believe it or not, I want to make them happy. I always have. Maybe he won't be too thrilled with me if it ends up not working out with this girl, but it feels like a new door is opening up anyway." Stella gave a little shrug, and her smile widened.

I nodded. I really was happy for her. I couldn't remember ever seeing her look as free as she did now, and I almost hated to change the subject, but I needed to be sure. "So he's okay with us going through with this? Isn't he worried about how this will screw up things between him and my parents?"

"He's not worried. He said your father cheats at poker, and he's always secretly hated the man. This feels like an appropriate punishment, according to my father."

"Remind me never to cheat your father in a game. And if he's okay with it, why is he looking at us like that?"

She glanced over at him and twinkled her fingers in a dainty wave. "He's been having stomach troubles the past few days. Gas and bloating."

I laughed. "Well. Okay."

"Richard," my father said loudly. He came up to Stella and me with a heavy slap on the back of my shoulder. "Good to see you, son."

I grimaced but hoped it would pass for a smile. As usual, my mother lurked a few steps behind him with her nose tilted up. I suspected she was withholding her relief until the moment she saw the marriage becoming official. True to form, she was planning to be disappointed. I wondered if intentionally disappointing her made me a good son in some twisted, confusing way. Probably not.

I'd given up any last desire to please them. Maybe before Kira and all this mayhem, I'd still held some deep-seated desire to patch over my relationship with them. Now, that was gone. I just wanted them out of my life so I could move on with my future.

"Quite the venue, isn't it?" my father asked, as if he'd been the one to choose it.

"Quite," I agreed.

"Stella, what do you think of it?"

"Yes, it's beautiful," she said.

He gave her a close-lipped smile, and then his eyes shifted to where Kira was standing on the other end of the room. She had a glass of soda in her hand and was doing an adorably poor job of hiding the fact that she was watching us. She took a huge gulp of her drink and jerked her gaze away when she saw my father looking.

"What do you think of her being here?" my father asked. "It wasn't long ago that my son was ready to toss you aside for her, no?"

"Rich and I have moved on from that," Stella said. Her voice was icy.

"Of course. It's just strange that he would invite her, don't you think?"

Shit. Kira had been right, after all. I'd thought my parents were too dense to suspect anything at this point, but apparently I was wrong. It wouldn't matter. As long as the wedding happened, everything would be fine. Besides, if they managed to find a way to screw it up, we could always go to the media ourselves and announce we were together. But part of the reason I wanted to use the wedding to announce it was for the theatrics. The real game that had gone on wouldn't be lost on the people in my parents' social circle. They'd know my parents had tried to outmaneuver us and lost. It would mean any more attempts they made to sabotage us would be obvious acts of petty revenge, which would risk damaging their reputation even more.

No, it had to be like this.

"Strange?" Stella asked. "No. What's strange is that you think my soon-to-be husband would have actually held any real interest in a local girl. Think of it," she said, wrinkling her nose in a perfect impression of my mother. "Richard King with a local *teacher*. One who can't even hold a job, nonetheless."

211

I knew what she was doing, but I still bristled to hear Kira being talked about like that.

"Is that right, son?"

I gritted my teeth. I couldn't bring myself to agree or even nod, so I just glared straight at him.

My father's eyebrows twitched in response, and I wasn't sure if I was being paranoid, but I thought I saw some kind of resolution forming behind his eyes. "Well," he said quickly, and in a single word, all the tension had left the conversation. "I'll leave you two lovebirds to enjoy the festivities. I can't wait to see the ceremony. I'm sure it will be beautiful."

I waited inside a small, cramped closet for a few minutes before the door opened and shut quickly. It was nearly dark inside, but from the sweet, flowery smell, I knew it was Kira. I reached out in the dark and found her hands to pull her closer. "You okay?" I asked.

"The venue really is perfect," she said.

I could see only the vague outline of her body, and something about the lack of vision was giving me bad ideas. With her scent filling my nose and nothing but my hands to feel her, it was hard to keep myself focused.

"I think my father suspects something," I said. I waited for Kira to say she'd told me so, because she literally had.

"It's okay. We'll figure something out."

I blindly pulled her closer by the back of her head and bent my neck to kiss her forehead. It was a mistake, because her warmth against my lips stirred up even more dangerous thoughts. There was no lock on the closet door, I knew, and I had no reason to believe someone wouldn't stumble in here while looking for a restroom.

"And that's why it was so easy to fall in love with you," I said.

"What do you mean?"

"I mean you tried your hardest to convince me this was a bad idea, and as it turns out, you were right. But you're not going to rub it in my face. You're too kind for something like that."

She laughed softly. "Actually, I was totally fist pumping in my head because I was right. I just forced myself not to say anything obnoxious."

I grinned. "Even better. You're human, but a better human than me."

"Maybe in some ways." Her hands reached out for me and slid down my chest. From the sound of her voice and the way her hands were moving, I knew the dark closet was giving more than one of us some dirty ideas. "But I think you've got me beat in the fitness department. *And hotness.* When do you even work out anyway? Aren't muscular guys supposed to do nothing but chug protein shakes and live in the gym?"

"I wake up early. And I just eat a lot of meat. I always hated the taste of protein shakes. *And* if you give me a vote, I don't have you beat in any ways." I didn't plan to, but I found myself gripping her legs and hoisting her up to pin her against the wall as my voice turned into a growl. "You're fucking perfect."

"Tell that to the fact that I always sneeze twice in a row," she said.

I barely heard her. I was kissing her neck, and the distant thrill of knowing someone could walk in felt like it was intensifying every sensation.

"Or the fact that I snort when I cry. Or—"

I kissed her on the mouth, not to make her stop talking but because once I put my hands on her, something came over me. I'd get a million ideas of the things I wanted—*needed*—to do to her, and being able to do only one or two at a time felt almost maddening. It drove me into a kind of starving frenzy where my brain didn't have room for normal thoughts anymore. All that was left were the primal, basic instincts to take and claim every inch of her.

She made the sexiest sounds when she was turned on. Her legs were wrapped around me, and the dress she'd been wearing had to have been hiked up above her hips. Knowing her panties—probably soaked—were right there but I couldn't see them was hot. It was hotter than it should've been. I used my hands where my eyes would've normally worked. I felt in the darkness for her and found the soft skin of her inner thigh pinned against me. I felt my way upward until I hit the edge of her panties and then moved my fingers down until they found what I'd been looking for. Her hot, wet arousal.

"You love getting wet for me, don't you?"

"Absolutely," she said.

I couldn't help chuckling. For some reason, the more turned on Kira got, the bigger the words she used. Where I thought most people would've just grunted out a quick yes, Kira would say something like *I definitely do*. It was adorable, along with the way she couldn't seem to stop herself from moaning when she came.

I tried to think of something else to ask her, just because I wanted to know what kind of ridiculous response she'd give. She was already panting heavily as our bodies rubbed together, seeking friction wherever we could find it.

"How bad do you want it?" I asked.

"Astonishingly bad," she breathed.

I laughed again. I could practically see the crooked, amused glare she'd be aiming at me through the darkness. I let her down to her feet just long enough to start tugging at her clothes, which was harder to do in the dark than I expected, especially considering I couldn't just tear them off her. We were in a closet in the middle of a crowded wedding rehearsal, after all.

After struggling to find a zipper on her dress for a few seconds, I decided to just yank her panties down. I accidentally did it a little too enthusiastically and heard the sound of fabric ripping.

"Damn it, Rich!"

"Sorry. No, wait. I forgot we're supposed to pull out our thesauruses during sex. My sincere regrets and deepest apologies, madam." When there was no sound for a few seconds, I grinned. "You're glaring, aren't you?"

"Yes. I can't help it, you know."

"Good. Because I like it. Now let me fuck you, because it won't be long before someone comes looking for me."

When I reached to find her in the dark, I could feel that she had her palms on the wall and her ass facing me. *Damn.* My cock was already rock-hard, and now it felt like it was going to burst from the pressure if I didn't get it inside her soon.

I unzipped my pants and pushed them down in a rush. I took the base of my cock in my hands and her hip in the other. She was so amazingly hot and wet for me. I groaned with pleasure at the first touch of her pussy to the head of my cock. I had to take it slow with her. An inch at a time as her walls relaxed enough for me to get deeper.

She was already gasping with her hand pressed to her lips from the sound of it within seconds. I wasn't doing much better. Despite my best efforts, I was grunting every time I slid inside her and felt the soft pressure of her warmth relaxing to let me in just a little deeper.

Kira had been a virgin, even if she still didn't want to admit it to me. I'd been taking it slow with her, and I didn't want to force her out of her comfort zone. I had all the time in the world, after all. So it was the first time I'd taken her from behind, and the fact that it had been *her* idea was turning me on way more than it had any right to. She was an amazing blend of shy, reserved, and shockingly dirty. I loved the unpredictability of it.

I took her hips in both hands and pulled her into me with each thrust. Her ass slapped against my hips in an increasingly rapid pattern. Despite the music playing outside the closet, I had a feeling her gasping moans were probably traveling farther than they should have.

I turned her around, lifted her by the backs of her thighs, and managed to slide myself back inside her warmth without a hand to guide myself. I kissed her deeply, swallowing up her moans. She gasped into my mouth again and again. I didn't have a condom with me, but I felt myself getting close to coming.

Sex had a way of making very stupid ideas seem reasonable, and I started to seriously consider asking her if she wanted me to come inside her. I came to my senses, if only barely. We had enough problems without adding a child to the mix. *For now.*

I did my best to put my mind somewhere else for a few minutes to hold out as long as I could. I wanted to feel her tighten around me as she came. I pulled my mouth from hers just long enough to whisper in her ear. "You feel so fucking amazing." I put my mouth back to hers, and it was just in time. Her body convulsed against me, and her pussy clenched around my length. I held off my own climax for as long as I could before I slid out of her and let it come.

"Goddamn," I groaned.

She said nothing, but I heard a little bit of rustling clothing as she was undoubtedly pulling her skirt back down.

I made a mental note to come in here when the coast was clear and clean up whatever mess we'd made.

Just as I was finishing zipping myself up, the door swung open. I moved as quickly as I could to stand in front of Kira, but then I saw who was standing at the door.

Cade.

He was wearing a shit-eating grin too. "You two done yet? I thought since maybe the ear-piercing moans had stopped, it might mean you two animals were done rutting in there."

"What the hell are you doing?" I whispered. Once the door was open, I realized there was some sort of commotion going on in the living room.

"Saving your ass is all." He nodded toward where Nick was lying on the ground next to spilled drinks and an overturned coffee table. Everyone was kneeling around him while someone was pressing ice to his face.

"I practically had to kill Nick to distract everyone from the sounds you two horndogs were making. I hope it was worth it. And if you made a baby in there, you're naming it Cade. You're welcome. Now hurry up and get out of there before people start looking. And you had better just go," he said to Kira.

For once, I couldn't disagree with him. Kira hurried out toward the parking lot, and I went with Cade toward an unoccupied room.

"Is Nick okay?" I asked.

"Mostly," Cade said. "He was pretty confused when I attacked him, though. I honestly feel a little bad. I didn't have time to explain the plan to him."

I shook my head in disbelief. "So you heard moans coming from the closet and assumed it was us?"

"No. I saw you two idiots go into the closet a few minutes apart. I heard moans and *knew* it was you. People started looking around, and I did what I do best. I made a genius plan and put it into action before anyone could tell me not to."

"Well, I can't believe I'm saying this. But good job. And thank you."

"That's what brothers are for. Also, you owe me now. So you bet your ass I'm going to call in the favor eventually."

Chapter 27
KIRA

Iris and Miranda helped me get my hair and makeup done at my condo. They also helped squeeze me into my dress, which might have become more snug from some of the stress eating I'd been doing the past few days.

Prepping for my wedding in my cramped little condo had never been how I imagined it, but I didn't care. The most important part of my dream wedding was the man I'd be standing next to at the altar. I had my dream man, so I'd live without everything else going exactly as planned.

"You look like a sexy librarian in a wedding dress," Iris said when we'd finished.

I rolled my eyes at her. "Would you stop with that already? It wasn't funny the first time."

"It's not humor. It's just how you look."

"Well, you look like Tinker Bell if she dyed her hair black and had an obsession with nightsticks."

"Thank you," Iris said with a wiggle of her eyebrows.

Clearly I'd missed the mark with my insult.

"We should get going," Miranda said. "I'm illegally parked, so the faster the better."

Iris and Miranda had me wait by the stairs in the hallway of my condo while they went to get Miranda's car. If the wrong person spotted me in a wedding dress right now, we weren't sure how fast word would travel, so we were going to play it safe.

But when Iris and Miranda came back inside a few minutes later, I could tell something was wrong.

"I can't find my car," Miranda said.

"What do you mean? You are the most organized person I know. You've never even lost your keys. How can you not find your car?"

"It's just gone. Maybe I got towed?"

I put my hands to my face, resisting the urge to run them through my hair. We'd spent nearly an hour getting me all done up for the wedding, after all. "Okay. It's fine. We'll just take mine then. Here." I took the keys off the rack by the door and extended them to Miranda.

"That's the other thing. Did your car have slashed tires the last time you drove it, or are we correct in assuming somebody else pulled that one off?" Iris asked.

I sank down to sit on the steps, which wasn't easy in my dress. I struggled with the fabric, got frustrated, and ended up lifting it as high as I could so I could flop down while it all bunched up around me. "How many miles away is the venue again?"

"Fifteen," Miranda said. "It's a twenty-minute drive. The wedding would be over by the time we walked there."

"Iris. You can call the station. Have someone send a car or something, right?"

Iris sighed and rubbed the back of her neck. "If everyone there didn't kind of hate me? Yeah. Maybe. But . . ."

I felt bad for asking. I knew she'd been having trouble fitting in, and I'd been so preoccupied with my own issues that I hadn't even asked her about it in weeks. "It's not a big deal," I said. "We can call an Uber."

Of the three of us, only Miranda had actually ever used Uber. It wasn't nearly as common in small towns as it was in cities, but she had traveled for her job and used it on trips.

Someone knocked at the door a few minutes after Miranda called the Uber. The three of us were all bunched together in the crowded space between the stairs and the door. We exchanged confused looks before Iris opened the door a crack to look out. "Yes?" she said.

"I'm your driver. You called a cab, right?"

"Uber, actually," Iris said. "But how did—"

I heard the man outside laugh. "Right. I used to drive for a cab company, so I always say it wrong. Yeah, I'm your Uber driver."

Miranda moved to Iris's side. "Since when do you guys come up to the house? And why did it say you were going to be driving a Ford Explorer? That's not even an SUV."

The guy glanced over his shoulder as if he needed to verify what she'd just said. He laughed and made a show of knocking himself on the head and rolling his eyes. "I'm always forgetting to update it when I take my wife's car. And coming to the door is just a courtesy thing. Don't forget to review me. Helps me out loads."

"Uh, just a second," Miranda said with a tight smile. She slammed the door in his face and showed me her phone. "That's not our Uber driver."

"What? How do you know?" I asked.

"Because our Uber driver is still fifteen miles away and apparently parked at a gas station."

"Who the hell is that guy, then?"

Miranda threw her arms up. "A serial killer, probably?"

"A serial killer with a car," Iris said. "If we don't go, we're going to be helping you file for divorce papers instead of stopping a wedding."

I frowned. "You're not suggesting we actually get in a car with someone we *know* is shady."

To my surprise, Miranda looked to Iris like she was waiting for a final judgment call.

Iris smirked. "What would be the point of having a cop friend if you couldn't flirt with danger every now and then?"

"Point taken," I said, "but isn't this more like letting danger put a roofie in your drink and watching?"

"Do you want to royally crash this wedding or not?"

That was when I knew I really had fallen deep for Rich, because the hundreds of rational, logical reasons I should've run for the hills remained unspoken. I nodded and said a silent prayer that I would actually be alive to regret this later.

"Right on," Miranda said. She took a deep breath and opened the door with a big smile. "Well, we're ready, Mr. Uber Driver."

The man looked a little confused but seemed eager enough to get us moving that he didn't care.

"Wow. On our way to a wedding, are we?" the man asked when he noticed my dress. He was squat and maybe in his forties.

My friends and I all shared another round of nervous glances but got in the car.

I settled in and reminded myself that Iris *was* a cop, and even though she didn't have her trusty nightstick with her this time, I knew she had pepper spray in her purse. She'd complained for weeks about having to get sprayed with it to get her certification and claimed she'd never leave home without it after that experience.

"The wedding is at an old property in the hills," I said. I scribbled the address down on a piece of paper and handed it to him.

"He already has it. From the app," Miranda said. "Right?"

I shot her a look. We already knew the guy was full of it, but she didn't need to provoke him.

"I know where it is," the driver confirmed.

I sank back in my seat and tried to clear my mind, despite the obvious ringing alarms that we were doing something very stupid because we were in such a rush to get to the wedding. I hadn't done much thinking about what it was actually going to be like walking out in front of so many people and shocking them. I was about as far from the confrontational type as you could get, and it didn't get much more confrontational than this.

My heart rate spiked, and for a few seconds, I thought I might actually have a panic attack.

Calm down, Kira. Only Rich's parents would be pissed. To everyone else, it would probably be a really fun story they could tell their friends. And Stella knew what was happening, so it wasn't like I was about to break some poor woman's heart in the process. *It was going to be okay.* As long as this creepy driver got us there on time.

When he peeked up at us in the rearview for about the tenth time in two minutes, I started regretting how I'd ignored my instincts and said it was okay to take a ride with this guy.

Iris ducked her head and started typing something on her phone after a few minutes. She tapped send and my phone buzzed.

Iris: He's taking us the opposite direction. Don't worry. You two sit back and watch. Countless hours of highly sophisticated police training have turned me into a human weapon. I got this.

I stared at her in disbelief. Before I had time to type back a reply, we'd stopped at a red light, and Iris, the human weapon, had leaped into action.

Chapter 28

RICH

I stood at the altar. I'd gone over the plan a dozen times with everyone we had working on our side of the scheme. Stella had been getting prepped in a wedding dress and makeup all morning so no one would be suspicious, but the plan was when everyone stood for the bride and her father, Kira would be the one to walk down the aisle.

Cade and Nick stood behind me as my groomsmen, and Stella had two family friends as bridesmaids. The other part of the plan was for Iris and Miranda to walk behind Kira down the aisle and trade spots with Stella's bridesmaids.

But as everyone got to their feet for the bride to come down the aisle, I had to do a double take when I saw Stella coming around the corner with her father's hand on her arm.

Oh shit.

"That's not good," I heard Cade mutter.

Stella looked like she was trying to figure out if she could simply turn and run full speed in the opposite direction. When they reached the altar, her father gave me a wink before turning away. Stella took her spot across from me and mouthed something I couldn't understand.

"What?" I said.

"Where is she?" Stella whispered.

The pastor started talking, ignoring our hurried whispers.

"She was supposed to be here. Did she not show up?"

"Obviously not."

The pastor cleared his throat finally, urging us to stop interrupting.

I swallowed hard. My mind was racing with all the possibilities. Had Kira decided not to marry me, after all? Had something happened to her? Had my—

I turned my head toward the crowd and scanned it until I spotted my parents. It took only one glance at the smug expressions on their faces to know they'd done something.

I closed my eyes, desperate to think of something I could do or say to fix this before it spiraled out of control. I realized I had only two choices. I could call the wedding off before the vows, or I could buy time and hope Kira managed to find a way to get here despite whatever my parents tried.

"Do you, Richard King, take—"

"Wait," Cade said loudly. He stepped forward so he was between us and the crowd.

Everyone gasped at the sudden interruption, but as usual, Cade didn't seem bothered by the attention.

"Aren't you going to ask if anyone objects to this union? When does that part come?"

"After the couple says 'I do,'" the pastor said through gritted teeth.

"Well, I can't let it go that far. I, sir, have an objection. A big, fat, throbbing objection." He paused, grinned like an idiot, and continued. For some reason, Cade's voice began to take on the slight hint of a southern preacher's accent. "My brother here. He's a good man. Despite his many faults—poorly endowed, underdeveloped sense of humor, small, girly calves, and the way he thinks macaroni and cheese is better if you don't add milk like God intended. Many faults. So many faults. My brother, he's not a perfect man."

I watched Cade in utter disbelief. While I'd been silently praying for some kind of distraction, I was already starting to think I'd like to change my heavenly request to a well-placed lightning bolt right between Cade's legs.

"He's bad at video games!" Cade shouted. He spread his arms and looked around, as if this was going to draw some kind of gasp of shock. Everyone was already muttering or watching with slack jaws. I was fairly sure no one was even listening to what he was saying. They were just shocked that my idiot brother had wandered in front of the ceremony and started this rant.

"I wish I could say it didn't get worse, but friends? It does. It gets much worse. Let me tell you a little story. How am I on time, Pastor?" he said quickly, as if he was giving some kind of planned interlude.

The pastor was too stunned to respond, so Cade took his silence as approval.

"Perfect, thanks." He shot the man a wink and turned back to the crowd. "Let me tell you about the incident of December the eighteenth. If my recollections serve me, it was a cold day. The date was . . . *wait*, what *was* the date?" He stroked his chin theatrically, and that was when I knew I was getting much more than a little extra time. Cade was ready to buy hours, if needed.

Chapter 29

KIRA

Our "Uber" driver was slumped in the passenger seat and whimpering quietly to himself when we arrived at the venue. I had nearly suffered a heart attack when we stopped at a red light and Iris threw herself into the front of the car with a catlike war cry. Everything happened so fast that I wasn't sure which parts I was making up and which parts I actually saw, but I was pretty sure Iris had spun in midair and landed a direct shot of pepper spray across the guy's eyes. Unfortunately, his reaction had been to slam on the gas and smash us into the car in front of us.

Miranda and I helped move him to the passenger seat so Iris could drive. She shouted out the window to the other driver we'd crashed into that she didn't have to worry, because Iris was a cop. I wasn't sure how that was supposed to help the woman, but Iris didn't give her time to complain.

And now we were here. *My wedding.* I stepped out of the car in a kind of daze. We were late, and I didn't have time to take in the decorations. If everything still went according to plan, I'd be able to look at them on the way to the reception, I figured.

Iris and Miranda followed me down the long driveway. The venue was a huge colonial-style farmhouse in the hills. The lawn stretched out as far as you could see and was peppered with peach trees and oaks.

I burst through the doors and headed straight for the backyard, where the ceremony was taking place. White wood trellises, archways, and decorative ivy had been put up everywhere. What had to be at least two hundred people sat in matching white wooden chairs on the freshly cut grass.

For some reason, Cade was sweaty, red-faced, and shouting in front of the altar. Everyone in the crowd looked somewhere between stunned, shocked, and amused.

"He told me to look down the barrel," Cade said. "'Tell me if you can see a spark,' he says!"

Nobody, including Cade, even saw us coming. To my surprise, many of them looked engrossed in his story.

"And when he flicked the igniter, all I saw was a fireball," Cade continued, his volume increasing with every sentence. "Eyebrows gone. Eyelashes melted together. It was horrible. *Oh.* Hi, Kira."

Two hundred wooden chairs creaked in unison when everyone turned to face me. I didn't pay attention to them. I saw Rich standing there at the altar. An irrational, jealous part of me leaped up in my throat when I saw Stella too. She was wearing a wedding dress, and for a split second I wanted to deck her. But she must have had to come out when I didn't show up on time. And Cade. Cade must have been stalling for time.

Rich signaled to the piano player, who had been adding a kind of dramatic soundtrack to Cade's story a moment ago. He switched the song to the classic "Here Comes the Bride" tune.

I'd taken about two steps down the aisle before Rich's parents stood up. I kept walking, but braced myself for an outburst. The driver admitted they'd been the ones to send him, after all. They knew what was coming, and they hadn't expected me to actually arrive in time.

My parents were only a few seats from Edna and Harper King. They were staring in openmouthed shock.

"What the hell are you doing, Kira?" my father asked. He had rushed to the edge of the aisle. When he tried to grab my arm, Iris slid between us and pushed his hand away.

"She's getting married to a guy she loves. *And I bet they're going to have amazing sex tonight,*" she added.

Holding back a smile took monumental effort. Iris and my dad had never gotten along. I could only imagine how much she enjoyed that. I expected my dad to shake her off and make some proclamation about how he was the mayor and would do what he wanted. Instead, he gave me a funny, searching look. It was such a different expression than I'd ever seen on his face that it nearly took my breath away. I realized it was because for the first time I could remember, it felt like he was seeing me—actually seeing *me* and not just the chess piece he'd drag around to parties to make himself look like a family man.

"Well, if you're not going to ask me to walk you down the aisle, I'm going to invite myself." He pushed his way into the aisle and took my arm in his, then gave me a familiar nudge. "This doesn't mean I approve, you know," he whispered to me.

"Good. This would feel a lot less exciting if I knew my dad was okay with it."

To my surprise, nobody else said a word as we made our way up to the altar. My dad kissed me on the forehead, which he hadn't done since I was a little girl, and gave my back a quick pat before he moved away to leave me standing in front of Rich and Stella.

I was finally able to tune the rest of them out and really look at Rich for the first time. He wasn't smiling. It actually looked like he was thinking about having a repeat of our encounter in the closet at the rehearsal.

Stella dipped her chin at me. "Be good to him. He's actually not such a bad guy."

"Thank you." I hugged her before she left.

I stole a glance at the crowd and saw more excitement than I'd expected. When I imagined how everyone would react, I thought the most likely possibility was outrage. Apparently, people just liked a good show. Almost everyone had a cell phone out and was recording. So much for Edna and Harper King covering this one up.

Miranda and Iris took their places behind us, and Cade reluctantly gave up his microphone before going to stand back by Nick.

"You can continue," Rich said to the pastor.

The pastor threw his hands up, as if to say, *Why not?*

I barely heard anything he said. Rich's hands were in mine, and we were in front of everyone for the first time in what felt like forever. I didn't have to hide the fact that I loved him.

"Sorry I'm late," I mouthed to him.

"You will be," he mouthed back.

The pastor walked us through our vows, had us say our I do's, and then asked if anyone had any reason we shouldn't be wed.

"Actually," Cade said loudly.

Nick put him in a headlock from behind and signaled for the pastor to continue. Cade was choking out something that sounded like *I was kidding*, but Nick didn't let him go.

"Then you may kiss the bride."

I may not have remembered much of what the pastor said or even all the decorations I'd spent so much mental effort deciding on. But as soon as his lips touched mine, I knew I'd remember that kiss for the rest of my life.

Chapter 30
RICH

I carried a slightly drunken Kira into our hotel room that night. I had her under the legs and arms in the traditional over-the-threshold position. I paused once I saw the inside of the room.

"Jesus. You're sure this is where you want to stay tonight? We could use the plane and go to a five-star hotel, get checked in, and be in our beds in less than an hour."

"I'm sure," she said. "Throw me on the bed, *big boy*." She giggled at herself and blushed a beautiful shade of red.

How was I supposed to argue with that?

I lobbed her a few feet—probably a few too many—into the air. She flopped down on the bed in a laughing heap. "It's perfect."

"Remind me why we're staying at the cheapest, most run-down hotel in West Valley?"

"Come here," she growled. She beckoned me forward with her index finger. She still wore her wedding dress, and the combination of blushing red cheeks and the drunken, wild light in her eyes was both adorable and sexy. It was even more adorable when I considered that it had taken only two glasses of wine to get her to this level of intoxication.

I kicked off my shoes and crawled on the bed to lie beside her.

She bit her lip and touched her finger to my chin. "I wanted to have our wedding night in a rinky-dink hotel, because I don't ever want you to think I care about your money. I want our first real memory as a married couple to be somewhere shitty like this, because it doesn't matter if we're in a shitty hotel or a luxury suite." She laughed at herself. "Apparently I get sappy when I'm drunk."

"This isn't drunk," I said. "You're tipsy. Another glass or two, and maybe that would be drunk. For you."

She wiggled her eyebrows. "Is that a challenge?"

"No. I want you sober for tonight. And once I get you going, it'll clear some of the alcohol from your system."

"You're sure you don't mind being here?" she asked. "I know it probably sounds stupid, but—"

I put my finger to her lips, partly because I wanted to touch them. They looked so impossibly soft. "It's not stupid. And I think it's incredibly sweet that you want to make sure I don't think you're a gold digger."

"I never said gold digger. Do you think I'm a gold digger?"

I laughed. "No. It's a common term. I'm just saying it was considerate of you to think of that. So thank you."

"You're welcome. And you have to admit, it's kind of fun being in a cheap hotel, right?"

I looked around. "I mean, the carpet is interesting," I said. "It's kind of like they picked a pattern so ugly and busy that you wouldn't even know if it had blood or any other bodily fluids on it."

"Ew," Kira said. "Don't say *bodily fluids*."

"You mean I shouldn't say there are probably people's bodily fluids on this comforter, or the sheets?"

Kira sat up a little straighter and grimaced. "I'm not even a germophobe. Why is this working on me?"

"Because it's not germs. It's *bodily fluids*."

Kira groaned. "You know what? You can try your little games on me. I don't care. This is my fantasy wedding night, and I'm getting what I want. *So there*."

"Hey, whether it's in a rat-infested cardboard box or silk sheets, I'll take you where I can get you."

She gripped my cheeks and pulled me down into a kiss. "I can't tell if that was romantic, or I'm just so tipsy that I thought it was."

"Then I get the final vote. It was so romantic that you should reward your new husband."

"What kind of reward did you have in mind?"

"Sex. I had sex in mind."

Kira laughed. "That was direct."

I crawled on top of her and pulled one strap of her dress down her shoulder. "I'm in a direct kind of mood."

♥ ♥ ♥

Kira stood outside my parents' house with me two days after our wedding. She was wearing a hilariously formal pantsuit.

"You know this isn't a legal briefing, right?" I asked.

"I dress up when I get nervous," she whispered out of the side of her mouth.

"Don't be nervous. They'll—"

The door swung open. My father was holding a glass of liquor, even though it was barely noon. "Come in," he said, waving us in.

I had to take Kira by the hand to get her to actually come inside. My mother was sitting on the couch with a glass of wine beside her.

"Come on, sit," my father urged.

Kira and I took a seat on the couch across from my mother.

"Want anything to drink? I've got a brandy fresh out of—"

"No, thank you," I said. "We're fine."

He muttered something, held up his nearly empty glass, and shuffled off toward the kitchen.

My mother looked to be holding her liquor better than my father was.

"Come to gloat, I presume?" my mother asked.

"We're here because we want to know if we should be looking over our shoulders, or if the two of you are ready to stop meddling."

She waved off the question, blinking in annoyance. "You've already done enough damage, Richard. You think your father and I would resort to petty revenge?" She sniffed. "No. There's nothing to be gained from wasting our time with you or her anymore. You've won. Is that what you wanted to hear me say?"

Kira leaned forward with surprising quickness. She was speaking before I could stop her.

"You're damn right we did," Kira half shouted. Her eyes went a little wide a second later, and she sat back against the couch. "Sorry," she muttered.

My father returned with a fresh glass and plopped down on the couch. "Did I miss the victory speech? What a shame."

"No victory speech. We were just looking for a truce," I said.

My father sputtered a laugh. "A truce? How about a son who doesn't look at me like I'm a worthless sack of air all the time?"

There was a twinge of real emotion in his voice. My eyebrows pulled together. "Since when do you care what I think of you?"

"You think a father wants his son to think he's useless?"

"Harper," my mother said softly, "you're drunk, sweetheart. And you're embarrassing yourself."

"Maybe he's being honest," Kira said.

"You're damn right I am," my father barked. "I've always wanted your respect, Richard. Clearly, I fucked the pooch on that one."

I snorted a surprised laugh. "It's *screwed the pooch*. And I'm not making any promises, but if you can manage to stop hatching maniacal plans, we might be able to work something out."

"No more maniacal plans from us," my father said.

I reached over the coffee table between us and squeezed his shoulder. I knew I'd never have a picture-perfect relationship with my parents, but I could live with that. For once, it seemed like my dad was actually trying. My mom was my mom, of course, but it was enough to know that we weren't directly at odds for once.

"How touching," my mother spat. "And I'm supposed to promise I'll behave and be a good little girl from now on? *Fuck. That.* I'll do as I please, and I'll do it when it pleases me."

Kira was like a dog on the scent of prey when it came to my mother. Just the sound of her voice seemed to set her off, and I could feel the tension building in Kira before she spoke.

"Then you can watch your back, assuming you're flexible enough to turn your neck that far. *Old hag*," she muttered under her breath.

I choked back laughter. "Well," I said before my mother and Kira could get into a full-blown shouting match. "This has been productive, Mother," I said icily. "And Dad," I said, pulling my dad in and giving him the first hug—albeit a quick one—I'd given him in as long as I could remember.

Epilogue
KIRA

One Month Later

I parked my new car at the top of Overlook Point. Despite weeks of protest, Rich had finally had my old car towed and bought me a reasonably priced new car. He claimed my old car was "a deteriorating death trap." Even marriage hadn't completely taken away my weirdness about the whole billionaire thing.

I knew if I pushed too hard to keep our finances separate, it would cause more problems than it would solve. So I didn't. I let him pick up the tab when we ate out together, and I let him give me rides on his private jet—small consolations, I know. But I still worked every day. I paid for everything I could on my own. I got the groceries, and I still kept a budget. It was important to me to live something like a normal life, even though Rich and his money let him live outside the rules most normal people had to live within. I just wasn't ready to fully dive into that. Not yet, at least.

Rich got out and came to stand beside me. "This is, uh, underwhelming?"

Our view was pretty much as I remembered it, if not a little worse. The school blocked most of everything, meaning we could see only some stars overhead and a few lights from downtown if we craned our necks to the side.

I shrugged. "If you lean just right, the view is kind of nice."

Rich tilted his upper body until his head was sideways. "Hmm. Yeah, I guess so."

"I still can't believe the play went so well," I said. I couldn't help smiling when I thought about it. Rich had helped convince Principal Lockett that neither my parents nor Rich's would try to crucify him for rehiring me. I'd had two weeks to get the kids back on track and make sure the play still happened.

"Yeah," Rich said. "It's almost like it couldn't have possibly happened without such a talented codirector."

I laughed. "I really did appreciate your help."

"Yeah. Without my back rubs, which incidentally always seemed to lead to sex, there's no way you could've pulled it off."

"Right. Can you imagine how hard it would've been to put on the play if my sex-crazed husband hadn't been dragging me into every dark corner, closet, and bed he could find at all hours of the day?"

Rich pulled me in close and kissed the top of my head. His voice was a low rumble that I could feel through his chest. "I've never had you on the hood of a car, you know."

"Not tonight. Not yet, at least. I actually brought you here because this was where me, Iris, and Miranda made our little oath to stay away from you and your brothers. I realized I'd never taken you up here. It felt like I should, just to break the spell or something."

"Break the spell, huh? You don't think marrying me broke it?" He leaned in a little closer until his lips tickled my earlobe. "And you don't think fucking me all those times might have been a slight violation?"

"Ass." I laughed.

"Please," he said, reaching and squeezing two handfuls of my rear.

I squealed and swatted at him, but I was no match when I was laughing. He tackled me to the ground and then rolled off me so we were both lying on our backs. "You're a child," I said.

"Then you're a pedophile."

I groaned. "You know, sometimes I actually wonder if you and your brother switch places without telling anyone. One minute you can be so serious and so smart, and then the next you're just a complete goof."

"Cade's not really that different. I think everybody hides behind something. For him, it's humor."

"What does he have to hide?"

"Maybe you can ask him someday."

I slapped Rich's arm. "I'm your wife. Are you sure you're allowed to keep secrets from me?"

"Cade and Nick are the only ones with a right to tell you their stories, if they ever choose to."

"I wasn't really being serious," I said. I felt bad when I saw how intense Rich looked. "I mean, I was curious, but when—"

"It's not a big deal. You know what *is* a big deal, though? I don't think I've ever seen what you look like when you're naked in the moonlight."

"Rich," I said with a hint of warning. "Not the best idea."

He stood. "What? Why not." Rich yanked his shirt over his head and tossed it to the grass.

"Rich!" I said, hurrying to try to cover him back up.

"Too late!" He pulled his pants down until he was only in his boxers.

That was exactly the moment when Iris and Miranda pulled up.

Rich dove face-first to the ground for his shirt and tried to get it on, but he ended up getting his head stuck in one of the armholes as Miranda and Iris came out of their car. Conveniently, they had parked so their headlights were still glaring on my half-naked husband.

"I get it now," Iris said. "You invited us up here because you're exhibitionists now? You wanted us to watch you two go wild out here or something?" She looked at Rich, who was hopping on one leg with his head completely trapped in the armhole of his shirt. "Or maybe this is an interpretive dance thing?"

"If that's Rich's version of dancing, he really is a perfect match for Kira."

I helped Rich get his clothes back on while Iris and Miranda watched with amused little smirks.

"Okay," I said, looking between everyone to make sure I had their attention. "I wanted everyone to come here because we never officially nullified the promise."

"Seriously?" Miranda asked. "Don't you think this is a bit dramatic?"

"No. Because Rich is my husband now, which means his brothers are my brothers-in-law. Which means I need my best friends to not be like hissing cats around my brothers-in-law, because I don't need any more awkward in my life."

Iris rolled her eyes. "I'm fine nullifying the promise, but it doesn't mean I'm not going to whack Cade in the balls with my nightstick the next time he tries to talk to me."

Miranda crossed her arms and glared at the grass.

"Miranda . . . ," I said.

"Fine. It doesn't really matter either way. It's just an old, stupid promise we made."

"It wasn't stupid when you two were beating me over the head with it a couple months ago."

"Fair point," Iris said.

"I'm not here to be a human sacrifice or something, am I?" Rich asked.

"No," I said. "You're here because you're my husband, and I don't like doing things alone anymore. I needed a car ride, buddy."

Rich pursed his lips. "I see."

"Okay, so . . . do we all unswear it?" I asked.

"That's what we're going with?" Iris asked. "Unswear? Seems kind of second grade."

"If you have a better word, feel free to jump in."

Iris thought on that for a second. "I abolish my former promise." She spoke with a smug, self-satisfied smile. "Don't worry, it's legal-speak. Police stuff. I don't expect you to understand it, but it's much more formal than *unswear*."

"I take back the promise," Miranda said.

"Me too. Obviously," I said with a nod toward Rich. "Well! Feels good, right? Now we can all put the past behind us?"

"Yahoo," Iris droned. "By the way, what are the chances you'll tell me the story behind this violent pooper legend I've heard whispers of?"

I could already feel my cheeks burning at the memory. "The chances are zero. I'll never talk about it again."

Iris scoffed but seemed to accept that she wouldn't get the story out of me.

"As fun as this is, I gotta head out," Miranda said.

"Yeah. Catch you guys later," Iris said.

Rich came up behind me once they were gone, and we were alone again. "Did that go how you wanted?"

"Kind of? I think they'll come around. It'll be like it was with you. They're just stubborn."

"What is it you're hoping will happen if they come around, exactly?" He turned me gently toward him by pressing his fingertip against my chin and moving my face up. I thought he might kiss me any second, but he was just watching me with those heavy, all-consuming eyes of his.

"Nothing. I just don't want it to be weird anymore."

"You're sure some part of you isn't trying to play matchmaker? Do you realize what kind of chaos we'd be dealing with if my brothers were dating Iris and Miranda? Can you imagine holidays?"

I felt my eyes widen a little. "You're right. What the hell am I doing?"

He kissed my forehead. "You're being you. Being adorable and thoughtful. And a little reckless. You're being the girl I couldn't resist marrying."

It didn't matter how many times he kissed me or how many displays of affection he showed. I always melted inside. There was something inherently sexy and heartwarming about a man as big and imposing as Rich could be showing tenderness.

"Speaking of adorable and thoughtful," I said. "I was lying when I said I just brought you up here to be a driving buddy. I actually wanted to do something kind of sappy."

Rich grinned. "I like you when you get sappy."

"Well, since this was where I promised I'd never date you again, I thought this would be an appropriate place to promise I'll always love you." I felt sort of silly as soon as I said it, and it didn't help that Rich looked like he was holding back laughter. "What?" I demanded. I swatted at his chest in annoyance that he'd laugh at me when I was putting myself out there like that, but of course, he caught my hand.

"It's just that your last promise up here didn't go so well. How about we start a new tradition and say *fuck all the promises*. We don't need them. We've got each other, and we've got the way we feel. We'll always have that."

"Damn it," I said under my breath. "That was way better than my sappy thing."

Rich laughed. "It was a competition?"

"No. But I wanted to win."

"Too bad. And as the honorary winner, I'm ready to claim my prize."

Rich took me by the waist and lifted me. I squealed in surprise as he carried me to the hood of the car and set me down on my ass. "There. You're mine now. *All mine.*"

AUTHOR'S NOTE

Thank you so much for reading *Anyone but Rich*! This was the first book I've ever worked on with Montlake Romance or any traditional publisher, and I absolutely loved the experience. So I want to extend a sincere thank-you to everyone at Montlake who helped with editing and marketing and who also let me stretch my deadlines once or twice to make *Anyone but Rich* happen. I also want to thank them for believing in my writing enough to trust me to write not just one book with them, but three.

Please don't forget to review on Amazon, whether you loved the book or not. Also, keep an eye out for *Anyone but Cade* and *Anyone but Nick*, which will be coming up next!

Sign up for my mailing list to be notified when I have new releases (https://landing.mailerlite.com/webforms/landing/a0y7m1).

Follow me on Facebook (www.facebook.com/PenelopeBloomRomance).

And check out my website for my blog posts (www.penelope-bloom.com).

It has been an absolutely crazy, up-and-down journey that has left me thinking I'd made a terrible mistake more than once. Whether my books do well or not, I always try to learn something from the last book and improve on it in the next. Every book is an opportunity to get better and grow as an author, and I'll never waste that chance.

I'll never stop being grateful to every single person who has read my books and helped me turn this crazy dream of mine into a reality. I'll always appreciate that when my daughters are old enough to understand, I'll be able to *show* them what happens when you set aside your fears and go after what you want. I stop almost every day just to look around and let it sink in: I'm an author. My "job" is to write books, entertain people, and take my imagination for a spin. I get to wear socks all day—pants optional—and I get to spend more time with my family than I could in any other career.

When you read my book, you played a part in making that happen, and I hope I was able to return the favor by telling you a great story. Thank you so much!

—Penelope Bloom

ABOUT THE AUTHOR

Penelope Bloom is a *USA Today*, Amazon, and *Washington Post* best-selling author whose books have been translated into seven languages. Her popular romances include *His Banana, Her Cherry, Savage*, and *Punished.*

Her writing career started when she left her job as a high school teacher to pursue her dream. She loves taking her imagination for a spin and writing romances she'd want to live. She likes a man with a mind as dirty as sin and a heart of gold he keeps hidden away. Her favorite things include getting to wear socks all day—pants optional—and being a positive example for her girls. Showing her daughters that no dream is too big, no matter what anyone tells them, is worth all the late nights, doubts, and fears that come with being a writer.

Stay connected! For giveaways, goodies, updates, and extras, join the mailing list at https://landing.mailerlite.com/webforms/landing/a0y7m1. Follow her on Facebook at PenelopeBloomRomance, and check out her website at www.penelope-bloom.com.